Jame

The Mettle of the Pasture

James Lane Allen

The Mettle of the Pasture

1st Edition | ISBN: 978-3-73406-748-8

Place of Publication: Frankfurt am Main, Germany

Year of Publication: 2019

Outlook Verlag GmbH, Germany.

THE METTLE OF THE PASTURE

BY

JAMES LANE ALLEN

Author of "The Choir Invisible," "A Kentucky Cardinal," etc., etc.

New York, 1903

To My Sister

1

PART FIRST

I

She did not wish any supper and she sank forgetfully back into the stately oak chair. One of her hands lay palm upward on her white lap; in the other, which drooped over the arm of the chair, she clasped a young rose dark red amid its leaves—an inverted torch of love.

Old-fashioned glass doors behind her reached from a high ceiling to the floor; they had been thrown open and the curtains looped apart. Stone steps outside led downward to the turf in the rear of the house. This turf covered a lawn unroughened by plant or weed; but over it at majestic intervals grew clumps of gray pines and dim-blue, ever wintry firs. Beyond lawn and evergreens a flower garden bloomed; and beyond the high fence enclosing this, tree-tops and house-tops of the town could be seen; and beyond these—away in the west—the sky was naming now with the falling sun.

A few bars of dusty gold hung poised across the darkening spaces of the supper room. Ripples of the evening air, entering through the windows, flowed over her, lifting the thick curling locks at the nape of her neck, creeping forward over her shoulders and passing along her round arms under the thin fabric of her sleeves.

They aroused her, these vanishing beams of the day, these arriving breezes of the night; they became secret invitations to escape from the house into the privacy of the garden, where she could be alone with thoughts of her great happiness now fast approaching.

A servant entered noiselessly, bringing a silver bowl of frozen cream. Beside this, at the head of the table before her grandmother, he placed scarlet strawberries gathered that morning under white dews. She availed herself of the slight interruption and rose with an apology; but even when love bade her go, love also bade her linger; she could scarce bear to be with them, but she could scarce bear to be alone. She paused at her grandmother's chair to stroke the dry bronze puffs on her temples—a unique impulse; she hesitated compassionately a moment beside her aunt, who had never married; then, passing around to the opposite side of the table, she took between her palms the sunburnt cheeks of a youth, her cousin, and buried her own tingling cheek in his hair. Instinct at that moment drew her most to him because he was young as she was young, having life and love before him as she had; only, for him love stayed far in the future; for her it came to-night.

When she had crossed the room and reached the hall, she paused and glanced back, held by the tension of cords which she dreaded to break. She felt that nothing would ever be the same again in the home of her childhood. Until marriage she would remain under its dear honored roof, and there would be no outward interruption of its familiar routine; but for her all the bonds of life would have become loosened from old ties and united in him alone whom this evening she was to choose as her lot and destiny. Under the influence of that fresh fondness, therefore, which wells up so strangely within us at the thought of parting from home and home people, even though we may not greatly care for them, she now stood gazing at the picture they formed as though she were already calling it back through the distances of memory and the changes of future years.

They, too, had shifted their positions and were looking at her with one undisguised expression of pride and love; and they smiled as she smiled radiantly back at them, waving a last adieu with her spray of rose and turning quickly in a dread of foolish tears.

"Isabel."

It was the youthful voice of her grandmother. She faced them again with a little frown of feigned impatience.

"If you are going into the garden, throw something around your shoulders."

"Thank you, grandmother; I have my lace."

Crossing the hall, she went into the front parlor, took from a damask sofa a rare shawl of white lace and, walking to a mirror, threw it over her head, absently noting the effect in profile. She lifted this off and, breaking the rose from part of its stem, pinned that on her breast. Then, stepping aside to one of the large lofty windows, she stood there under the droop of the curtains, sunk into reverie again and looking out upon the yard and the street beyond.

Hardly a sound disturbed the twilight stillness. A lamplighter passed, torching the grim lamps. A sauntering carrier threw the evening newspaper over the gate, with his unintelligible cry. A dog-cart rumbled by, and later, a brougham; people were not yet returned from driving on the country turnpikes. Once, some belated girls clattered past on ponies. But already little children, bare-armed, bare-necked, swinging lanterns, and attended by proud young mothers, were on their way to a summer-night festival in the park. Up and down the street family groups were forming on the verandas. The red disks of cigars could be seen, and the laughter of happy women was wafted across the dividing fences and shrubbery, and vines.

Breaking again through her reverie, which seemed to envelop her, wherever she went, like a beautiful cloud, she left the window and appeared at the front door. Palms stood on each side of the granite steps, and these arched their tropical leaves far over toward her quiet feet as she passed down. Along the pavement were set huge green boxes, in which white oleanders grew, and flaming pomegranates, and crepe myrtle thickly roofed with pink. She was used to hover about them at this hour, but she strolled past, unmindful now, the daily habit obliterated, the dumb little tie quite broken. The twisted newspaper lay white on the shadowed pavement before her eyes and she did not see that. She walked on until she reached the gate and, folding her hands about one of the brass globes surmounting the iron spikes, leaned over and probed with impatient eyes the long dusk of the street; as far as he could be seen coming she wished to see him.

It was too early. So she filled her eyes with pictures of the daylight fading over woods and fields far out in the country. But the entire flock of wistful thoughts settled at last about a large house situated on a wooded hill some miles from town. A lawn sloped upward to it from the turnpike, and there was a gravelled driveway. She unlatched the gate, approached the house, passed through the wide hall, ascended the stairs, stood at the door of his room— waiting. Why did he not come? How could he linger?

Dreamily she turned back; and following a narrow walk, passed to the rear of the house and thence across the lawn of turf toward the garden.

A shower had fallen early in the day and the grass had been cut afterwards. Afternoon sunshine had drunk the moisture, leaving the fragrance released and floating. The warmth of the cooling earth reached her foot through the sole of her slipper. On the plume of a pine, a bird was sending its last call after the bright hours, while out of the firs came the tumult of plainer kinds as they mingled for common sleep. The heavy cry of the bullbat fell from far above, and looking up quickly for a sight of his winnowing wings under the vast purpling vault she beheld the earliest stars.

Thus, everywhere, under her feet, over her head, and beyond the reach of vision, because inhabiting that realm into which the spirit alone can send its aspiration and its prayer, was one influence, one spell: the warmth of the good

4

wholesome earth, its breath of sweetness, its voices of peace and love and rest, the majesty of its flashing dome; and holding all these safe as in the hollow of a hand the Eternal Guardianship of the world.

As she strolled around the garden under the cloudy flush of the evening sky dressed in white, a shawl of white lace over one arm, a rose on her breast, she had the exquisiteness of a long past, during which women have been chosen in marriage for health and beauty and children and the power to charm. The very curve of her neck implied generations of mothers who had valued grace. Generations of forefathers had imparted to her walk and bearing their courage and their pride. The precision of the eyebrow, the chiselled perfection of the nostril, the loveliness of the short red lip; the well-arched feet, small, but sure of themselves; the eyes that were kind and truthful and thoughtful; the sheen of her hair, the fineness of her skin, her nobly cast figure,—all these were evidences of descent from a people, that had reached in her the purity, without having lost the vigor, of one of its highest types.

She had supposed that when he came the servant would receive him and announce his arrival, but in a little while the sound of a step on the gravel reached her ear; she paused and listened. It was familiar, but it was unnatural —she remembered this afterwards.

She began to walk away from him, her beautiful head suddenly arched far forward, her bosom rising and falling under her clasped hands, her eyes filling with wonderful light. Then regaining composure because losing consciousness of herself in the thought of him, she turned and with divine simplicity of soul advanced to meet him.

Near the centre of the garden there was an open spot where two pathways crossed; and it was here, emerging from the shrubbery, that they came in sight of each other. Neither spoke. Neither made in advance a sign of greeting. When they were a few yards apart she paused, flushing through her whiteness; and he, dropping his hat from his hand, stepped quickly forward, gathered her hands into his and stood looking down on her in silence. He was very pale and barely controlled himself.

"Isabel!" It was all he could say.

"Rowan!" she answered at length. She spoke under her breath and stood before him with her head drooping, her eyes on the ground. Then he released her and she led the way at once out of the garden.

When they had reached the front of the house, sounds of conversation on the veranda warned them that there were guests, and without concealing their desire to be alone they passed to a rustic bench under one of the old trees, standing between the house and the street; they were used to sitting there;

5

they had known each other all their lives.

A long time they forced themselves to talk of common and trivial things, the one great meaning of the hour being avoided by each. Meanwhile it was growing very late. The children had long before returned drowsily home held by the hand, their lanterns dropped on the way or still clung to, torn and darkened. No groups laughed on the verandas; but gas-jets had been lighted and turned low as people undressed for bed. The guests of the family had gone. Even Isabel's grandmother had not been able further to put away sleep from her plotting brain in order to send out to them a final inquisitive thought —the last reconnoitring bee of all the In-gathered hive. Now, at length, as absolutely as he could have wished, he was alone with her and secure from interruption.

The moon had sunk so low that its rays fell in a silvery stream on her white figure; only a waving bough of the tree overhead still brushed with shadow her neck and face. As the evening waned, she had less to say to him, growing always more silent in new dignity, more mute with happiness.

He pushed himself abruptly away from her side and bending over touched his lips reverently to the back of one of her hands, as they lay on the shawl in her lap.

"Isabel," and then he hesitated.

"Yes," she answered sweetly. She paused likewise, requiring nothing more; it was enough that he should speak her name.

He changed his position and sat looking ahead. Presently he began again, choosing his words as a man might search among terrible weapons for the least deadly.

"When I wrote and asked you to marry me, I said I should come to-night and receive your answer from your own lips. If your answer had been different, I should never have spoken to you of my past. It would not have been my duty. I should not have had the right. I repeat, Isabel, that until you had confessed your love for me, I should have had no right to speak to you about my past. But now there is something you ought to be told at once."

She glanced up quickly with a rebuking smile. How could he wander so far from the happiness of moments too soon to end? What was his past to her?

He went on more guardedly.

"Ever since I have loved you, I have realized what I should have to tell you if you ever returned my love. Sometimes duty has seemed one thing, sometimes another. This is why I have waited so long—more than two years; the way was not clear. Isabel, it will never be clear. I believe now it is wrong to tell you; I believe It is wrong not to tell you. I have thought and thought—it is wrong either way. But the least wrong to you and to myself—that is what I have always tried to see, and as I understand my duty, now that you are willing to unite your life with mine, there is something you must know."

He added the last words as though he had reached a difficult position and were announcing his purpose to hold it. But he paused gloomily again.

She had scarcely heard him through wonderment that he could so change at such a moment. Her happiness began to falter and darken like departing sunbeams. She remained for a space uncertain of herself, knowing neither what was needed nor what was best; then she spoke with resolute deprecation:

"Why discuss with me your past life? Have I not known you always?"

These were not the words of girlhood. She spoke from the emotions of womanhood, beginning to-night in the plighting of her troth.

"You have trusted me too much, Isabel."

Repulsed a second time, she now fixed her large eyes upon him with surprise. The next moment she had crossed lightly once more the widening chasm.

"Rowan," she said more gravely and with slight reproach, "I have not waited so long and then not known the man whom I have chosen."

"Ah," he cried, with a gesture of distress.

Thus they sat: she silent with new thoughts; he speechless with his old ones. Again she was the first to speak. More deeply moved by the sight of his increasing excitement, she took one of his hands into both of hers, pressing it with a delicate tenderness.

"What is it that troubles you, Rowan? Tell me! It is my duty to listen. I have the right to know."

He shrank from what he had never heard in her voice before—disappointment in him. And it was neither girlhood nor womanhood which had spoken now: it was comradeship which is possible to girlhood and to womanhood through wifehood alone: she was taking their future for granted. He caught her hand and lifted it again and again to his lips; then he turned away from her.

Thus shut out from him again, she sat looking out into the night.

But in a woman's complete love of a man there is something deeper than girlhood or womanhood or wifehood: it is the maternal—that dependence on his strength when he is well and strong, that passion of protection and defence when he is frail or stricken. Into her mood and feeling toward him even the

7

maternal had forced its way. She would have found some expression for it but he anticipated her.

"I am thinking of you, of my duty to you, of your happiness."

She realized at last some terrible hidden import in all that he had been trying to confess. A shrouded mysterious Shape of Evil was suddenly disclosed as already standing on the threshold of the House of Life which they were about to enter together. The night being warm, she had not used her shawl. Now she threw it over her head and gathered the weblike folds tightly under her throat as though she were growing cold. The next instant, with a swift movement, she tore it from her head and pushed herself as far as possible away from him out into the moonlight; and she sat there looking at him, wild with distrust and fear.

He caught sight of her face.

"Oh, I am doing wrong," he cried miserably. "I must not tell you this!"

He sprang up and hurried over to the pavement and began to walk to and fro. He walked to and fro a long time; and after waiting for him to return, she came quickly and stood in his path. But when he drew near her he put out his hand.

"I cannot!" he repeated, shaking his head and turning away.

Still she waited, and when he approached and was turning away again, she stepped forward and laid on his arm her quivering finger-tips.

"You must," she said. "You *shall* tell me!" and if there was anger in her voice, if there was anguish in it, there was the authority likewise of holy and sovereign rights. But he thrust her all but rudely away, and going to the lower end of the pavement, walked there backward and forward with his hat pulled low over his eyes—walked slowly, always more slowly. Twice he laid his hand on the gate as though he would have passed out. At last he stopped and looked back to where she waited in the light, her face set immovably, commandingly, toward him. Then he came back and stood before her.

The moon, now sinking low, shone full on his face, pale, sad, very quiet; and into his eyes, mournful as she had never known any eyes to be. He had taken off his hat and held it in his hand, and a light wind blew his thick hair about his forehead and temples. She, looking at him with senses preternaturally aroused, afterwards remembered all this.

Before he began to speak he saw rush over her face a look of final entreaty that he would not strike her too cruel a blow. This, when he had ceased speaking, was succeeded by the expression of one who has received a shock beyond all imagination. Thus they stood looking into each other's eyes; then she shrank back and started toward the house.

He sprang after her.

"You are leaving me!" he cried horribly.

She walked straight on, neither quickening nor slackening her pace nor swerving, although his body began unsteadily to intercept hers.

He kept beside her.

"Don't! Isabel!" he prayed out of his agony. "Don't leave me like this—!"

She walked on and reached the steps of the veranda. Crying out in his longing he threw his arms around her and held her close.

"You must not! You shall not! Do you know what you are doing, Isabel?"

She made not the least reply, not the least effort to extricate herself. But she closed her eyes and shuddered and twisted her body away from him as a bird of the air bends its neck and head as far as possible from a repulsive captor; and like the heart of such a bird, he could feel the throbbing of her heart.

Her mute submission to his violence stung him: he let her go. She spread out her arms as though in a rising flight of her nature and the shawl, tossed backward from her shoulders, fell to the ground: it was as if she cast off the garment he had touched. Then she went quickly up the steps. Before she could reach the door he confronted her again; he pressed his back against it. She stretched out her hand and rang the bell. He stepped aside very quickly— proudly. She entered, closing and locking noiselessly the door that no sound might reach the servant she had summoned. As she did so she heard him try the knob and call to her in an undertone of last reproach and last entreaty:

"*Isabel!—Isabel!—Isabel!*"

Hurrying through the hall, she ran silently up the stairs to her room and shut herself in.

Her first feeling was joy that she was there safe from him and from every one else for the night. Her instant need was to be alone. It was this feeling also that caused her to go on tiptoe around the room and draw down the blinds, as though the glimmering windows were large eyes peering at her with intrusive wounding stare. Then taking her position close to a front window, she listened. He was walking slowly backward and forward on the pavement reluctantly, doubtfully; finally he passed through the gate. As it clanged heavily behind him, Isabel pressed her hands convulsively to her heart as though it also had gates which had closed, never to reopen.

9

Then she lighted the gas-jets beside the bureau and when she caught sight of herself the thought came how unchanged she looked. She stood there, just as she had stood before going down to supper, nowhere a sign of all the deep displacement and destruction that had gone on within.

But she said to herself that what he had told her would reveal itself in time. It would lie in the first furrows deepening down her cheeks; it would be the earliest frost of years upon her hair.

A long while she sat on the edge of the couch in the middle of the room under the brilliant gaslight, her hands forgotten in her lap, her brows arched high, her eyes on the floor. Then her head beginning to ache, a new sensation for her, she thought she should bind a wet handkerchief to it as she had often done for her aunt; but the water which the maid had placed in the room had become warm. She must go down to the ewer in the hall. As she did so, she recollected her shawl.

It was lying on the wet grass where it had fallen. There was a half-framed accusing thought that he might have gone for it; but she put the thought away; the time had passed for courtesies from him. When she stooped for the shawl, an owl flew viciously at her, snapping its bill close to her face and stirring the air with its wings. Unnerved, she ran back into the porch, but stopped there ashamed and looking kindly toward the tree in which it made its home.

An old vine of darkest green had wreathed itself about the pillars of the veranda on that side; and it was at a frame-like opening in the massive foliage of this that the upper part of her pure white figure now stood revealed in the last low, silvery, mystical light. The sinking of the moon was like a great death on the horizon, leaving the pall of darkness, the void of infinite loss.

She hung upon this far spectacle of nature with sad intensity, figuring from it some counterpart of the tragedy taking place within her own mind.

II

Isabel slept soundly, the regular habit of healthy years being too firmly entrenched to give way at once. Meanwhile deep changes were wrought out in her.

When we fall asleep, we do not lay aside the thoughts of the day, as the hand its physical work; nor upon awakening return to the activity of these as it to the renewal of its toil, finding them undisturbed. Our most piercing insight yields no deeper conception of life than that of perpetual building and unbuilding; and during what we call our rest, it is often most active in executing its inscrutable will. All along the dark chimneys of the brain, clinging like myriads of swallows deep-buried and slumbrous in quiet and in soot, are the countless thoughts which lately winged the wide heaven of conscious day. Alike through dreaming and through dreamless hours Life moves among these, handling and considering each of the unredeemable multitude; and when morning light strikes the dark chimneys again and they rush forth, some that entered young have matured; some of the old have become infirm; many of which have dropped in singly issue as companies; and young broods flutter forth, unaccountable nestlings of a night, which were not in yesterday's blue at all. Then there are the missing—those that went in with the rest at nightfall but were struck from the walls forever. So all are altered, for while we have slept we have still been subject to that on-moving energy of the world which incessantly renews us yet transmutes us—double mystery of our permanence and our change.

It was thus that nature dealt with Isabel on this night: hours of swift difficult transition from her former life to that upon which she was now to enter. She fell asleep overwhelmed amid the ruins of the old; she awoke already engaged with the duties of the new. At sundown she was a girl who had never confessed her love; at sunrise she was a woman who had discarded the man she had just accepted. Rising at once and dressing with despatch, she entered upon preparations for completing her spiritual separation from Rowan in every material way.

The books he had lent her—these she made ready to return this morning. Other things, also, trifles in themselves but until now so freighted with significance. Then his letters and notes, how many, how many they were! Thus ever about her rooms she moved on this mournful occupation until the last thing had been disposed of as either to be sent back or to be destroyed.

And then while Isabel waited for breakfast to be announced, always she was realizing how familiar seemed Rowan's terrible confession, already lying far from her across the fields of memory—with a path worn deep between it and herself as though she had been traversing the distance for years; so old can sorrow grow during a little sleep. When she went down they were seated as she had left them the evening before, grandmother, aunt, cousin; and they looked up with the same pride and fondness. But affection has so different a quality in the morning. Then the full soundless rides which come in at nightfall have receded; and in their stead is the glittering beach with thin waves that give no rest to the ear or to the shore—thin noisy edge of the deeps of the soul.

This fresh morning mood now ruled them; no such wholesome relief had come to her. So that their laughter and high spirits jarred upon her strangely. She had said to herself upon leaving them the evening before that never again could they be the same to her or she the same to them. But then she had expected to return isolated by incommunicable happiness; now she had returned isolated by incommunicable grief. Nevertheless she glided Into her seat with feigned cheerfulness, taking a natural part in their conversation; and she rose at last, smiling with the rest.

But she immediately quitted the house, eager to be out of doors surrounded by things that she loved but that could not observe her or question her in return— alone with things that know not evil.

These were the last days of May. The rush of Summer had already carried it far northward over the boundaries of Spring, and on this Sunday morning it filled the grounds of Isabel's home with early warmth. Quickened by the heat, summoned by the blue, drenched with showers and dews, all things which have been made repositories of the great presence of Life were engaged in realizing the utmost that it meant to them.

It was in the midst of this splendor of light and air, fragrance, colors, shapes, movements, melodies and joys that Isabel, the loftiest receptacle of life among them all, soon sat in a secluded spot, motionless and listless with her unstanched and desperate wound. Everything seemed happy but herself; the very brilliancy of the day only deepened the shadow under which she brooded. As she had slipped away from the house, she would soon have escaped from the garden had there been any further retreat.

It was not necessary long to wait for one. Borne across the brown roofs and red chimneys of the town and exploding in the crystal air above her head like balls of mellow music, came the sounds of the first church bells, the bells of Christ Church.

They had never conveyed other meaning to her than that proclaimed by the town clock: they sounded the hour. She had been too untroubled during her young life to understand their aged argument and invitation.

Held In the arms of her father, when a babe, she had been duly christened. His death had occurred soon afterwards, then her mother's. Under the nurture of a grandmother to whom religion was a convenience and social form, she had received the strictest ceremonial but in no wise any spiritual training. The first conscious awakening of this beautiful unearthly sense had not taken place until the night of her confirmation—a wet April evening when the early green of the earth was bowed to the ground, and the lilies-of-the-valley in the yard had chilled her fingers as she had plucked them (chosen flower of her consecration); she and they but rising alike into their higher lives out of the same mysterious Mother.

That night she had knelt among the others at the chancel and the bishop who had been a friend of her father's, having approached her in the long line of young and old, had laid his hands the more softly for his memories upon her brow with the impersonal prayer:

"Defend, O Lord, this thy child with thy heavenly grace, that she may continue thine forever, and daily increase in thy Holy Spirit more and more, until she come unto thy Everlasting Kingdom."

For days afterwards a steady radiance seemed to Isabel to rest upon her wherever she went, shed straight from Eternity. She had avoided her grandmother, secluded herself from the closest companions, been very thoughtful.

Years had elapsed since. But no experience of the soul is ever wasted or effaceable; and as the sound of the bells now reached her across the garden, they reawoke the spiritual impulses which had stirred within her at confirmation. First heard whispering then, the sacred annunciation now more eloquently urged that in her church, the hour of real need being come, she would find refuge, help, more than earthly counsellor.

She returned unobserved to the house and after quick simple preparation, was on her way.

When she slipped shrinkingly into her pew, scarce any one had arrived. Several women in mourning were there and two or three aged men. It is the sorrowful and the old who head the human host in its march toward Paradise: Youth and Happiness loiter far behind and are satisfied with the earth. Isabel looked around with a poignant realization of the broken company over into which she had so swiftly crossed.

She had never before been in the church when it was empty. How hushed and solemn it waited in its noonday twilight—the Divine already there, faithful keeper of the ancient compact; the human not yet arrived. Here indeed was the refuge she had craved; here the wounded eye of the soul could open unhurt and unafraid; and she sank to her knees with a quick prayer of the heart, scarce of the lips, for Isabel knew nothing about prayer in her own words—that she might have peace of mind during these guarded hours: there would be so much time afterwards in which to remember—so many years in which to remember!

How still it was! At first she started at every sound: the barely audible opening and shutting of a pew door by some careful hand; the grating of wheels on the cobblestones outside as a carriage was driven to the entrance; the love-calls of sparrows building in the climbing oak around the Gothic windows.

Soon, however, her ear became sealed to all outward disturbance. She had fled to the church, driven by many young impulses, but among them was the keen hope that her new Sorrow, which had begun to follow her everywhere since she awoke, would wait outside when she entered those doors: so dark a spirit would surely not stalk behind her into the very splendor of the Spotless. But as she now let her eyes wander down the isle to the chancel railing where she had knelt at confirmation, where bridal couples knelt in receiving the benediction, Isabel felt that this new Care faced her from there as from its appointed shrine; she even fancied that in effect it addressed to her a solemn warning:

"Isabel, think not to escape me in this place! It is here that Rowan must seem to you most unworthy and most false; to have wronged you most cruelly. For it was here, at this altar, that you had expected to kneel beside him and be blessed in your marriage. In years to come, sitting where you now sit, you may live to see him kneel here with another, making her his wife. But for you, Isabel, this spot must ever mean the renunciation of marriage, the bier of love. Then do not think to escape me here, me, who am Remembrance."

And Isabel, as though a command had been laid upon her, with her eyes fixed on the altar over which the lights of the stained glass windows were joyously playing, gave herself up to memories of all the innocent years that she had known Rowan and of the blind years that she had loved him.

She was not herself aware that marriage was the only sacrament of religion that had ever possessed interest for her. Recollection told her no story of how even as a child she had liked to go to the crowded church with other children and watch the procession of the brides—all mysterious under their white veils, and following one and another so closely during springs and autumns that in truth they were almost a procession. Or with what excitement she had watched each walk out, leaning on the arm of the man she had chosen and henceforth to be called his in ail things to the end while the loud crash of the wedding march closed their separate pasts with a single melody.

But there were mothers in the church who, attracted by the child's expression, would say to each other a little sadly perhaps, that love and marriage were destined to be the one overshadowing or overshining experience in life to this most human and poetic soul.

After she had learned of Rowan's love for her and had begun to return his love, the altar had thenceforth become the more personal symbol of their destined happiness. Every marriage that she witnessed bound her more sacredly to him. Only a few months before this, at the wedding of the Osborns —Kate being her closest friend, and George Osborn being Rowan's—he and she had been the only attendants; and she knew how many persons in the church were thinking that they might be the next to plight their vows; with crimsoning cheeks she had thought it herself.

Now there returned before Isabel's eyes the once radiant procession of the brides—but how changed! And bitter questioning she addressed to each! Had any such confession been made to any one of them—either before marriage or afterwards—by the man she had loved? Was it for some such reason that one had been content to fold her hands over her breast before the birth of her child? Was this why another lived on, sad young wife, motherless? Was this why in the town there were women who refused to marry at all? So does a little knowledge of evil move backward and darken for us even the bright years in which it had no place.

The congregation were assembling rapidly. Among those who passed further down were several of the girls of Isabel's set. How fresh and sweet they looked as they drifted gracefully down the aisles this summer morning! How light-hearted! How far away from her in her new wretchedness! Some, after they were seated, glanced back with a smile. She avoided their eyes.

A little later the Osborns entered, the bride and groom of a few months before. Their pew was immediately in front of hers. Kate wore mourning for her mother. As she seated herself, she lifted her veil halfway, turned and slipped a hand over the pew into Isabel's. The tremulous pressure of the fingers spoke of present trouble; and as Isabel returned it with a quick response of her own, a tear fell from the hidden eyes.

The young groom's eyes were also red and swollen, but for other reasons; and he sat in the opposite end of the pew as far as possible from his wife's side. When she a few moments later leaned toward him with timidity and hesitation, offering him an open prayer-book, he took it coldly and laid it between them on the cushion. Isabel shuddered: her new knowledge of evil so cruelly opened her eyes to the full understanding of so much.

Little rime was left for sympathy with Kate. Nearer the pulpit was another pew from which her thoughts had never been wholly withdrawn. She had watched it with the fascination of abhorrence; and once, feeling that she could not bear to see him come in with his mother and younger brother, she had started to leave the church. But just then her grandmother had bustled richly in, followed by her aunt; and more powerful with Isabel already than any other feeling was the wish to bury her secret—Rowan's secret—in the deepest vault of consciousness, to seal it up forever from the knowledge of the world.

The next moment what she so dreaded took place. He walked quietly down the aisle as usual, opened the pew for his mother and brother with the same courtesy, and the three bent their heads together in prayer.

"Grandmother," she whispered quickly, "will you let me pass! I am not very well, I think I shall go home."

Her grandmother, not heeding and with her eyes fixed upon the same pew, whispered in return;

"The Merediths are here," and continued her satisfying scrutiny of persons seated around.

Isabel herself had no sooner suffered the words to escape than she regretted them. Resolved to control herself from this time on, she unclasped her prayer-book, found the appointed reading, and directed her thoughts to the service soon to begin.

It was part of the confession of David that reached her, sounding across how many centuries. Wrung from him who had been a young man himself and knew what a young man is. With time enough afterwards to think of this as soldier, priest, prophet, care-worn king, and fallible judge over men—with time enough to think of what his days of nature had been when he tended sheep grazing the pastures of Bethlehem or abided solitary with the flock by night, lowly despised work, under the herded stars. Thus converting a young man's memories into an older man's remorses.

As she began to read, the first outcry gripped and cramped her heart like physical pain; where all her life she had been repeating mere words, she now with eyes tragically opened discerned forbidden meanings:

"Thou art about my path and about my bed ... the darkness is no darkness to thee.... . Thine eyes did see my substance being yet imperfect ... look well if there be any wickedness in me; and lead me in the way everlasting ... haste thee unto me ... when I cry unto thee. O let not my heart be inclined to an evil

thing."

She was startled by a general movement throughout the congregation. The minister had advanced to the reading desk and begun to read:

"I will arise and go to my father and will say unto him: Father, I have sinned against heaven and before thee and am no more worthy to be called thy son."

Ages stretched their human wastes between these words of the New Testament and those other words of the Old; but the parable of Christ really finished the prayer of David: in each there was the same young prodigal—the ever-falling youth of humanity.

Another moment and the whole congregation knelt and began the confession. Isabel also from long custom sank upon her knees and started to repeat the words, "We have erred and strayed from thy ways like lost sheep." Then she stopped. She declined to make that confession with Rowan or to join in any service that he shared and appropriated.

The Commandments now remained and for the first time she shrank from them as being so awful and so near. All our lives we placidly say over to ourselves that man is mortal; but not until death knocks at the threshold and enters do we realize the terrors of our mortality. All our lives we repeat with dull indifference that man is erring; but only when the soul most loved and trusted has gone astray, do we begin to realize the tragedy of human imperfection. So Isabel had been used to go through the service, with bowed head murmuring at each response, *"Lord have mercy upon us and incline our hearts to keep this law."*

But the laws themselves had been no more to her than pious archaic statements, as far removed as the cherubim, the candlesticks and the cedar of Solomon's temple. If her thoughts had been forced to the subject, she would have perhaps admitted the necessity of these rules for men and women ages ago. Some one of them might have meant much to a girl in those dim days: to Rebecca pondering who knows what temptation at the well; to Ruth tempted who knows how in the corn and thinking of Boaz and the barn; to Judith plotting in the camp; to Jephtha's daughter out on the wailing mountains.

But to-day, sitting in an Episcopal church in the closing years of the nineteenth century, holding a copy of those old laws, and thinking of Rowan as the breaker of the greatest of them, Isabel for the first time awoke to realization of how close they are still—those voices from the far land of Shinar; how all the men and women around her in that church still waged their moral battles over those few texts of righteousness; how the sad and sublime wandering caravans of the whole race forever pitch their nightly tents beneath that same mountain of command.

Thick and low sounded the response of the worshippers. She could hear her grandmother's sonorous voice, a mingling of worldly triumph and indifference; her aunt's plaintive and aggrieved. She could hear Kate's needy and wounded. In imagination she could hear his proud, noble mother's; his younger brother's. Against the sound of his responses she closed all hearing; and there low on her knees, in the ear of Heaven itself, she recorded against him her unforgiveness and her dismissal forever.

An organ melody followed, thrillingly sweet; and borne outward on it the beseeching of the All-Merciful:

> "'Art thou weary, art thou languid,
> Art thou sore distressed?
> Come to me!' saith one; 'and, coming,
> Be at rest!'"

It was this hymn that brought her in a passion to her feet.

With whatsoever other feelings she had sought the church, it was at least with the hope that it had a message for her. She had indeed listened to a personal message, but it was a message delivered to the wrong person; for at every stage of the worship she, the innocent, had been forgotten and slighted; Rowan, the guilty, had been considered and comforted. David had his like in mind and besought pardon for him; the prophet of old knew of a case like his and blessed him; the apostle centuries afterward looked on and did not condemn; Christ himself had in a way told the multitude the same story that Rowan had told her,—counselling forgiveness. The very hymns of the church were on Rowan's side—every one gone in search of the wanderer. For on this day Religion, universal mother of needy souls and a minister of all comforts, was in the mood to deal only with youth and human frailty.

She rebelled. It was like commanding her to dishonor a woman's strongest and purest instincts. It called upon her to sympathize with the evil that had blighted her life. And Rowan himself!—in her anger and suffering she could think of him in no other way than as enjoying this immortal chorus of anxiety on his account; as hearing it all with complacency and self-approval. It had to her distorted imagination the effect of offering a reward to him for having sinned; he would have received no such attention had he remained innocent.

With one act of complete revulsion she spurned it all: the moral casuistry that beguiled him, the church that cloaked him; spurned psalm and prophet and apostle, Christ and parable and song.

"Grandmother," she whispered, "I shall not wait for the sermon."

A moment later she issued from the church doors and took her way slowly homeward through the deserted streets, under the lonely blue of the unanswering sky.

III

The Conyers homestead was situated in a quiet street on the southern edge of the town. All the houses in that block had been built by people of English descent near the close of the eighteenth or at the beginning of the nineteenth century. Each was set apart from each by lawns, yards and gardens, and further screened by shrubs and vines in accordance with old English custom. Where they grew had once been the heart of a wilderness; and above each house stood a few old forest trees, indifferent guardsmen of the camping generations.

The architects had given to the buildings good strong characters; the family living in each for a hundred years or more had long since imparted reputation. Out of the windows girlish brides had looked on reddening springs and whitening winters until they had become silver-haired grandmothers themselves; then had looked no more; and succeeding eyes had watched the swift pageants of the earth, and the swifter pageants of mortal hope and passion. Out of the front doors, sons, grandsons, and great-grandsons had gone away to the cotton and sugar and rice plantations of the South, to new farm lands of the West, to the professions in cities of the North. The mirrors within held long vistas of wavering forms and vanishing faces; against the walls of the rooms had beaten unremembered tides of strong and of gentle voices. In the parlors what scenes of lights and music, sheen of satins, flashing of gems; in the dining rooms what feastings as in hale England, with all the robust humors of the warm land, of the warm heart.

Near the middle of the block and shaded by forest trees, stood with its heirlooms and treasures the home of Isabel's grandmother. Known to be heiress to this though rich in her own right was Isabel herself, that grandmother's idol, the only one of its beautiful women remaining yet to be married; and to celebrate with magnificence in this house Isabel's marriage to Rowan Meredith had long been planned by the grandmother as the last scene of her own splendid social drama: having achieved that, she felt she should be willing to retire from the stage—and to play only behind the curtain.

It was the middle of the afternoon of the same Sunday. In the parlors extending along the eastern side of the house there was a single sound: the audible but healthful breathing of a sleeper lying on a sofa in the coolest corner. It was Isabel's grandmother nearing the end of her customary nap.

Sometimes there are households in which two members suggest the single canvas of a mediaeval painter, depicting scenes that represent a higher and a lower world: above may be peaks, clouds, sublimity, the Transfiguration; underneath, the pursuits and passions of local worldly life—some story of loaves and fishes and of a being possessed by a devil. Isabel and her grandmother were related as parts of some such painting: the grandmother was the bottom of the canvas.

In a little while she awoke and uncoiling her figure, rolled softly over on her back and stretched like some drowsy feline of the jungle; then sitting up with lithe grace she looked down at the print of her head on the pillow and deftly smoothed it out. The action was characteristic: she was careful to hide the traces of her behavior, and the habit was so strong that it extended to things innocent as slumber. Letting her hands drop to the sofa, she yawned and shook her head from side to side with that short laugh by which we express amusement at our own comfort and well- being.

Beside the sofa, toe by toe and heel by heel, sat her slippers—the pads of this leopardess of the parlors. She peered over and worked her nimble feet into these. On a little table at the end of the sofa lay her glasses, her fan, and a small bell. She passed her fingers along her temples in search of small disorders in the scant tufts of her hair, put on her glasses, and took the fan. Then she glided across the room to one of the front windows, sat down and raised the blind a few inches in order to peep out: so the well-fed, well-fanged leopardess with lowered head gazes idly through her green leaves.

It was very hot. With her nostrils close to the opening In the shutters, she inhaled the heated air of the yard of drying grass. On the white window-sill just outside, a bronze wasp was whirling excitedly, that cautious stinger which never arrives until summer is sure. The oleanders in the big green tubs looked wilted though abundantly watered that morning.

She shot a furtive glance at the doors and windows of the houses across the street. All were closed; and she formed her own pictures of how people inside were sleeping, lounging, idly reading until evening coolness should invite them again to the verandas and the streets.

No one passed but gay strolling negroes. She was seventy years old, but her interest in life was insatiable; and it was in part, perhaps, the secret of her amazing vitality and youthfulness that her surroundings never bored her; she derived instant pleasure from the nearest spectacle, always exercising her powers humorously upon the world, never upon herself. For lack of other entertainment she now fell upon these vulnerable figures, and began to criticise and to laugh at them: she did not have to descend far to reach this level. Her undimmed eyes swept everything—walk, imitative manners, imitative dress.

Suddenly she withdrew her face from the blinds; young Meredith had entered the gate and was coming up the pavement. If anything could greatly have increased her happiness at this moment it would have been the sight of him. He had been with Isabel until late the night before; he had attended morning service and afterward gone home with his mother and brother (she had watched the carriage as it rolled away down the street); he had returned at this unusual hour. Such eagerness had her approval; and coupling it with Isabel's demeanor upon leaving the table the previous evening, never before so radiant with love, she felt that she had ground for believing the final ambition of her life near its fulfilment.

As he advanced, the worldly passions other nature—the jungle passions—she had no others—saluted him with enthusiasm. His head and neck and bearing, stature and figure, family and family history, house and lands—she inventoried them all once more and discovered no lack. When he had rung the bell, she leaned back; in her chair and eavesdropped with sparkling eyes.

"Is Miss Conyers at home?"

The maid replied apologetically:

"She wished to be excused to-day, Mr. Meredith."

A short silence followed. Then he spoke as a man long conscious of a peculiar footing:

"Will you tell her Mr. Meredith would like to see her," and without waiting to be invited he walked into the library across the hall.

She heard the maid go upstairs with hesitating step.

Some time passed before she came down. She brought a note and handed it to him, saying with some embarrassment:

"She asked me to give you this note, Mr. Meredith."

Listening with sudden tenseness of attention, Mrs. Conyers heard him draw the sheet from the envelope and a moment later crush it.

She placed her eyes against the shutters and watched him as he walked away; then she leaned back in her chair, thoughtful and surprised. What was the meaning of this? The events of the day were rapidly reviewed: that Isabel had not spoken with her after breakfast; that she had gone to service at an unusual hour and had left the church before the sermon; that she had effaced herself at dinner and at once thereafter had gone up to her rooms, where she still remained.

Returning to the sofa she lay down, having first rung her bell. When the maid appeared, she rubbed her eyelids and sat sleepily up as though just awakened:

she remembered that she had eavesdropped, and the maid must be persuaded that she had not. Guilt is a bad logician.

"Where is your Miss Isabel?"

"She is in her room, Miss Henrietta."

"Go up and tell her that I say come down into the parlors: it is cooler down here. And ask her whether she'd like some sherbet. And bring me some—bring it before you go."

A few moments later the maid reentered with the sherbet. She lifted the cut-glass dish from the silver waiter with soft purrings of the palate, and began to attack the minute snow mountain around the base and up the sides with eager jabs and stabs, depositing the spoonfuls upon a tongue as fresh as a child's. Momentarily she forgot even her annoyance; food instantly absorbed and placated her as it does the carnivora.

The maid reentered.

"She says she doesn't wish any sherbet, Miss Henrietta."

"Did she say she would come down?"

"She did not say, Miss Henrietta."

"Go back and tell her I'd like to see her: ask her to come down into the parlors." Then she hurried hack to the sherbet. She wanted her granddaughter, but she wanted that first.

Her thoughts ascended meantime to Isabel in the room above. She finished the sherbet. She waited. Impatience darkened to uneasiness and anger. Still she waited; and her finger nails began to scratch audibly at the mahogany of her chair and a light to burn in the tawny eyes.

In the room overhead Isabel's thoughts all this time were descending to her grandmother. Before the message was delivered it had been her intention to go down. Once she had even reached the head of the staircase; but then had faltered and shrunk back. When the message came, it rendered her less inclined to risk the interview. Coming at such an hour, that message was suspicious. She, moreover, naturally had learned to dread her grandmother's words when they looked most innocent. Thus she, too, waited—lacking the resolution to descend.

As she walked homeward from church she realized that she must take steps at once to discard Rowan as the duty of her social position. And here tangible perplexities instantly wove themselves across her path. Conscience had promptly arraigned him at the altar of religion. It was easy to condemn him there. And no one had the right to question that arraignment and that

23

condemnation. But public severance of all relations with him in her social world—how should she accomplish that and withhold her justification?

Her own kindred would wish to understand the reason. The branches of these scattered far and near were prominent each in its sphere, and all were intimately bound together by the one passion of clannish allegiance to the family past. She knew that Rowan's attentions had continued so long and had been so marked, that her grandmother had accepted marriage between them as a foregone conclusion, and in letters had disseminated these prophecies through the family connection. Other letters had even come back to Isabel, containing evidence only too plain that Rowan had been discussed and accepted in domestic councils. Against all inward protests of delicacy, she had been forced to receive congratulations that in this marriage she would preserve the traditions of the family by bringing into it a man of good blood and of unspotted name; the two idols of all the far separated hearthstones.

To the pride of all these relatives she added her own pride—the highest. She was the last of the women in the direct line yet unwedded, and she was sensitive that her choice should not in honor and in worth fall short of the alliances that had preceded hers. Involved in this sense of pride she felt that she owed a duty to the generations who had borne her family name in this country and to the still earlier generations who had given it distinction in England—land of her womanly ideals. To discard now without a word of explanation the man whose suit she had long been understood to favor would create wide disappointment and provoke keen question.

Further difficulties confronted her from Rowan's side. His own family and kindred were people strong and not to be trifled with, proud and conservative like her own. Corresponding resentments would be aroused among them, questions would be asked that had no answers. She felt that her life in its most private and sacred relation would be publicly arraigned and have open judgment passed upon it by conflicting interests and passions—and that the mystery which contained her justification must also forever conceal it.

Nevertheless Rowan must be discarded; she must act quickly and for the best.

On the very threshold one painful necessity faced her: the reserve of years must be laid aside and her grandmother admitted to confidence in her plans. Anything that she might do could not escape those watchful eyes long since grown impatient. Moreover despite differences of character, she and her grandmother had always lived together, and they must now stand together before their world in regard to this step.

"Did you wish to see me about anything, grandmother?"

Mrs. Conyers had not heard Isabel's quiet entrance. She was at the window still: she turned softly in her chair and looked across the darkened room to where Isabel sat facing her—a barely discernible white figure.

From any other member other family she would roughly have demanded the explanation she desired. She was the mother of strong men (they were living far from her now), and even in his manhood no one of them had ever crossed her will without bearing away the scars of her anger, and always of her revenge. But before this grandchild, whom she had reared from infancy, she felt the brute cowardice which is often the only tribute that a debased nature can pay to the incorruptible. Her love must have its basis in some abject emotion: it took its origin from fear.

An unforeseen incident, occurring when Isabel was yet a child and all but daily putting forth new growths of nature, rendered very clear even then the developing antagonism and prospective relationship of these two characters. In a company of ladies the grandmother, drawing the conversation to herself, remarked with a suggestive laugh that as there were no men present she would tell a certain story. "Grandmother," interposed Isabel, vaguely startled, "please do not say anything that you would not say before a man;" and for an instant, amid the hush, the child and the woman looked at each other like two repellent intelligences, accidentally meeting out of the heavens and the pit.

This had been the first of a long series of antagonism and recoils, and as the child had matured, the purity and loftiness of her nature had by this very contact grown chilled toward austerity. Thus nature lends a gradual protective hardening to a tender surface during abrasion with a coarser thing. It left Isabel more reserved with her grandmother than with any one else of all the persons who entered into her life.

For this reason Mrs. Conyers now foresaw that this interview would be specially difficult. She had never enjoyed Isabel's confidence in regard to her love affairs—and the girl had had her share of these; every attempt to gain it had been met by rebuffs so courteous but decisive that they had always wounded her pride and sometimes had lashed her to secret fury.

"Did you wish to see me about anything, grandmother?"

The reply came very quickly: "I wanted to know whether you were well."

"I am perfectly well. Why did you think of asking?"

"You did not seem well in church."

"I had forgotten. I was not well in church."

Mrs. Conyers bent over and drew a chair in front of her own. She wished to watch Isabel's face. She had been a close student of women's faces—and of many men's.

"Sit here. There is a breeze through the window."

"Thank you. I'd rather sit here."

Another pause ensued.

"Did you ever know the last of May to be so hot?"

"I cannot remember now."

"Can you imagine any one calling on such an afternoon?"

There was no reply.

"I am glad no one has been here. While I was asleep I thought I heard the bell."

There was no reply.

"You were wise not to stay for the sermon." Mrs. Conyers' voice trembled with anger as she passed on and on, seeking a penetrable point for conversation. "I do not believe in using the church to teach young men that they should blame their fathers for their own misdeeds. If I have done any good in this world, I do not expect my father and mother to be rewarded for it in the next; if I have done wrong, I do not expect my children to be punished. I shall claim the reward and I shall stand the punishment, and that is the end of it. Teaching young men to blame their parents because they are prodigals is nonsense, and injurious nonsense. I hope you do not imagine," she said, with a stroke of characteristic coarseness, "that you get any of your faults from me."

"I have never held you responsible, grandmother."

Mrs. Conyers could wait no longer.

"Isabel," she asked sharply, "why did you not see Rowan when he called a few minutes ago?"

"Grandmother, you know that I do not answer such questions."

How often in years gone by such had been Isabel's answer! The grandmother awaited it now. To her surprise Isabel after some moments of hesitation replied without resentment:

"I did not wish to see him."

There was a momentary pause; then this unexpected weakness was met with a blow.

"You were eager enough to see him last night."

"I can only hope," murmured Isabel aloud though wholly to herself, "that I did not make this plain to him."

"But what has happened since?"

Nothing was said for a while. The two women had been unable to see each other clearly. A moment later Isabel crossed the room quickly and taking the chair in front of her grandmother, searched that treacherous face imploringly for something better in it than she had ever seen there. Could she trust the untrustworthy? Would falseness itself for once be true?

"Grandmother," she said, and her voice betrayed how she shrank from her own words, "before you sent for me I was about to come down. I wished to speak with you about a very delicate matter, a very serious matter. You have often reproached me for not taking you into my confidence. I am going to give you my confidence now."

At any other moment the distrust and indignity contained in the tone of this avowal would not have escaped Mrs. Conyers. But surprise riveted her attention. Isabel gave her no time further:

"A thing has occurred in regard to which we must act together for our own sakes—on account of the servants in the house—on account of our friends, so that there may be no gossip, no scandal."

Nothing at times so startles us as our own words. As the girl uttered the word "scandal," she rose frightened as though it faced her and began to walk excitedly backward and forward. Scandal had never touched her life. She had never talked scandal; had never thought scandal. Dwelling under the same roof with it as the master passion of a life and forced to encounter it in so many repulsive ways, she had needed little virtue to regard it with abhorrence.

Now she perceived that it might be perilously near herself. When all questions were asked and no reasons were given, would not the seeds of gossip fly and sprout and bear their kinds about her path: and the truth could never be told. She must walk on through the years, possibly misjudged, giving no sign.

After a while she returned to her seat.

"You must promise me one thing," she said with white and trembling lips. "I give you my confidence as far as I can; beyond that I will not go. And you shall not ask. You are not to try to find out from me or any one else more than I tell you. You must give me your word of honor!"

She bent forward and looked her grandmother wretchedly in the eyes.

Mrs. Conyers pushed her chair back as though a hand had struck her rudely in the face.

27

"Isabel," she cried, "do you forget to whom you are speaking?"

"Ah, grandmother," exclaimed Isabel, reckless of her words by reason of suffering, "it is too late for us to be sensitive about our characters."

Mrs. Conyers rose with insulted pride: "Do not come to me with your confidence until you can give it."

Isabel recrossed the room and sank into the seat she had quitted. Mrs. Conyers remained standing a moment and furtively resumed hers.

Whatever her failings had been—one might well say her crimes—Isabel had always treated her from the level of her own high nature. But Mrs. Conyers had accepted this dutiful demeanor of the years as a tribute to her own virtues. Now that Isabel, the one person whose respect she most desired, had openly avowed deep distrust of her, the shock was as real as anything life could have dealt.

She glanced narrowly at Isabel: the girl had forgotten her.

Mrs. Conyers could shift as the wind shifts; and one of her characteristic resources in life had been to conquer by feigning defeat: she often scaled her mountains by seeming to take a path which led to the valleys. She now crossed over and sat down with a peace-making laugh. She attempted to take Isabel's hand, but it was quickly withdrawn. Fearing that this movement indicated a receding confidence Mrs. Conyers ignored the rebuff and pressed her inquiry in a new, entirely practical, and pleasant tone:

"What is the meaning of all this, Isabel?"

Isabel turned upon her again a silent, searching, wretched look of appeal.

Mrs. Conyers realized that it could not be ignored: "You know that I promise anything. What did I ever refuse you?"

Isabel sat up but still remained silent. Mrs. Conyers noted the indecision and shrugged her shoulders with a careless dismissal of the whole subject:

"Let us drop the subject, then. Do you think it will rain?"

"Grandmother, Rowan must not come here any more." Isabel stopped abruptly. "That is all."

... "I merely wanted you to understand this at once. We must not invite him here any more."

... "If we meet him at the houses of our friends, we must do what we can not to be discourteous to them if he is their guest."

... "If we meet Rowan alone anywhere, we must let him know that he is not

28

on the list of our acquaintances any longer. That is all."

Isabel wrung her hands.

Mrs. Conyers had more than one of the traits of the jungle: she knew when to lie silent and how to wait. She waited longer now, but Isabel had relapsed into her own thoughts. For her the interview was at an end; to Mrs. Conyers it was beginning. Isabel's words and manner had revealed a situation far more serious than she had believed to exist. A sense of personal slights and wounds gave way to apprehension. The need of the moment was not passion and resentment, but tact and coolness and apparent unconcern.

"What is the meaning of this, Isabel?" She spoke in a tone of frank and cordial interest as though the way were clear at last for the establishment of complete confidence between them.

"Grandmother, did you not give me your word?" said Isabel, sternly. Mrs. Conyers grew indignant: "But remember in what a light you place me! I did not expect you to require me to be unreasonable and unjust. Do you really wish me to be kept in the dark in a matter like this? Must I refuse to speak to Rowan and have no reason? Close the house to him and not know why? Cut him in public without his having offended me? If he should ask why I treat him in this way, what am I to tell him?"

"He will never ask," said Isabel with mournful abstraction.

"But tell *me* why you wish me to act so strangely."

"Believe that I have reasons."

"But ought I not to know what these reasons are if I must act upon them as though they were my own?"

Isabel saw the stirrings of a mind that brushed away honor as an obstacle and that was not to be quieted until it had been satisfied. She sank back into her chair, saying very simply with deep disappointment and with deeper sorrow:

"Ah, I might have known!"

Mrs. Conyers pressed forward with gathering determination:

"What happened last night?"

"I might have known that it was of no use," repeated Isabel.

Mrs. Conyers waited several moments and then suddenly changing her course feigned the dismissal of the whole subject: "I shall pay no attention to this. I shall continue to treat Rowan as I have always treated him."

Isabel started up: "Grandmother, if you do, you will regret it." Her voice rang clear with hidden meaning and with hidden warning.

It fell upon the ear of the other with threatening import. For her there seemed to be in it indeed the ruin of a cherished plan, the loss of years of hope and waiting. Before such a possibility tact and coolness and apparent unconcern were swept away by passion, brutal and unreckoning: "Do you mean that you have refused Rowan? Or have you found out at last that he has no intention of marrying you—has never had any?"

Isabel rose: "Excuse me," she said proudly and turned away. She reached the door and pausing there put out one of her hands against the lintel as if with weakness and raised the other to her forehead as though with bewilderment and indecision.

Then she came unsteadily back, sank upon her knees, and hid her face in her grandmother's lap, murmuring through her fingers: "I have been rude to you, grandmother! Forgive me! I do not know what I have been saying. But any little trouble between us is nothing, nothing! And do as I beg you—let this be sacred and secret! And leave everything to me!"

She crept closer and lifting her face looked up into her grandmother's. She shrank back shuddering from what she saw there, burying her face in her hands; then rising she hurried from the room,

Mrs. Conyers sat motionless.

Was it true then that the desire and the work of years for this marriage had come to nothing? And was it true that this grandchild, for whom she had planned and plotted, did not even respect her and could tell her so to her face?

Those insulting words rang in her ears still: "*You must give me your word of honor ... it is too late to be sensitive about our characters.*"

She sat perfectly still: and in the parlors there might have been heard at intervals the scratching of her sharp finger nails against the wood of the chair.

IV

The hot day ended. Toward sunset a thunder-shower drenched the earth, and the night had begun cool and refreshing.

Mrs. Conyers was sitting on the front veranda, waiting for her regular Sunday evening visitor. She was no longer the self-revealed woman of the afternoon, but seemingly an affable, harmless old lady of the night on the boundary of her social world. She was dressed with unfailing: elegance—and her taste lavished itself especially on black silk and the richest lace. The shade of heliotrope satin harmonized with the yellowish folds of her hair. Her small, warm, unwrinkled hands were without rings, being too delicately beautiful. In one she held a tiny fan, white and soft like the wing of a moth; on her lap lay a handkerchief as light as smoke or a web of gossamer.

She rocked softly. She unfolded and folded the night-moth fan softly. She touched the handkerchief to her rosy youthful lips softly. The south wind blew in her face softly. Everything about her was softness, all her movements were delicate and refined. Even the early soft beauty of her figure was not yet lost. (When a girl of nineteen, she had measured herself by the proportions of the ideal Venus; and the ordeal had left her with a girdle of golden reflections.)

But if some limner had been told the whole truth of what she was and been requested to imagine a fitting body for such a soul, he would never have painted Mrs. Conyers as she looked. Nature is not frank in her characterizations, lest we remain infants in discernment. She allows foul to appear fair, and bids us become educated in the hardy virtues of insight and prudence. Education as yet had advanced but little; and the deepest students in the botany of women have been able to describe so few kinds that no man, walking through the perfumed enchanted wood, knows at what moment he may step upon or take hold of some unknown deadly variety.

As the moments passed, she stopped rocking and peered toward the front gate under the lamp-post, saying to herself:

"He is late."

At last the gate was gently opened and gently shut.

"Ah," she cried, leaning back in her chair smiling and satisfied. Then she sat up rigid. A change passed over her such as comes over a bird of prey when it draws its feathers in flat against its body to lessen friction in the swoop. She unconsciously closed the little fan, the little handkerchief disappeared somewhere.

As the gate had opened and closed, on the bricks of the pavement was heard only the tap of his stout walking-stick; for he was gouty and wore loose low shoes of the softest calfskin, and these made no noise except the slurring sound of slippers.

Once he stopped, and planting his cane far out in the grass, reached stiffly over and with undisguised ejaculations of discomfort snipped off a piece of heliotrope in one of the tubs of oleander. He shook away the raindrops and drew it through his buttonhole, and she could hear his low "Ah! ah! ah!" as he thrust his nose down into it.

"There's nothing like it," he said aloud as though he had consenting listeners, "it outsmells creation."

He stopped at another tub of flowers where a humming-bird moth was gathering honey and jabbed his stick sharply at it, taking care that the stick did not reach perilously near.

"Get away, sir," he said; "you've had enough, sir. Get away, sir."

Having reached a gravel walk that diverged from the pavement, he turned off and went over to a rose-bush and walked around tapping the roses on their heads as he counted them—cloth-of-gold roses. "Very well done," he said, "a large family—a good sign."

Thus he loitered along his way with leisure to enjoy all the chance trifles that gladdened it; for he was one of the old who return at the end of life to the simple innocent things that pleased them as children.

She had risen and advanced to the edge of the veranda.

"Did you come to see me or did you come to see my flowers?" she called out charmingly.

"I came to see the flowers, madam," he called back. "Most of all, the century plant: how is she?"

She laughed delightedly: "Still harping on my age, I see."

"Still harping, but harping your praises. Century plants are not necessarily old: they are all young at the beginning! I merely meant you'd be blooming at a hundred."

"You are a sly old fox," she retorted with a spirit. "You give a woman a dig on her age and then try to make her think it a compliment."

"I gave myself a dig that time: the remark had to be excavated," he said aloud but as though confidentially to himself. Open disrespect marked his speech and manner with her always; and sooner or later she exacted full punishment.

Meantime he had reached the steps. There he stopped and taking off his straw hat looked up and shook it reproachfully at the heavens.

"What a night, what a night!" he exclaimed. "And what an injustice to a man wading up to his knees in life's winters."

"How do you do," she said impatiently, always finding it hard to put up with his lingerings and delays. "Are you coming in?"

"Thank you, I believe I am. But no, wait. I'll not come in until I have made a speech. It never occurred to me before and it will never again. It's now or never.

"The life of man should last a single year. He should have one spring for birth and childhood, for play and growth, for the ending of his dreams and the beginning of his love. One summer for strife and toil and passion. One autumn in which to gather the fruits of his deeds and to live upon them, be they sweet or bitter. One winter in which to come to an end and wrap himself with resignation in the snows of nature. Thus he should never know the pain of seeing spring return when there was nothing within himself to bud or be sown. Summer would never rage and he have no conflicts nor passions. Autumn would not pass and he with idle hands neither give nor gather. And winter should not end without extinguishing his tormenting fires, and leaving him the peace of eternal cold."

"Really," she cried, "I have never heard anything as fine as that since I used to write compositions at boarding-school."

"It may be part of one of mine!" he replied. "We forget ourselves, you know, and then we think we are original."

"Second childhood," she suggested. "Are you really coming in?"

"I am, madam," he replied. "And guided by your suggestion, I come as a second child."

When he had reached the top step, he laid his hat and cane on the porch and took her hands in his—pressing them abstemiously.

"Excuse me if I do not press harder," he said, lowering his voice as though he fancied they might be overheard. "I know you are sensitive in these little matters; but while I dislike to appear lukewarm, really, you know it is too late to be ardent," and he looked at her ardently.

She twisted her fingers out of his with coy shame.

"What an old fox," she repeated gayly.

"Well, you know what goes with the fox—the foxess, or the foxina."

She had placed his chair not quite beside hers yet designedly near, where the light of the chandelier in the hall would fall out upon him and passers could see that he was there: she liked to have him appear devoted. For his part he was too little devoted to care whether he sat far or near, in front or behind. As the light streamed out upon him, it illumined his noble head of soft, silvery hair, which fell over his ears and forehead, forgotten and disordered, like a romping boy's. His complexion was ruddy—too ruddy with high living; his clean-shaven face beautiful with candor, gayety, and sweetness; and his eyes, the eyes of a kind heart—saddened. He had on a big loose shirt collar such as men wore in Thackeray's time and a snow-white lawn tie. In the bosom of his broad-pleated shirt, made glossy with paraffin starch, there was set an old-fashioned cluster-diamond stud—so enormous that it looked like a large family of young diamonds in a golden nest.

As he took his seat, he planted his big gold-headed ebony cane between his knees, put his hat on the head of his cane, gave it a twirl, and looking over sidewise at her, smiled with an equal mixture of real liking and settled abhorrence.

For a good many years these two had been—not friends: she was incapable of so true a passion; he was too capable to misapply it so unerringly. Their association had assumed the character of one of those belated intimacies, which sometimes spring up in the lives of aged men and women when each wants companionship but has been left companionless.

Time was when he could not have believed that any tie whatsoever would ever exist between them. Her first husband had been his first law partner; and from what he had been forced to observe concerning his partner's fireside wretchedness during his few years of married life, he had learned to fear and to hate her. With his quick temper and honest way he made no pretence of hiding his feeling—declined her invitations—cut her openly in society—and said why. When his partner died, not killed indeed but broken-spirited, he spoke his mind on the subject more publicly and plainly still.

She brewed the poison of revenge and waited.

A year or two later when his engagement was announced her opportunity came. In a single day it was done—so quietly, so perfectly, that no one knew by whom. Scandal was set running—Scandal, which no pursuing messengers of truth and justice can ever overtake and drag backward along its path. His engagement was broken; she whom he was to wed in time married one of his friends; and for years his own life all but went to pieces.

Time is naught, existence a span. One evening when she was old Mrs. Conyers, and he old Judge Morris, she sixty and he sixty-five, they met at an evening party. In all those years he had never spoken to her, nurturing his original dislike and rather suspecting that it was she who had so ruined him. But on this night there had been a great supper and with him a great supper was a great weakness: there had been wine, and wine was not a weakness at all, but a glass merely made him more than happy, more than kind. Soon after supper therefore he was strolling through the emptied rooms in a rather lonesome way, his face like a red moon in a fog, beseeching only that it might shed its rays impartially on any approachable darkness.

Men with wives and children can well afford to turn hard cold faces to the outside world: the warmth and tenderness of which they are capable they can exercise within their own restricted enclosures. No doubt some of them consciously enjoy the contrast in their two selves—the one as seen abroad and the other as understood at home. But a wifeless, childless man—wandering at large on the heart's bleak common—has much the same reason to smile on all that he has to smile on any: there is no domestic enclosure for him: his affections must embrace humanity.

As he strolled through the rooms, then, in his appealing way, seeking whom he could attach himself to, he came upon her seated in a doorway connecting two rooms. She sat alone on a short sofa, possibly by design, her train so arranged that he must step over it if he advanced—the only being in the world that he hated. In the embarrassment of turning his back upon her or of trampling her train, he hesitated; smiling with lowered eyelids she motioned him to a seat by her side.

"What a vivacious, agreeable old woman," he soliloquized with enthusiasm as he was driven home that night, sitting in the middle of the carriage cushions with one arm swung impartially through the strap on each side. "And she has invited me to Sunday evening supper. Me!—after all these years—in that house! I'll not go."

But he went.

"I'll not go again," he declared as he reached home that night and thought it over. "She is a bad woman."

But the following Sunday evening he reached for his hat and cane: "I must go somewhere," he complained resentfully. "The saints of my generation are enjoying the saint's rest. Nobody is left but a few long-lived sinners, of whom I am a great part. They are the best I can find, and I suppose they are the best I deserve."

Those who live long miss many. Without exception his former associates at the bar had been summoned to appear before the Judge who accepts no bribe.

The ablest of the middle-aged lawyers often hurried over to consult him in difficult cases. All of them could occasionally listen while he, praiser of a bygone time, recalled the great period of practice when he was the favorite criminal lawyer of the first families, defending their sons against the commonwealth which he always insisted was the greater criminal. The young men about town knew him and were ready to chat with him on street corners —but never very long at a time. In his old law offices he could spend part of every day, guiding or guying his nephew Barbee, who had just begun to practice. But when all his social resources were reckoned, his days contained great voids and his nights were lonelier still. The society of women remained a necessity of his life; and the only woman in town, always bright, always full of ideas, and always glad to see him (the main difficulty) was Mrs. Conyers.

So that for years now he had been going regularly on Sunday evenings. He kept up apologies to his conscience regularly also; but it must have become clear that his conscience was not a fire to make him boil; it was merely a few coals to keep him bubbling.

In this acceptance of her at the end of life there was of course mournful evidence of his own deterioration. During the years between being a young man and being an old one he had so far descended toward her level, that upon renewing acquaintance with her he actually thought that she had improved.

Youth with its white-flaming ideals is the great separator; by middle age most of us have become so shaken down, on life's rough road, to a certain equality of bearing and forbearing, that miscellaneous comradeship becomes easy and rather comforting; while extremely aged people are as compatible and as miserable as disabled old eagles, grouped with a few inches of each other's beaks and claws on the sleek perches of a cage.

This evening therefore, as he took his seat and looked across at her, so richly dressed, so youthful, soft, and rosy, he all but thanked heaven out loud that she was at home.

"Madam," he cried, "you are a wonderful and bewitching old lady"—it was on the tip of his tongue to say "beldam."

"I know it," she replied briskly, "have you been so long in finding it out?"

"It is a fresh discovery every time I come."

"Then you forget me in the meanwhile."

"I never forget you unless I am thinking of Miss Isabel. How is she?"

"Not well."

"Then I'm not well! No one is well! Everybody must suffer if she is suffering.

The universe sympathizes."

"She is not ill. She is in trouble."

"But she must not be in trouble! She has done nothing to be in trouble about. Who troubles her? What troubles her?"

"She will not tell."

"Ah!" he cried, checking himself gravely and dropping the subject.

She noted the decisive change of tone: it was not by this direct route that she would be able to enter his confidence.

"What did you think of the sermon this morning?"

"The sermon on the prodigal? Well, it is too late for such sermons to be levelled at me; and I never listen to those aimed at other people."

"At what other people do you suppose this one could have been directed?" She asked the question most carelessly, lifting her imponderable handkerchief and letting it drop into her lap as a sign of how little her interest weighed.

"It is not my duty to judge."

"We cannot help our thoughts, you know."

"I think we can, madam; and I also think we can hold our tongues," and he laughed at her very good-naturedly. "Sometimes we can even help to hold other people's—if they are long."

"Oh, what a rude speech to a lady!" she exclaimed gallantly. "Did you see the Osborns at church? And did you notice him? What an unhappy marriage! He is breaking Kate's heart. And to think that his character—or the lack of it— should have been discovered only when it was too late! How can you men so cloak yourselves before marriage? Why not tell women the truth then instead of leaving them to find it out afterward? Are he and Rowan as good friends as ever?" The question was asked with the air of guilelessness.

"I know nothing about that," he replied dryly. "I never knew Rowan to drop his friends because they had failings: it would break up all friendships, I imagine."

"Well, I cannot help *my* thoughts, and I think George Osborn was the prodigal aimed at in the sermon. Everybody thought so."

"How does she know what everybody thought?" commented the Judge to himself. He tapped the porch nervously with his cane, sniffed his heliotrope and said irrelevantly:

"Ah me, what a beautiful night! What a beautiful night!"

The implied rebuff provoked her. Irritation winged a venomous little shaft:

"At least no woman has ever held *you* responsible for her unhappiness."

"You are quite right, madam," he replied, "the only irreproachable husband in this world is the man who has no wife."

"By the way," she continued, "in all these years you have not told me why you never married. Come now, confess!"

How well she knew! How often as she had driven through the streets and observed him sitting alone in the door of his office or walking aimlessly about, she had leaned back and laughed.

"Madam," he replied, for he did not like the question, "neither have you ever told me why you married three times. Come now, confess."

It would soon be time for him to leave; and still she had not gained her point.

"Rowan was here this afternoon," she remarked carelessly. He was sitting so that the light fell sidewise on his face. She noted how alert it became, but he said nothing.

"Isabel refused to see him."

He wheeled round and faced her with pain and surprise.

"Refused to see him!"

"She has told me since that she never intends to see him."

"Never intends to see Rowan again!" he repeated the incredible words, "not see Rowan again!"

"She says we are to drop him from the list of our acquaintances."

"Ah!" he cried with impetuous sadness, "they must not quarrel! They *must* not!"

"But they *have* quarrelled," she replied, revealing her own anxiety. "Now they must be reconciled. That is why I come to you. I am Isabel's guardian; you were Rowan's. Each of us wishes this marriage. Isabel loves Rowan. I know that; therefore it is not her fault. Therefore it is Rowan's fault. Therefore he has said something or he has done something to offend her deeply. Therefore if you do not know what this Is, you must find out. And you must come and tell me. May I depend upon you?"

He had become grave. At length he said: "I shall go straight to Rowan and ask him."

"No!" she cried, laying her hand heavily on his arm, "Isabel bound me to secrecy. She does not wish this to be known."

"Ah!" he exclaimed, angry at being entrapped into a broken confidence, "then Miss Isabel binds me also: I shall honor her wish," and he rose.

She kept her seat but yawned so that he might notice it. "You are not going?"

"Yes, I am going. I have stayed too long already. Good night! Good night!" He spoke curtly over his shoulders as he hurried down the steps.

She had forgotten him before he reached the street, having no need just then to keep him longer in mind. She had threshed out the one grain of wheat, the single compact little truth, that she wanted. This was the certainty that Judge Morris, who was the old family lawyer of the Merediths, and had been Rowan's guardian, and had indeed known him intimately from childhood, was in ignorance of any reason for the present trouble; otherwise he would not have said that he should go to Rowan and ask the explanation. She knew him to be incapable of duplicity; in truth she rather despised him because he had never cultivated a taste for the delights and resources of hypocrisy.

Her next step must be to talk at once with the other person vitally interested— Rowan's mother. She felt no especial admiration for that grave, earnest, and rather sombre lady; but neither did she feel admiration for her sterling knife and fork: still she made them serviceable for the ulterior ends of being.

Her plan then embraced a visit to Mrs. Meredith in the morning with the view of discovering whether she was aware of the estrangement, and if aware whether she would in any unintentional way throw light upon the cause of it. Moreover—and this was kept clearly in view—there would be the chance of meeting Rowan himself, whom she also determined to see as soon as possible: she might find him at home, or she might encounter him on the road or riding over his farm. But this visit must be made without Isabel's knowledge. It must further be made to appear incidental to Mrs. Meredith herself—or to Rowan. She arranged therefore with that tortuous and superfluous calculation of which hypocrisy is such a master—and mistress— that she would at breakfast, in Isabel's presence, order the carriage, and announce her intention of going out to the farm of Ambrose Webb. Ambrose Webb was a close neighbor of the Merediths. He owned a small estate, most of which was good grass-land that was usually rented for pasture. She had for years kept her cows there when dry. This arrangement furnished her the opportunity for more trips to the farm than interest in her dairy warranted; it made her Mrs. Meredith's most frequent incidental visitor.

Having thus determined upon her immediate course for the prompt unravelling of this mysterious matter, she dismissed it from her mind, passed into her bedroom and was soon asleep: a smile played over the sweet old face.

The Judge walked slowly across the town in the moonlight.

It was his rule to get home to his rooms by ten o'clock; and people living on the several streets leading that way were used to hearing him come tapping along before that hour. If they sat in their doorways and the night was dark, they gave him a pleasant greeting through the darkness; if there was a moon or if he could be seen under a lamp post, they added smiles. No one loved him supremely, but every one liked him a little—on the whole, a stable state for a man. For his part he accosted every one that he could see in a bright cheery way and with a quick inquiring glance as though every heart had its trouble and needed just a little kindness. He was reasonably sure that the old had their troubles already and that the children would have theirs some day; so that it was merely the difference between sympathizing with the present and sympathizing with the future. As he careened along night after night, then, friendly little gusts of salutation blew the desolate drifting figure over the homeward course.

His rooms were near the heart of the town, In a shady street well filled with law offices: these were of red brick with green shutters—green when not white with dust. The fire department was in the same block, though he himself did not need to be safeguarded from conflagrations: the fires which had always troubled him could not have been reached with ladder and hose. There were two or three livery stables also, the chairs of which he patronized liberally, but not the vehicles. And there was a grocery, where he sometimes bought crystallized citron and Brazil nuts, a curious kind of condiment of his own devising: a pound of citron to a pound of nuts, if all were sound. He used to keep little brown paper bags of these locked in his drawer with legal papers and munched them sometimes while preparing murder cases.

At the upper corner of the block, opposite each other, were a saloon and the jail, two establishments which contributed little to each other's support, though well inclined to do so. The law offices seemed of old to have started in a compact procession for the jail, but at a certain point to have paused with the understanding that none should seek undue advantage by greater proximity. Issuing from this street at one end and turning to the left, you came to the courthouse—the bar of chancery; issuing from it at the other end and turning to the right, you came to the hotel—the bar of corn. The lawyers were usually solicitors at large and impartial practitioners at each bar. In the court room they sometimes tried to prove an alibi for their clients; at the hotel they often succeeded in proving one for themselves.

These law offices were raised a foot or two above the level of the street. The front rooms could be used for clients who were so important that they should be seen; the back rooms were for such as brought business, but not necessarily fame. Driving through this street, the wives of the lawyers could lean forward in their carriages and if their husbands were busy, they could smile and bow; if their husbands were idle, they could look straight ahead.

He passed under the shadow of the old court-house where in his prime he had fought his legal battles against the commonwealth. He had been a great lawyer and he knew it (if he had married he might have been Chief Justice). Then he turned the corner and entered the street of jurisprudence and the gaol. About midway he reached the staircase opening from the sidewalk; to his rooms above.

He was not poor and he could have lived richly had he wished. But when a man does not marry there are so many other things that he never espouses; and he was not wedded to luxury. As he lighted the chandelier over the centre-table in his sitting room, the light revealed an establishment every article of which, if it had no virtues, at least possessed habits: certainly everything had its own way. He put his hat and cane on the table, not caring to go back to the hatrack in his little hall, and seated himself in his olive morocco chair. As he did so, everything in the room—the chairs, the curtains, the rugs, the card-table, the punch-bowl, the other walking-sticks, and the rubbers and umbrellas—seemed to say in an affectionate chorus: "Well, now that you are in safe for the night, we feel relieved. So good night and pleasant dreams to you, for we are going to sleep;" and to sleep they went.

The gas alone flared up and said, "I'll stay up with him."

He drew out and wiped his glasses and reached for the local Sunday paper, his Sunday evening Bible. He had read it in the morning, but he always gleaned at night: he met so many of his friends by reading their advertisements. But to-night he spread it across his knees and turning to the table lifted the top of a box of cigars, an orderly responsive family; the paper slipped to the floor and lay forgotten behind his heels.

He leaned back in the chair with his cigar in his mouth and his eyes directed toward the opposite wall, where in an oval frame hung the life-size portrait of an old bulldog. The eyes were blue and watery and as full of suffering as a seats; from the extremity of the lower jaw a tooth stood up like a shoemaker's peg; and over the entire face was stamped the majesty, the patience, and the manly woes of a nature that had lived deeply and too long. The Judge's eyes rested on this comrade face.

The events of the day had left him troubled. Any sermon on the prodigal always touches men; even if it does not prick their memories, it can always stir their imaginations. Whenever he heard one, his mind went back to the years when she who afterwards became Rowan's mother had cast him off, so settling life for him. For after that experience he had put away the thought of marriage. "To be so treated once is enough," he had said sternly and proudly. True, in after years she had come back to him as far as friendship could bring her back, since she was then the wife of another; but every year of knowing her thus had only served to deepen the sense of his loss. He had long since fallen into the habit of thinking this over of Sunday evenings before going to bed, and as the end of life closed in upon him, he dwelt upon it more and more.

These familiar thoughts swarmed back to-night, but with them were mingled new depressing ones. Nothing now perhaps could have caused him such distress as the thought that Rowan and Isabel would never marry. All the love that he had any right to pour into any life, he had always poured with passionate and useless yearnings into Rowan's—son, of the only woman he had ever loved—the boy that should have been his own.

There came an interruption. A light quick step was heard mounting the stairs. A latch key was impatiently inserted in the hall door. A bamboo cane was dropped loudly into the holder of the hat-rack; a soft hat was thrown down carelessly somewhere—it sounded like a wet mop flung into a corner; and there entered a young man straight, slender, keen-faced, with red hair, a freckled skin, large thin red ears, and a strong red mouth. As he stepped forward into the light, he paused, parting the haircut of his eyes and blinking.

"Good evening, uncle," he said in a shrill key.

"Well, sir."

Barbee looked the Judge carefully over; he took the Judge's hat and cane from the table and hung them in the hall; he walked over and picked up the newspaper from between the Judge's legs and placed it at his elbow; he set the ash tray near the edge of the table within easy reach of the cigar. Then he threw himself into a chair across the room, lighted a cigarette, blew the smoke toward the ceiling like the steam of a little whistle signalling to stop work.

"Well, uncle," he said in a tone in which a lawyer might announce to his partner the settlement of a long-disputed point, "Marguerite is in love with me!"

The Judge smoked on, his eyes resting on the wall.

"Yes, sir; in love with me. The truth had to come out sometime, and it came out to-night. And now the joy of life is gone for me! As soon as a woman falls in love with a man, his peace is at an end. But I am determined that it shall not interfere with my practice."

"What practice?"

"The practice of my profession, sir! The profession of yourself and of the great men of the past: such places have to be filled."

"Filled, but not filled with the same thing."

"You should have seen the other hapless wretches there to-night! Pining for a smile! Moths begging the candle to scorch them! And the candle was as cold as the north star and as distant."

Barbee rose and took a turn across the room and returning to his chair stood before it.

"If Marguerite had only waited, had concealed herself a little longer! Why did she not keep me in doubt until I had won some great case! Think of a scene like this: a crowded court room some afternoon; people outside the doors and windows craning their necks to see and hear me; the judge nervous and excited; the members of the bar beside themselves with jealousy as I arise and confront the criminal and jury. Marguerite is seated just behind the jury; I know why she chose that seat: she wished to study me to the best advantage. I try to catch her eye; she will not look at me. For three hours my eloquence storms. The judge acknowledges to a tear, the jurors reach for their handkerchiefs, the people in the court room sob like the skies of autumn. As I finish, the accused arises and addresses the court: 'May it please your honor, in the face of such a masterly prosecution, I can no longer pretend to be innocent. Sir (addressing me), I congratulate you upon your magnificent service to the commonwealth. Gentlemen of the jury, you need not retire to bring in any verdict: I bring it in myself, I am guilty, and my only wish is to be hanged. I suggest that you have it done at once in order that nothing may mar the success of this occasion!' That night Marguerite sends for me: that would have been the time for declaration! I have a notion that if I can extricate myself without wounding this poor little innocent, to forswear matrimony and march on to fame."

"March on to bed."

"Marguerite is going to give a ball, uncle, a brilliant ball merely to celebrate this irrepressible efflux and panorama of her emotions. Watch me at that ball, uncle! Mark the rising Romeo of the firm when Marguerite, the youthful Juliet of this town—"

A hand waved him quietly toward his bedroom.

"Well, good night, sir, good night. When the lark sings at heaven's gate I'll greet thee, uncle. My poor Marguerite!—Good night, uncle, good night."

He was only nineteen.

The Judge returned to his thoughts.

He must have thought a long time: the clock not far away struck twelve. He took off his glasses, putting them negligently on the edge of the ash tray which tipped over beneath their weight and fell to the floor: he picked up his glasses, but let the ashes lie. Then he stooped down to take off his shoes, not without sounds of bodily discomfort.

Aroused by these sounds or for other reasons not to be discovered, there emerged from under a table on which was piled "The Lives of the Chief Justices" a bulldog, cylindrical and rigid with years. Having reached a decorous position before the Judge, by the slow action of the necessary machinery he lowered the posterior end of the cylinder to the floor and watched him.

"Well, did I get them off about right?"

The dog with a private glance of sympathy up into the Judge's face returned to his black goatskin rug under the Chief Justices; and the Judge, turning off the burners in the chandelier and striking a match, groped his way in his sock feet to his bedroom—to the bed with its one pillow.

V

Out in the country next morning it was not yet break of dawn. The stars, thickly flung about, were flashing low and yellow as at midnight, but on the horizon the great change had begun. Not with colors of rose or pearl but as the mysterious foreknowledge of the morning, when a vast swift herald rushes up from the east and sweeps onward across high space, bidding the earth be in readiness for the drama of the sun.

The land, heavy with life, lay wrapped in silence, steeped in rest. Not a bird in wet hedge or evergreen had drawn nimble head from nimble wing. In meadow and pasture fold and herd had sunk down satisfied. A black brook brawling through a distant wood sounded loud in the stillness. Under the forest trees around the home of the Merediths only drops of dew might have been heard splashing downward from leaf to leaf. In the house all slept. The mind, wakefullest of happy or of suffering things, had lost consciousness of joy and care save as these had been crowded down into the chamber which lies beneath our sleep, whence they made themselves audible through the thin flooring as the noise of dreams.

Among the parts of the day during which man may match the elements of the world within him to the world without—his songs with its sunrises, toil with noontide, prayer with nightfall, slumber with dark—there is one to stir within him the greatest sense of responsibility: the hour of dawn.

If he awaken then and be alone, he is earliest to enter the silent empty theatre of the earth where the human drama is soon to recommence. Not a mummer has stalked forth; not an auditor sits waiting. He himself, as one of the characters in this ancient miracle play of nature, pauses at the point of separation between all that he has enacted and all that he will enact. Yesterday he was in the thick of action. Between then and now lies the night, stretching like a bar of verdure across wearying sands. In that verdure he has rested; he has drunk forgetfulness and self-renewal from those deep wells of sleep. Soon the play will be ordered on again and he must take his place for parts that are new and confusing to all. The servitors of the morning have entered and hung wall and ceiling with gorgeous draperies; the dust has been sprinkled; fresh airs are blowing; and there is music, the living orchestra of the living earth. Well for the waker then if he can look back upon the role he has played with a quiet conscience, and as naturally as the earth greets the sun step forth upon the stage to continue or to end his brief part in the long drama of destiny.

The horizon had hardly begun to turn red when a young man, stretched on his bed by an open window, awoke from troubled sleep. He lay for a few moments without moving, then he sat up on the edge of the bed. His hands rested listlessly on his kneecaps and his eyes were fixed on the sky-line crimsoning above his distant woods.

After a while he went over and sat at one of the windows, his eyes still fixed on the path of the coming sun; and a great tragedy of men sat there within him: the tragedy that has wandered long and that wanders ever, showing its face in all lands, retaining its youth in all ages; the tragedy of love that heeds not law, and the tragedy of law forever punishing heedless love.

Gradually the sounds of life began. From the shrubs under his window, from the orchard and the wet weeds of fence corners, the birds reentered upon their lives. Far off in the meadows the cattle rose from their warm dry places, stretched themselves and awoke the echoes of the wide rolling land with peaceful lowing. A brood mare in a grazing lot sent forth her quick nostril call to the foal capering too wildly about her, and nozzled it with rebuking affection. On the rosy hillsides white lambs were leaping and bleating, or running down out of sight under the white sea-fog of the valleys. A milk cart rattled along the turnpike toward the town.

It had become broad day.

He started up and crossed the hall to the bedroom opposite, and stood looking down at his younger brother. How quiet Dent's sleep was; how clear the current of his life had run and would run always! No tragedy would ever separate him and the woman he loved.

When he went downstairs the perfect orderliness of his mother's housekeeping had been before him. Doors and windows had been opened to the morning freshness, sweeping and dusting had been done, not a servant was in sight. His setters lay waiting on the porch and as he stepped out they hurried up with glistening eyes and soft barkings and followed him as he passed around to the barn. Work was in progress there: the play of currycombs, the whirl of the cutting-box, the noise of the mangers, the bellowing of calves, the rich streamy sounds of the milking. He called his men to him one after another, laying out the work of the day.

When he returned to the house he saw his mother walking on the front pavement; she held flowers freshly plucked for the breakfast table: a woman of large mould, grave, proud, noble; an ideal of her place and time.

"Is the lord of the manor ready for his breakfast?" she asked as she came forward, smiling.

"I am ready, mother," he replied without smiling, touching his lips to her cheek.

She linked her arm in his as they ascended the steps. At the top she drew him gently around until they faced the landscape rolling wide before them.

"It is so beautiful!" she exclaimed with a deep narrow love of her land. "I never see it without thinking of it as it will be years hence. I can see you riding over it then and your children playing around the house and some one sitting here where we stand, watching them at their play and watching you in the distance at your work. But I have been waiting a long time for her to take my place—and to take her own," and she leaned heavily on his arm as a sign of her dependence but out of weakness also (for she did not tell him all). "I am impatient to hear the voice of your children, Rowan. Do you never wish to hear them yourself?"

As they stood silent, footsteps approached through the hall and turning they saw Dent with a book in his hand.

"Are you grand people never coming to breakfast?" he asked, frowning with pretended impatience, "so that a laboring man may go to his work?"

He was of short but well-knit figure. Spectacles and a thoughtful face of great refinement gave him the student's stamp. His undergraduate course at college would end in a few weeks. Postgraduate work was to begin during the summer. An assistant professorship, then a full professorship—these were successive stations already marked by him on the clear track of life; and he was now moving toward them with straight and steady aim. Sometimes we encounter personalities which seem to move through the discords of this life as though guided by laws of harmony; they know neither outward check nor inward swerving, and are endowed with that peaceful passion for toil which does the world's work and is one of the marks of genius.

He was one of these—a growth of the new time not comprehended by his mother. She could neither understand it nor him. The pain which this had given him at first he had soon outgrown; and what might have been a tragedy to another nature melted away in the steady sunlight of his entire reasonableness. Perhaps he realized that the scientific son can never be the idol of a household until he is born of scientific parents.

As mother and elder son now turned to greet him, the mother was not herself aware that she still leaned upon the arm of Rowan and that Dent walked into the breakfast room alone.

Less than usual was said during the meal. They were a reserved household, inclined to the small nobilities of silence. (It is questionable whether talkative families ever have much to say.) This morning each had especial reason for self-communing.

When they had finished breakfast and came out into the hall. Dent paused at one of the parlor doors.

"Mother" he said simply, "come into the parlor a moment, will you? And Rowan, I should like to see you also."

They followed him with surprise and all seated themselves.

"Mother," he said, addressing Her with a clear beautiful light in his gray eyes, yet not without the reserve which he always felt and always inspired, "I wish to tell you that I am engaged to Pansy Vaughan. And to tell you also, Rowan. You know that I finish college this year; she does also. We came to an understanding yesterday afternoon and I wish you both to know it at once. We expect to be married in the autumn as soon as I am of age and a man in my own right. Mother, Pansy is coming to see you; and Rowan, I hope you will go to see Pansy. Both of you will like her and be proud of her when you know her."

He rose as though he had rounded his communication to a perfect shape. "Now I must get to my work. Good morning," and with a smile for each he walked quietly out of the room. He knew that he could not expect their congratulations at that moment and that further conference would be awkward for all. He could merely tell them the truth and leave the rest to the argument of time.

"But I cannot believe it, Rowan! I cannot!"

Mrs. Meredith sat regarding' her elder son with incredulity and distress. The shock of the news was for certain reasons even greater to him; so that he could not yet command himself sufficiently to comfort her. After a few moments she resumed: "I did not know that Dent had begun to think about girls. He never said so. He has never cared for society. He has seemed absorbed in his studies. And now—Dent in love. Dent engaged, Dent to be married in the autumn—why, Rowan, am I dreaming, am I in my senses? And to this girl! She has entrapped him—poor, innocent, unsuspecting Dent! My poor, little, short-sighted bookworm." Tears sprang to her eyes, but she laughed also. She had a mother's hope that this trouble would turn to comedy. She went on quickly: "Did you know anything about this? Has he ever spoken to you about it?"

"No, I am just as much surprised. But then Dent never speaks in advance."

She looked at him a little timidly: "I thought perhaps it was this that has been troubling you. You have been trying to hide it from me."

He dropped his eyes quickly and made no reply.

"And do you suppose he is in earnest, Rowan?"

"He would never jest on such a subject."

"I mean, do you think he knows his own mind?"

"He always does."

"But would he marry against my wishes?"

"He takes it for granted that you will be pleased: he said so."

"But how can he think I'll be pleased? I have never spoken to this girl in my life. I have never seen her except when we have passed them on the turnpike. I never spoke to her father but once and that was years ago when he came here one cold winter afternoon to buy a shock of fodder from your father."

She was a white character; but even the whiteness of ermine gains by being necked with blackness. "How can he treat me with so little consideration? It is just as if he had said: 'Good morning, mother. I am going to disgrace the family by my marriage, but I know you will be delighted—-good morning.'"

"You forget that Dent does not think he will disgrace the family.
He said you would be proud of her."

"Well, when the day comes for me to be proud of this, there will not be much left to be ashamed of. Rowan, for once I shall interfere."

"How can you interfere?"

"Then you must: you are his guardian."

"I shall not be his guardian by the autumn. Dent has arranged this perfectly, mother, as he always arranges everything."

She returned to her point. "But he *must* be kept from making such a mistake! Talk to him as a man. Advise him, show him that he will tie a millstone around his neck, ruin his whole life. I am willing to leave myself out and to forget what is due me, what is due you, what is due the memory of his father and of my father: for his own sake he must not marry this girl."

He shook his head slowly. "It is settled, mother," he added consolingly, "and I have so much confidence in Dent that I believe what he says: we shall be proud of her when we know her."

She sat awhile in despair. Then she said with fresh access of conviction: "This is what comes of so much science: it always tends to make a man common in his social tastes. You need not smile at me in that pitying way, for it is true: it destroys aristocratic feeling; and there is more need of aristocratic feeling in a democracy than anywhere else: because it is the only thing that can be aristocratic. That is what science has done for Dent! And this girl I—the public school has tried to make her uncommon, and the Girl's College has attempted, to make her more uncommon; and now I suppose she actually thinks she *is* uncommon: otherwise she would never have imagined that she could marry a son of mine. Smile on, I know I amuse you! You think I am not abreast of the times. I am glad I am not. I prefer my own. Dent should have studied for the church—with his love of books, and his splendid mind, and his grave, beautiful character. Then he would never have thought of marrying beneath him socially; he would have realized that if he did, he could never rise. Once in the church and with the right kind of wife, he might some day have become a bishop: I have always wanted a bishop in the family. But he set his heart upon a professorship, and I suppose a professor does not have to be particular about whom he marries."

"A professor has to be particular only to please himself—and the woman. His choice is not regulated by salaries and congregations."

She returned to her point: "You breed fine cattle and fine sheep, and you try to improve the strain of your setters. You know how you do it. What right has Dent to injure his children in the race for life by giving them an inferior mother? Are not children to be as much regarded in their rights of descent as rams and poodles?"

"You forget that the first families in all civilizations have kept themselves alive and at the summit by intermarriage with good, clean, rich blood of people whom they have considered beneath them."

"But certainly my family is not among these. It is certainly alive and it is certainly not dying out. I cannot discuss the subject with you, if you once begin that argument. Are you going to call on her?"

"Certainly. It was Dent's wish and it is right that I should."

"Then I think I shall go with you, Rowan. Dent said she was coming to see me; but I think I should rather go to see her. Whenever I wished to leave, I could get away, but if she came here, I couldn't."

"When should you like to go?"

"Oh, don't hurry me! I shall need time—a great deal of time! Do you suppose they have a parlor? I am afraid I shall not shine in the kitchen in comparison with the tins."

She had a wry face; then her brow cleared and she added with relief:

"But I must put this whole trouble out of my mind at present! It is too close to me, I cannot even see it. I shall call on the girl with you and then I shall talk quietly with Dent. Until then I must try to forget it. Besides, I got up this morning with something else on my mind. It is not Dent's unwisdom that distresses me."

Her tone indicated that she had passed to a more important topic. If any one had told her that her sons were not equally dear, the wound of such injustice would never have healed. In all that she could do for both there had never been maternal discrimination; but the heart of a woman cannot help feeling things that the heart of a mother does not; and she discriminated as a woman. This was evident now as she waived her young son's affairs.

"It is not Dent that I have been thinking of this morning," she repeated. "Why is it not you that come to tell me of your engagement? Why have you not set Dent an example as to the kind of woman he ought to marry? How many more years must he and I wait?"

They were seated opposite each other. He was ready for riding out on the farm, his hat on his crossed knees, gloves and whip in hand. Her heart yearned over him as he pulled at his gloves, his head dropped forward so that his face was hidden.

"Now that the subject has come up in this unexpected way, I want to tell you how long I have wished to see you married. I have never spoken because my idea is that a mother should not advise unless she believes it necessary. And in your case it has not been necessary. I have known your choice, and long before it became yours, it became mine. She is my ideal among them all. I know women, Rowan, and I know she is worthy of you and I could not say more. She is-high-minded and that quality is so rare in either sex. Without it what is any wife worth to a high-minded man? And I have watched her. With all her pride and modesty I have discovered her secret—she loves you. Then why have you waited? Why do you still wait?"

He did not answer and she continued with deeper feeling:

"Life is so uncertain to all of us and of course to me! I want to see you wedded to her, see her brought here as mistress of this house, and live to hear the laughter of your children." She finished with solemn emotion: "It has been my prayer, Rowan."

She became silent with her recollections of her own early life for a moment and then resumed:

"Nothing ever makes up for the loss of such years—the first years of happy marriage. If we have had these, no matter what happens afterward, we have not lived for nothing. It becomes easier for us to be kind and good afterward, to take an interest in life, to believe in our fellow-creatures, and in God."

He sprang up.

"Mother, I cannot speak with you about this now." He turned quickly and stood with his back to her, looking out of doors; and he spoke over his shoulder and his voice was broken: "You have had one disappointment this morning: it is enough. But do not think of my marrying—of my ever marrying. Dent must take my place at the head of the house. It is all over with me! But I cannot speak with you about this now," and he started quickly to leave the parlors. She rose and put her arm around his waist, walking beside him.

"You do not mind my speaking to, you about this, Rowan?" she said, sore at having touched some trouble which she felt that he had long been hiding from her, and with full respect for the privacies of his life.

"No, no, no!" he cried, choking with emotion. "Ah, mother, mother!"—and he gently disengaged himself from her arms.

She watched him as he rode out of sight. Then she returned and sat in the chair which he had, quitted, folding her hands in her lap.

For her it was one of the moments when we are reminded that our lives are not in our keeping, and that whatsoever is to befall us originates in sources beyond our power. Our wills may indeed reach the length of our arms or as far as our voices can penetrate space; but without us and within us moves one universe that saves us or ruins us only for its own purposes; and we are no more free amid its laws than the leaves of the forest are free to decide their own shapes and season of unfolding, to order the showers by which they are to be nourished and the storms which shall scatter them at last.

Above every other she had cherished the wish for a marriage between Rowan and Isabel Conyers; now for reasons unknown to her it seemed that this desire was never to be realized. She did not know the meaning of what Rowan had just said to her; but she did not doubt there was meaning behind it, grave meaning. Her next most serious concern would have been that in time Dent likewise should choose a wife wisely; now he had announced to her his intention to wed prematurely and most foolishly; she could not altogether shake off the conviction that he would do what he had said he should.

As for Dent it was well-nigh the first anxiety that he had ever caused her. If her affection for him was less poignant, being tenderness stored rather than tenderness exercised, this resulted from the very absence of his demand for it. He had always needed her so little, had always needed every one so little, unfolding his life from the first and drawing from the impersonal universe whatever it required with the quietude and efficiency of a prospering plant. She lacked imagination, or she might have thought of Dent as a filial sunflower, which turned the blossom of its life always faithfully and beautifully toward her, but stood rooted in the soil of knowledge that she could not supply.

What she had always believed she could see in him was the perpetuation under a new form of his father and the men of his father's line.

These had for generations been grave mental workers: ministers, lawyers, professors in theological seminaries; narrow-minded, strong-minded; upright, unbending; black-browed, black-coated; with a passion always for dealing in justice and dealing out justice, human or heavenly; most of all, gratified when in theological seminaries, when they could assert themselves as inerrant interpreters of the Most High. The portraits of two of them hung in the dining room now, placed there as if to watch the table and see that grace was never left unsaid, that there be no levity at meat nor heresy taken in with the pudding. Other portraits were also in other rooms—they always had themselves painted for posterity, seldom or never their wives.

Some of the books they had written were in the library, lucid explanations of the First Cause and of how the Judge of all the earth should be looked at from without and from within. Some that they had most loved to read were likewise there: "Pollock's Course of Time"; the slow outpourings of Young, sad sectary; Milton, with the passages on Hell approvingly underscored—not as great poetry, but as great doctrine; nowhere in the bookcases a sign of the "Areopagitica," of "Comus," and "L'Allegro"; but most prominent the writings of Jonathan Edwards, hoarsest of the whole flock of New World theological ravens.

Her marriage into this family had caused universal surprise. It had followed closely upon the scandals in regard to the wild young Ravenel Morris, the man she loved, the man she had promised to marry. These scandals had driven her to the opposite extreme from her first choice by one of life's familiar reactions; and in her wounded flight she had thrown herself into the arms of a man whom people called irreproachable. He was a grave lawyer, one of the best of his kind; nevertheless he and she, when joined for the one voyage of two human spirits, were like a funeral barge lashed to some dancing boat, golden-oared, white-sailed, decked with flowers. Hope at the helm and Pleasure at the prow.

For she herself had sprung from a radically different stock: from sanguine, hot-blooded men; congressmen shaping the worldly history of their fellow-beings and leaving the non-worldly to take care of itself; soldiers illustrious in the army and navy; hale country gentlemen who took the lead in the country's hardy sports and pleasures; all sowing their wild oats early in life with hands that no power could stay; not always living to reap, but always leaving enough reaping to be done by the sad innocent who never sow; fathers of large families; and even when breaking the hearts of their wives, never losing their love; for with their large open frailties being men without crime and cowardice, tyrannies, meannesses.

With these two unlike hereditary strains before her she had, during the years, slowly devised the maternal philosophy of her sons.

Out of those grave mental workers had come Dent—her student. She loved to believe that in the making of him her own blood asserted itself by drawing him away from the tyrannical interpretation of God to the neutral investigation of the earth, from black theology to sunlit science—so leaving him at work and at peace, the ancestral antagonisms becoming neutralized by being blended.

But Rowan! while he was yet a little fellow, and she and her young husband would sit watching him at play, characteristics revealed themselves which led her to shake her head rebukingly and say: "He gets these traits from you." At other times contradictory characteristics appeared and the father, looking silently at her, would in effect inquire: "Whence does he derive these?" On both accounts she began to look with apprehension toward this son's maturing years. And always, as the years passed, evidence was forced more plainly upon her that in him the two natures he inherited were antagonistic still; each alternately uppermost; both in unceasing warfare; thus endowing him with a double nature which might in time lead him to a double life. So that even then she had begun to take upon herself the burden of dreading lest she should not only be the mother of his life, but the mother of his tragedies. She went over this again and again: "Am I to be the mother of his tragedies?"

As she sat this young summer morning after he had left her so strangely, all at once the world became autumn to her remembrance.

An autumn morning: the rays of the sun shining upon the silvery mists swathing the trees outside, upon the wet and many-colored leaves; a little frost on the dark grass here and there; the first fires lighted within; the carriage already waiting at the door; the breakfast hurriedly choked down—in silence; the mournful noise of his trunk being brought downstairs—his first trunk. Then the going out upon the veranda and the saying good-by to him; and then—the carriage disappearing in the silver mists, with a few red and yellow leaves whirled high from the wheels.

That was the last of the first Rowan,—youth at the threshold of manhood. Now off for college, to his university in New England. As his father and she stood side by side (he being too frail to take that chill morning ride with his son) he waved his hand protectingly after him, crying out: "He is a good boy." And she, having some wide vision of other mothers of the land who during these same autumn days were bidding God-speed to their idols—picked youth of the republic—she with some wide vision of this large fact stood a proud mother among them all, feeling sure that he would take foremost place in his college for good honest work and for high character and gentle manners and gallant bearing—with not a dark spot in him.

It was toward the close of the first session, after she had learned the one kind of letter he always wrote, that his letters changed. She could not have explained how they were changed, could not have held the pages up to the inspection of any one else and have said, "See! it is here." But she knew it was there, and it stayed there. She waited for his father to notice it; but if he ever noticed it, he never told her: nor did she ever confide her discovery to him.

When vacation came, it brought a request from Rowan that he might be allowed to spend the summer with college friends farther north—camping, fishing, hunting, sailing, seeing more of his country. His father's consent was more ready than her own. The second session passed and with the second vacation the request was renewed. "Why does he not come home? Why does he not wish to come home?" she said, wandering restlessly over the house with his letter in her hands; going up to his bedroom and sitting down in the silence of it and looking at his bed—which seemed so strangely white that day—looking at all the preparations she had made for his comfort. "Why does he not come?"

Near the close of the third session he came quickly enough, summoned by his father's short fatal illness.

Some time passed before she observed anything in him but natural changes after so long an absence and grief over his great loss. He shut himself in his room for some days, having it out alone with himself, a young man's first solemn accounting to a father who has become a memory. Gradually there began to emerge his new care of her, and tenderness, a boy's no more. And he stepped forward easily into his place as the head of affairs, as his brother's guardian. But as time wore on and she grew used to him as so much older in mere course of nature, and as graver by his loss and his fresh responsibilities, she made allowances for all these and brushed them away and beheld constantly beneath them that other change.

Often while she sat near him when they were reading, she would look up and note that unaware a shadow had stolen out on his face. She studied that shadow. And one consolation she drew: that whatsoever the cause, it was nothing by which he felt dishonored. At such moments her love broke over him with intolerable longings. She remembered things that her mother had told her about her father; she recalled the lives of her brothers, his uncles. She yearned to say: "What is it, Rowan? You can tell me anything, anything. I know so much more than you believe."

But some restraint dissuaded her from bridging that reserve. She may have had the feeling that she spared him a good deal by her not knowing.

For more than a year after his return he had kept aloof from society—going into town only when business demanded, and accepting no invitations to the gayeties of the neighborhood. He liked rather to have his friends come out to stay with him: sometimes he was off with them for days during the fishing and hunting seasons. Care of the farm and its stock occupied a good deal of his leisure, and there were times when he worked hard in the fields—she thought so unnecessarily. Incessant activity of some kind had become his craving—the only ease.

She became uneasy, she disapproved. For a while she allowed things to have their way, but later she interfered—though as always with her silent strength and irresistible gentleness. Making no comment upon his changed habits and altered tastes, giving no sign of her own purposes, she began the second year of his home-coming to accept invitations for herself and formally reentered her social world; reassumed her own leadership there; demanded him as her escort; often filled the house with young guests; made it for his generation what the home of her girlhood had been to her—in all sacrificing for him the gravity and love of seclusion which had settled over her during the solemn years, years which she knew to be parts of a still more solemn future.

She succeeded. She saw him again more nearly what he had been before the college days—more nearly developing that type of life which belonged to him and to his position.

Finally she saw him in love as she wished; and at this point she gradually withdrew from society again, feeling that he needed her no more.

VI

The noise of wheels on the gravel driveway of the lawn brought the reflections of Mrs. Meredith to an abrupt close. The sound was extremely unpleasant to her; she did not feel in a mood to entertain callers this morning. Rising with regret, she looked out. The brougham of Mrs. Conyers, flashing in the sun, was being driven toward the house—was being driven rapidly, as though speed meant an urgency.

If Mrs. Meredith desired no visitor at all, she particularly disliked the appearance of this one. Rowan's words to her were full of meaning that she did not understand; but they rendered it clear at least that his love affair had been interrupted, if not been ended. She could not believe this due to any fault of his; and friendly relations with the Conyers family was for her instantly at an end with any wrong done to him.

She summoned a maid and instructed her regarding the room in which the visitor was to be received (not in the parlors; they were too full of solemn memories this morning). Then she passed down the long hall to her bedchamber.

The intimacy between these ladies was susceptible of exact analysis; every element comprising it could have been valued as upon a quantitative scale. It did not involve any of those incalculable forces which constitute friendship—a noble mystery remaining forever beyond unravelling.

They found the first basis of their intimacy in a common wish for the union of their offsprings. This subject had never been mentioned between them. Mrs. Conyers would have discussed it had she dared; but she knew at least the attitude of the other. Furthermore, Mrs. Meredith brought to this association a beautiful weakness: she was endowed with all but preternatural insight into what is fine in human nature, but had slight power of discovering what is base; she seemed endowed with far-sightedness in high, clear, luminous atmospheres, but was short-sighted in moral twilights. She was, therefore, no judge of the character of her intimate. As for that lady's reputation, this was well known to her; but she screened herself against this reputation behind what she believed to be her own personal discovery of unsuspected virtues in the misjudged. She probably experienced as much pride in publicly declaring the misjudged a better woman than she was reputed, as that lady would have felt in secretly declaring her to be a worse one.

On the part of Mrs. Conyers, the motives which she brought to the association presented nothing that must be captured and brought down from the heights, she was usually to be explained by mining rather than mounting. Whatever else she might not have been, she was always ore; never rainbows.

Throughout bird and animal and insect life there runs what is recognized as the law of protective assimilation. It represents the necessity under which a creature lives to pretend to be something else as a condition of continuing to be itself. The rose-colored flamingo, curving its long neck in volutions that suggest the petals of a corolla, burying its head under its wing and lifting one leg out of sight, becomes a rank, marvellous flower, blooming on too slight a stalk in its marshes. An insect turns itself into one of the dried twigs of a dead stick. On the margin of a shadowed pool the frog is hued like moss— greenness beside greenness. Mrs. Conyers availed herself of a kind of protective assimilation when she exposed herself to the environment of Mrs. Meredith, adopting devices by which she would be taken for any object in nature but herself. Two familiar devices were applied to her habiliments and her conversations. Mrs. Meredith always dressed well to the natural limit of her bountiful years; Mrs. Conyers usually dressed more than well and more than a generation behind hers. On occasions when she visited Rowan's unconcealed mother, she allowed time to make regarding herself almost an honest declaration. Ordinarily she Was a rose nearly ready to drop, which is bound with a thread of its own color to look as much as possible like a bud that is nearly ready to open.

Her conversations were even more assiduously tinged and fashioned by the needs of accommodation. Sometimes she sat in Mrs. Meredith's parlors as a soul sick of the world's vanities, an urban spirit that hungered for country righteousness. During a walk one day through the gardens she paused under the boughs of a weeping willow and recited, "Cromwell, I charge thee fling away ambition—" She uniformly imparted to Mrs. Meredith the assurance that with her alone she could lay aside all disguises.

This morning she alighted from her carriage at the end of the pavement behind some tall evergreens. As she walked toward the house, though absorbed with a serious purpose, she continued to be as observant of everything as usual. Had an eye been observant of her, it would have been noticed that Mrs. Conyers in all her self-concealment did not conceal one thing—her walk. This one element of her conduct had its curious psychology. She had never been able to forget that certain scandals set going many years before, had altered the course of Mrs. Meredith's life and of the lives of some others. After a lapse of so long a time she had no fear now that she should be discovered. Nevertheless it was impossible for her ever to approach this house without "coming delicately." She "came delicately" in the same sense that Agag, king of Amalek, walked when he was on his way to Saul, who was about to hew him to pieces before the Lord in Gilgal.

She approached the house now, observant of everything as she tripped. Had a shutter been hung awry; if a window shade had been drawn too low or a pane of glass had not sparkled, or there had been loose paper on the ground or moulted feathers on the bricks, she would have discovered this with the victorious satisfaction of finding fault. But orderliness prevailed. No; the mat at the front door had been displaced by Rowan's foot as he had hurried from the house. (The impulse was irresistible: she adjusted it with her toe and planted herself on it with a sense of triumph.)

As she took out her own and Isabel's cards, she turned and looked out across the old estate. This was the home she had designed for Isabel: the land, the house, the silver, the glass, the memories, the distinction—they must all be Isabel's.

Some time passed before Mrs. Meredith appeared. Always a woman of dignity and reserve, she had never before in her life perhaps worn a demeanor so dignified and reserved. Her nature called for peace; but if Rowan had been wronged, then there was no peace—and a sacred war is a cruel one. The instant that the two ladies confronted each other, each realized that each concealed something from the other. This discovery instantly made Mrs. Meredith cooler still; it rendered Mrs. Conyers more cordial.

"Isabel regretted that she could not come."

"I am sorry." The tone called for the dismissal of the subject.

"This is scarcely a visit to you," Mrs. Conyers went on; "I have been paying one of my usual pastoral calls: I have been to Ambrose Webb's to see if my cows are ready to return to town. Strawberries are ripe and strawberries call for more cream, and more cream calls for more calves, and more calves call for—well, we have all heard them! I do not understand how a man who looks like Ambrose can so stimulate cattle. Of course my cows are not as fine and fat as Rowan's—that is not to be expected. The country is looking very beautiful. I never come for a drive without regretting that I live in town." (She would have found the country intolerable for the same reason that causes criminals to flock to cities.)

Constraint deepened as the visit was prolonged. Mrs. Conyers begged Mrs. Meredith for a recipe that she knew to be bad; and when Mrs. Meredith had left the room for it, she rose and looked eagerly out of the windows for any sign of Rowan. When Mrs. Meredith returned, for the same reason she asked to be taken into the garden, which was in its splendor of bloom. Mrs. Meredith culled for her a few of the most resplendent blossoms—she could not have offered to any one anything less. Mrs. Conyers was careful not to pin any one of these on; she had discovered that she possessed a peculiarity known to some florists and concealed by those women who suffer from it— that flowers soon wilt when worn by them.

Meanwhile as they walked she talked of flowers, of housekeeping; she discussed Marguerite's coming ball and Dent's brilliant graduation. She enlarged upon this, praising Dent to the disparagement of her own grandson Victor, now in retreat from college on account of an injury received as centre-rush in his football team. Victor, she protested, was above education; his college was a kind of dormitory to athletics.

When we are most earnest ourselves, we are surest to feel the lack of earnestness in others; sincerity stirred to the depths will tolerate nothing less. It thus becomes a new test of a companion. So a weak solution may not reveal a poison when a strong one will. Mrs. Meredith felt this morning as never before the real nature of the woman over whom for years she had tried to throw a concealing charity; and Mrs. Conyers saw as never before in what an impossible soil she had tried to plant poison oak and call it castle ivy.

The ladies parted with coldness. When she was once more seated in her carriage, Mrs. Conyers thrust her head through the window and told the coachman to drive slowly. She tossed the recipe into a pine tree and took in her head. Then she caught hold of a brown silk cord attached to a little brown silk curtain in the front of the brougham opposite her face. It sprang aside, revealing a little toilette mirror. On the cushion beside her lay something under a spread newspaper. She quickly drew off her sombre visiting gloves; and lifting the newspaper, revealed under it a fresh pair of gloves, pearl-colored. She worked her tinted hands nimbly into these. Then she took out a rose-colored scarf or shawl as light as a summer cloud. This she threw round her shoulders; it added no warmth, it added color, meaning. There were a few other youthward changes and additions; and then the brown silk curtain closed over the mirror.

Another woman leaned back in a corner of the brougham. By a trick of the face she had juggled away a generation of her years. The hands were moved backward on the horologe of mortality as we move backward the pointers on the dial of a clock: her face ticked at the hour of two in the afternoon of life instead of half-past five.

There was still time enough left to be malicious.

VII

One morning about a week later she entered her carriage and was driven rapidly away. A soft-faced, middle-aged woman with gray ringlets and nervous eyes stepped timorously upon the veranda and watched her departure with an expression of relief—Miss Harriet Crane, the unredeemed daughter of the household.

She had been the only fruit of her mother's first marriage and she still remained attached to the parental stem despite the most vigorous wavings and shakings of that stem to shed its own product. Nearly fifty years of wintry neglect and summer scorching had not availed to disjoin Harriet from organic dependence upon her mother. And of all conceivable failings in a child of hers that mother could have found none so hard to forgive as the failure to attract a man in a world full of men nearly all bent upon being attracted.

It was by no choice of Harriet's that she was born of a woman who valued children as a kind of social collateral, high-class investments to mature after long periods with at least reasonable profits for the original investors. Nor was it by any volition of hers that she had commended herself to her mother in the beginning by being a beautiful and healthful child: initial pledge that she could be relied upon to turn out lucrative in the end. The parent herself was secretly astounded that she had given birth to a child of so seraphic a disposition.

Trouble and disappointment began with education, for education is long stout resistance. You cannot polish highly a stone that is not hard enough to resist being highly polished. Harriet's soft nature gave way before the advance of the serried phalanxes of knowledge: learning passed her by; and she like the many "passed through school."

By this time her mother had grown alarmed and she brought Harriet out prematurely, that she might be wedded before, so to speak, she was discovered. Meantime Mrs. Crane herself had married a second and a third time, with daughters by the last husband who were little younger than her eldest; and she laughingly protested that nothing is more confusing to a woman than to have in the house children by two husbands. Hence further reason for desiring immediate nuptials: she could remove from the parlors the trace of bi-marital collaboration.

At first only the most brilliant matches were planned for Harriet; these one by one unaccountably came to naught. Later the mother began to fall back: upon those young men who should be glad to embrace such an opportunity; but these less desirable young men failed to take that peculiar view of their destinies. In the meanwhile the Misses Conyers had come on as debutantes and were soon bespoken. At the marriage of the youngest, Harriet's mother had her act as first bridesmaid and dressed her, already fading, as though she were the very spirit of April.

The other sisters were long since gone, scattered north and south with half-grown families; and the big house was almost empty save when they came in troops to visit it.

Harriet's downward career as an article of human merchandise had passed through what are perhaps not wholly unrecognizable stages. At first she had been displayed near the entrance for immediate purchase by the unwary. Then she had been marked down as something that might be secured at a reduced price; but intending buyers preferred to pay more. By and by even this label was taken off and she became a remnant of stock for which there was no convenient space—being moved from shelf to shelf, always a little more shop-worn, a little more out of style. What was really needed was an auction.

Mrs. Conyers did not take much to heart the teachings of her Bible; but it had at least defined for her one point of view: all creatures worth saving had been saved in pairs.

Bitter as were those years for Harriet, others more humiliating followed. The maternal attempts having been discontinued, she, desperate with slights and insults, had put forth some efforts of her own. But it was as though one had been placed in a boat without oars and told to row for life: the little boat under the influence of cosmic tides had merely drifted into shallows and now lay there—forgotten.

This morning as she sat idly rocking on the veranda, she felt that negative happiness which consists in the disappearance of a positively disagreeable thing. Then she began to study how she should spend the forenoon most agreeably. Isabel was upstairs; she would have been perfectly satisfied to talk with her; but for several mornings Isabel had shown unmistakable preference to be let alone; and in the school of life Harriet had attained the highest proficiency in one branch of knowledge at least—never to get in anybody's way. Victor Fielding lay under the trees with a pipe and a book, but she never ventured near him.

So Harriet bethought herself of a certain friend of hers on the other side of town, Miss Anna Hardage, who lived with her brother, Professor Hardage—two people to trust.

She put on her hat which unfortunately she had chosen to trim herself, tied a white veil across the upper part of her face and got out her second-best pair of gloves: Harriet kept her best gloves for her enemies. In the front yard she pulled a handful of white lilacs (there was some defect here or she would never have carried white lilacs in soiled white gloves); and passed out of the gate. Her eyes were lighted up with anticipations, but ill must have overtaken her in transit; for when she was seated with Miss Anna in a little side porch looking out on the little green yard, they were dimmed with tears.

"The same old story," she complained vehemently. "The same ridicule that has been dinned into my ears since I was a child."

"Ah, now, somebody has been teasing her about being an old maid," said Miss Anna to herself, recognizing the signs.

"This world is a very unprincipled place to live in," continued Harriet, her rage curdling into philosophy.

"Ah, but it is the best there is just yet," maintained Miss Anna, stoutly. "By and by we may all be able to do better—those of us who get the chance."

"What shall I care then?" said Harriet, scouting eternity as a palliative of contemporary woes.

"Wait! you are tired and you have lost your temper from thirst: children always do. I'll bring something to cure you, fresh from the country, fresh from Ambrose Webb's farm. Besides, you have a dark shade of the blues, my dear; and this remedy is capital for the blues. You have but to sip a glass slowly—and where are they?" And she hastened into the house.

She returned with two glasses of cool buttermilk.

The words and the deed were characteristic of one of the most wholesome women that ever helped to straighten out a crooked and to cool a feverish world. Miss Anna's very appearance allayed irritation and became a provocation to good health, to good sense. Her mission in life seemed not so much to distribute honey as to sprinkle salt, to render things salubrious, to enable them to keep their tonic naturalness. Not within the range of womankind could so marked a contrast have been found for Harriet as in this maiden lady of her own age, who was her most patient friend and who supported her clinging nature (which still could not resist the attempt to bloom) as an autumn cornstalk supports a frost-nipped morning-glory.

If words of love had ever been whispered into Miss Anna's ear, no human being knew it now: but perhaps her heart also had its under chamber sealed with tears. Women not even behind her back jested at her spinsterhood; and when that is true, a miracle takes place indeed. No doubt Miss Anna was a miracle, not belonging to any country, race, or age; being one of those offerings to the world which nature now and then draws from the deeps of womanhood: a pure gift of God.

The two old maids drained their rectifying beverage in the shady porch. Whether from Miss Anna's faith in it or from the simple health-giving of her presence, Harriet passed through a process of healing; and as she handed back the empty glass, she smiled gratefully into Miss Anna's sparkling brown eyes. Nature had been merciful to her in this, that she was as easily healed as wounded. She now returned to the subject which had so irritated her, as we rub pleasantly a spot from which a thorn has been extracted.

"What do I care?" she said, straightening her hat as if to complete her recovery. "But if there is one thing that can make me angry, Anna, it is the middle-aged, able-bodied unmarried men of this town. They are perfectly, *perfectly* contemptible."

"Oh, come now!" cried Miss Anna, "I am too old to talk about such silly things myself; but what does a woman care whether she is married or not if she has had offers? And you have had plenty of good offers, my dear."

"No, I haven't!" said Harriet, who would tell the truth about this rankling misfortune.

"Well, then, it was because the men knew you wouldn't have them."

"No, it wasn't!" said Harriet, "it was because they knew I would."

"Nonsense!" cried Miss Anna, impatiently. "You mustn't try to palm off so much mock modesty on me, Harriet."

"Ah, I am too old to fib about it, Anna! I leave *that* to my many sisters in misfortune."

Harriet looked at her friend's work curiously: she was darning Professor Hardage's socks.

"Why do you do that, Anna? Socks are dirt cheap. You might as well go out into the country and darn sheep."

"Ah, you have never had a brother—my brother! so you cannot understand. I can feel his heels pressing against my stitches when he is walking a mile away. And I know whenever his fingers touch the buttons I have put back. Besides, don't you like to see people make bad things good, and things with holes in them whole again? Why, that is half the work of the world, Harriet! It is not his feet that make these holes," continued Miss Anna, nicely, "it is his shoes, his big, coarse shoes. And his clothes wear out so soon. He has a tailor who misfits him so exactly from year to year that there is never the slightest deviation in the botch. I know beforehand exactly where all the creases will begin. So I darn and mend. The idea of his big, soft, strong feet making holes

66

in anything! but, then, you have never tucked him in bed at night, my dear, so you know nothing about his feet."

"Not I!" said Harriet, embarrassed but not shocked.

Miss Anna continued fondly in a lowered voice: "You should have heard him the other day when he pulled open a drawer: 'Why, Anna,' he cried, 'where on earth did I get all these new socks? The pair I left in here must have been alive: they've bred like rabbits.'—'Why, you've forgotten,' I said. 'It's your birthday; and I have made you over, so that you are as good as new—*me*!'"

"I never have to be reminded of my birthday," remarked Harriet, reflectively. "Anna, do you know that I have lived about one-eighth of the time since Columbus discovered America: doesn't that sound awful!"

"Ah, but you don't look it," said Miss Anna, artistically, "and that's the main object."

"Oh, I don't feel it," retorted Harriet, "and that's the main object too. I'm as young as I ever was when I'm away from home; but I declare, Anna, there are times when my mother can make me feel I'm about the oldest thing alive."

"Oh, come now! you mustn't begin to talk that way, or I'll have to give you more of the antidote. You are threatened with a relapse."

"No more," ordered Harriet with a forbidding hand, "and I repeat what I said. Of course you know I never gossip, Anna; but when I talk to you, I do not feel as though I were talking to anybody."

"Why, of course not," said Miss Anna, trying to make the most of the compliment, "I am nobody at all, just a mere nonentity, Harriet."

"Anna," said Harriet, after a pause of unusual length, "if it had not been for my mother, I should have been married long ago. Thousands of worse-looking women, and of actually worse women, marry every year in this world and marry reasonably well. It was because she tried to marry me off: that was the bottom of the deviltry—the men saw through her."

"I am afraid they did," admitted Miss Anna, affably, looking down into a hole.

"Of course I know I am not brilliant," conceded Harriet, "but then I am never commonplace."

"I should like to catch any one saying such a thing."

"Even if I were, commonplace women always make the best wives: do they not?"

"Oh, don't ask that question in this porch," exclaimed Miss Anna a little resentfully. "What do I know about it!"

"My mother thinks I am a weak woman," continued Harriet, musingly. "If my day ever comes, she will know that I am, strong, Anna, *strong*."

"Ah, now, you must forgive your mother," cried Miss Anna, having reached a familiar turn in this familiar dialogue. "Whatever she did, she did for the best. Certainly it was no fault of yours. But you could get married to-morrow if you wished and you know it, Harriet." (Miss Anna offered up the usual little prayer to be forgiven.)

The balm of those words worked through Harriet's veins like a poison of joy. So long as a single human being expresses faith in us, what matters an unbelieving world? Harriet regularly visited Miss Anna to hear these maddening syllables. She called for them as for the refilling of a prescription, which she preferred to get fresh every time rather than take home once for all and use as directed.

Among a primitive folk who seemed to have more moral troubles than any other and to feel greater need of dismissing them by artificial means, there grew up the custom of using a curious expedient. They chose a beast of the field and upon its head symbolically piled all the moral hard-headedness of the several tribes; after which the unoffending brute was banished to the wilderness and the guilty multitude felt relieved. However crude that ancient method of transferring mental and moral burdens, it had at least this redeeming feature: the early Hebrews heaped their sins upon a creature which they did not care for and sent it away. In modern times we pile our burdens upon our dearest fellow-creatures and keep them permanently near us for further use. What human being but has some other upon whom he nightly hangs his troubles as he hangs his different garments upon hooks and nails in the walls around him? Have we ever suspected that when once the habit of transferring our troubles has become pleasant to us, we thereafter hunt for troubles in order that we may have them to transfer, that we magnify the little ones in order to win the credit of having large ones, and that we are wonderfully refreshed by making other people despondent about us? Mercifully those upon whom the burdens are hung often become the better for their loads; they may not live so long, but they are more useful. Thus in turn the weak develop the strong.

For years Miss Anna had sacrificially demeaned herself in the service of Harriet, who would now have felt herself a recreant friend unless she had promptly detailed every annoyance of her life. She would go home, having left behind her the infinite little swarm of stinging things—having transferred them to the head of Miss Anna, around which they buzzed until they died.

There was this further peculiarity in Harriet's visits: that the most important moments were the last; Just as a doctor, after he has listened to the old story of his patient's symptoms, and has prescribed and bandaged and patted and soothed, and has reached the door, turns, and noting a light in the patient's eye hears him make a remark which shows that all the time he has really been thinking about something else.

Harriet now showed what was at the bottom of her own mind this morning:

"What I came to tell you about, Anna, is that for a week life at home has been unendurable. There is some trouble, some terrible trouble; and no matter what goes wrong, my mother always holds me responsible. Positively there are times when I wonder whether I, without my knowing it, may not be the Origin of Evil."

Miss Anna made no comment, having closed the personal subject, and Harriet continued:

"It has scarcely been possible for me to stay in the house. Fortunately mother has been there very little herself. She goes and goes and drives and drives. Strange things have been happening. You know that Judge Morris has not missed coming on Sunday evening for years. Last night mother sat on the veranda waiting for him and he did not come. I know, for I watched. What have I to do but watch other people's affairs?—I have none of my own. I believe the trouble is all between Isabel and Rowan."

Miss Anna dropped her work and looked at Harriet with sudden gravity.

"I can give you no idea of the real situation because it is very dramatic; and you know, Anna, I am not dramatic: I am merely historical: I tell my little tales. But at any rate Rowan has not been at the house for a week. He called last Sunday afternoon and Isabel refused to see him. I know; because what have I to do but to interest myself in people who have affairs of interest? Then Isabel had his picture in her room: it has been taken down. She had some of his books: they are gone. The house has virtually been closed to company. Isabel has excused herself to callers. Mother was to give a tea; the invitations were cancelled. At table Isabel and mother barely speak; but when I am not near, they talk a great deal to each other. And Isabel walks and walks and walks—in the garden, in her rooms. I have waked up two or three times at night and have seen her sitting at her window. She has always been very kind to me, Anna," Harriet's voice faltered, "she and you: and I cannot bear to see her so unhappy. You would never believe that a few days would make such a change in her. The other morning I went up to her room with a little bunch of violets which I had gathered for her myself. When she opened the door, I saw that she was packing her trunks. And the dress she had ordered for

Marguerite's ball was lying on the bed ready to be put in. As I gave her the flowers she stood looking at them a long time; then she kissed me without a word and quickly closed the door."

When Harriet had gone. Miss Anna sat awhile in her porch with a troubled face. Then she went softly into the library, the windows of which opened out upon the porch. Professor Hardage was standing on a short step-ladder before a bookcase, having just completed the arrangement of the top shelf.

"Are you never going to get down?" she asked, looking up at him fondly.

He closed the book with a snap and a sigh and descended. Her anxious look recalled his attention,

"Did I not hear Harriet harrowing you up again with her troubles?" he asked. "You poor, kind soul that try to bear everybody's!"

"Never mind about what I bear! What can you bear for dinner?"

"It is an outrage, Anna! What right has she to make herself happier by making you miserable, lengthening her life by shortening yours? For these worries always clip the thread of life at the end: that is where all the small debts are collected as one."

"Now you must not be down on Harriet! It makes her happier; and as to the end of my life, I shall be there to attend to that."

"Suppose I moved away with you to some other college entirely out of her reach?"

"I shall not suppose it because you will never do it. If you did, Harriet would simply find somebody else to confide in; she *must* tell *everything* to *somebody*. But if she told any one else, a good many of these stories would be all over town. She tells me and they get no further."

"What right have you to listen to scandal in order to suppress it?"

"I don't even listen always: I merely stop the stream at its source."

"I object to your offering your mind as the banks to such a stream. Still I'm glad that I live near the banks," and he kissed his hand to her.

"When one woman tells another anything and the other woman does not tell, remember it is not scandal—it is confidence."

"Then there is no such thing as confidence," he replied, laughing.

He turned toward his shelves.

"Now do rest," she pleaded, "you look worn out."

She had a secret notion that books instead of putting life into people took it out of them. At best they performed the function of grindstones: they made you sharper, but they made you thinner—gave you more edge and left you less substance.

"I wish every one of those books had a lock and I had the bunch of keys."

"Each has a lock and key; but the key cannot be put into your pocket, Anna, my dear; it is the unlocking mind. And you are not to speak of books as a collection of locks and keys; they make up the living tree of knowledge, though of course there is very little of the tree in this particular bookcase."

"I don't see any of it," she remarked with wholesome literalness.

"Well, here at the bottom are lexicons—think of them as roots and soil. Above them lie maps and atlases: consider them the surface. Then all books are history of course. But here is a great central trunk rising out of the surface which is called History in especial. On each side of that, running to the right and to the left, are main branches. Here for instance is the large limb of Philosophy—a very weighty limb indeed. Here is the branch of Criticism. Here is a bough consisting principally of leaves on which live unnamed venomous little insects that poison them and die on them: their appointed place in creation."

"And so there is no positive fruit anywhere," she insisted with her practical taste for the substantial.

"It is all food, Anna, edible and nourishing to different mouths and stomachs. Some very great men have lived on the roots of knowledge, the simplest roots. And here is poetry for dates and wild honey; and novels for cocoanuts and mushrooms. And here is Religion: that is for manna."

"What is at the very top?"

His eyes rested upon the highest row of books.

"These are some of the loftiest growths, new buds of the mind opening toward the unknown. Each in its way shows the best that man, the earth-animal, has been able to accomplish. Here is a little volume for instance which tells what he ought to be—and never is. This small volume deals with the noblest ideals of the greatest civilizations. Here is what one of the finest of the world's teachers had to say about justice. Aspiration is at that end. This little book is on the sad loveliness of Greek girls; and the volume beside it is about the brief human chaplets that Horace and some other Romans wore—and then trod on. Thus the long story of light and shadow girdles the globe. If you were nothing but a spirit, Anna, and could float in here some night, perhaps you would see a mysterious radiance streaming upward from this shelf of books like the northern lights from behind the world—starting no one knows where, sweeping away we know not whither—search-light of the mortal, turned on dark eternity."

She stood a little behind him and watched him in silence, hiding her tenderness.

"If I were a book," she said thoughtlessly, "where should I be?"

He drew the fingers of one hand lingeringly across the New Testament.

"Ah, now don't do that," she cried, "or you shall have no dinner. Here, turn round! look at the dust! look at this cravat on one end! look at these hands! March upstairs."

He laid his head over against hers.

"Stand up!" she exclaimed, and ran out of the room.

Some minutes later she came back and took a seat near the door. There was flour on her elbow; and she held a spoon in her hand.

"Now you look like yourself," she said, regarding him with approval as he sat reading before the bookcase. "I started to tell you what Harriet told me."

He looked over the top of his book at her.

"I thought you said you stopped the stream at its source. Now you propose to let it run down to me—or up to me: how do you know it will not run past me?"

"Now don't talk in that way," she said, "this is something you will want to know," and she related what Harriet had chronicled.

VIII

When she had left the room, he put back into its place the volume he was reading: its power over him was gone. All the voices of all his books, speaking to him from lands and ages, grew simultaneously hushed. He crossed the library to a front window opening upon the narrow rocky street and sat with his elbow on the window-sill, the large fingers of one large hand unconsciously searching his brow—that habit of men of thoughtful years, the smoothing out of the inner problems.

The home of Professor Hardage was not in one of the best parts of the town. There was no wealth here, no society as it impressively calls itself; there were merely well-to-do human beings of ordinary intelligence and of kindly and unkindly natures. The houses, constructed of frame or of brick, were crowded wall against wall along the sidewalk; in the rear were little gardens of flowers and of vegetables. The street itself was well shaded; and one forest tree, the roots of which bulged up through the mossy bricks of the pavement, hung its boughs before his windows. Throughout life he had found so many companions in the world outside of mere people, and this tree was one. From the month of leaves to the month of no leaves—the period of long hot vacations—when his eyes were tired and his brain and heart a little tired also, many a time it refreshed him by all that it was and all that it stood for—this green tent of the woods arching itself before his treasured shelves. In it for him were thoughts of cool solitudes and of far-away greenness; with tormenting visions also of old lands, the crystal-aired, purpling mountains of which, and valleys full of fable, he was used to trace out upon the map, but knew that he should never see or press with responsive feet.

For travel was impossible to him. Part of his small salary went to the family of a brother; part disappeared each year in the buying of books—at once his need and his passion; there were the expenses of living; and Miss Anna always exacted appropriations.

"I know we have not much, but then my little boys and girls have nothing; and the poor must help the poorer."

"Very well," he would reply, "but some day you will be a beggar yourself, Anna."

"Oh, well then, if I am, I do not doubt that I shall be a thrifty old mendicant. And I'll beg for *you*! So don't you be uneasy; and give me what I want."

She always looked like a middle-aged Madonna in the garb of a housekeeper.

Indeed, he was wont to call her the Madonna of the Dishes; but at these times, and in truth for all deeper ways, he thought of her as the Madonna of the Motherless. Nevertheless he was resolute that out of this many-portioned salary something must yet be saved.

"The time will come," he threatened, "when some younger man will want my professorship—and will deserve it. I shall either be put out or I shall go out; and then—decrepitude, uselessness, penury, unless something has been hoarded. So, Anna, out of the frail uncertain little basketful of the apples of life which the college authorities present to me once a year, we must save a few for what may prove a long hard winter."

Professor Hardage was a man somewhat past fifty, of ordinary stature and heavy figure, topped with an immense head. His was not what we call rather vaguely the American face. In Germany had he been seen issuing from the lecture rooms of a university, he would have been thought at home and his general status had been assumed: there being that about him which bespoke the scholar, one of those quiet self-effacing minds that have long since passed with entire humility into the service of vast themes. In social life the character of a noble master will in time stamp itself upon the look and manners of a domestic; and in time the student acquires the lofty hall-mark of what he serves.

It was this perhaps that immediately distinguished him and set him apart in every company. The appreciative observer said at once: "Here is a man who may not himself be great; but he is at least great enough to understand greatness; he is used to greatness."

As so often is the case with the strong American, he was self-made—that glory of our boasting. But we sometimes forget that an early life of hardship, while it may bring out what is best in a man, so often wastes up his strength and burns his ambition to ashes in the fierce fight against odds too great. So that the powers which should have carried him far carry him only a little distance or leave him standing exhausted where he began.

When Alfred Hardage was eighteen, he had turned his eyes toward a professorship in one of the great universities of his country; before he was thirty he had won a professorship in the small but respectable college of his native town; and now, when past fifty, he had never won anything more. For him ambition was like the deserted martin box in the corner of his yard: returning summers brought no more birds. Had his abilities been even more extraordinary, the result could not have been far otherwise. He had been compelled to forego for himself as a student the highest university training, and afterward to win such position as the world accorded him without the prestige of study abroad.

It became his duty in his place to teach the Greek language and its literature; sometimes were added classes in Latin. This was the easier problem. The more difficult problem grew out of the demand, that he should live intimately in a world of much littleness and not himself become little; feel interested in trivial minds at street corners, yet remain companion and critic of some of the greatest intellects of human kind; contend with occasional malice and jealousy in the college faculty, yet hold himself above these carrion passions; retain his intellectual manhood, yet have his courses of study narrowed and made superficial for him; be free yet submit to be patronized by some of his fellow-citizens, because they did him the honor to employ him for so much as a year as sage and moral exampler to their sons.

Usually one of two fates overtakes the obscure professional scholar in this country: either he shrinks to the dimensions of a true villager and deserts the vastness of his library; or he repudiates the village and becomes a cosmopolitan recluse—lonely toiler among his books. Few possess the breadth and equipoise which will enable them to pass from day to day along mental paths, which have the Forum of Augustus or the Groves of the Academy at one end and the babbling square of a modern town at the other; remaining equally at home amid ancient ideals and everyday realities.

It was the fate of the recluse that threatened him. He had been born with the scholar's temperament—this furnished the direction; before he had reached the age of twenty-five he had lost his wife and two sons—that furrowed the tendency. During the years immediately following he had tried to fill an immense void of the heart with immense labors of the intellect. The void remained; yet undoubtedly compensation for loneliness had been found in the fixing of his affections upon what can never die—the inexhaustible delight of learning.

Thus the life of the book-worm awaited him but for an interference excellent and salutary and irresistible. This was the constant companionship of a sister whose nature enabled her to find its complete universe in the only world that she had ever known: she walking ever broad-minded through the narrowness of her little town; remaining white though often threading its soiling ways; and from every life which touched hers, however crippled and confined, extracting its significance instead of its insignificance, shy harmonies instead of the easy discords which can so palpably be struck by any passing hand.

It was due to her influence, therefore, that his life achieved the twofold development which left him normal in the middle years; the fresh pursuing scholar still but a man practically welded to the people among whom he lived —receiving their best and giving his best.

But we cannot send our hearts out to play at large among our kind, without their coming to choose sooner or later playfellows to be loved more than the rest.

Two intimacies entered into the life of Professor Hardage. The first of these had been formed many years before with Judge Ravenel Morris. They had discovered each other by drifting as lonely men do in the world; each being without family ties, each loving literature, each having empty hours. The bond between them had strengthened, until it had become to each a bond of strength indeed, mighty and uplifting.

The other intimacy was one of those for which human speech will never, perhaps, be called upon to body forth its describing word. In the psychology of feeling there are states which we gladly choose to leave unlanguaged. Vast and deep-sounding as is the orchestra of words, there are scores which we never fling upon such instruments—realities that lie outside the possibility and the desirability of utterance as there are rays of the sun that fall outside the visible spectrum of solar light.

What description can be given in words of that bond between two, when the woman stands near the foot of the upward slope of life, and the man is already passing down on the sunset side, with lengthening afternoon shadows on the gray of his temples—between them the cold separating peaks of a generation?

Such a generation of toiling years separated Professor Hardage from Isabel Conyers. When, at the age of twenty, she returned after years of absence in an eastern college—it was a tradition of her family that its women should be brilliantly educated—he verged upon fifty. To his youthful desires that interval was nothing; but to his disciplined judgment it was everything.

"Even though it could be," he said to himself, "it should not be, and therefore it shall not."

His was an idealism that often leaves its holder poor indeed save in the possession of its own incorruptible wealth. No doubt also the life-long study of the ideals of classic time came to his guidance now with their admonitions of exquisite balance, their moderation and essential justness.

But after he had given up all hope of her, he did not hesitate to draw her to him in other ways; and there was that which drew her unfathomably to him— all the more securely since in her mind there was no thought that the bond between them would ever involve the possibility of love and marriage.

His library became another home to her. One winter she read Greek with him —authors not in her college course. Afterward he read much more Greek to her. Then they laid Greek aside, and he took her through the history of its literature and through that other noble one, its deathless twin.

When she was not actually present, he yet took her with him through the wide regions of his studies—-set her figure in old Greek landscapes and surrounded it with dim shapes of loveliness—saw her sometimes as the perfection that went into marble—made her a portion of legend and story, linking her with Nausicaa and Andromache and the lost others. Then quitting antiquity with her altogether, he passed downward with her into the days of chivalry, brought her to Arthur's court, and invested her with one character after another, trying her by the ladies of knightly ideals—reading her between the lines in all the king's idyls.

But last and best, seeing her in the clear white light of her own country and time—as the spirit of American girlhood, pure, refined, faultlessly proportioned in mental and physical health, full of kindness, full of happiness, made for love, made for motherhood. All this he did in his hopeless and idealizing worship of her; and all this and more he hid away: for he too had his crypt.

So watching her and watching vainly over her, he was the first to see that she was loved and that her nature was turning away from him, from all that he could offer—subdued by that one other call.

"Now, Fates," he said, "by whatsoever names men have blindly prayed to you; you that love to strike at perfection, and pass over a multitude of the ordinary to reach the rare, stand off for a few years! Let them be happy together in their love, their marriage, and their young children. Let the threads run freely and be joyously interwoven. Have mercy at least for a few years!"

A carriage turned a corner of the street and was driven to the door. Isabel got out, and entered the hall without ringing.

He met her there and as she laid her hands in his without a word, he held them and looked at her without a word. He could scarcely believe that in a few days her life could so have drooped as under a dreadful blight.

"I have come to say good-by," and with a quiver of the lips she turned her face aside and brushed past him, entering the library.

He drew his own chair close to hers when she had seated herself.

"I thought you and your grandmother were going later: is not this unexpected?"

"Yes, it is very unexpected."

"But of course she is going with you?"

"No, I am going alone."

"For the summer?"

"Yes, for the summer. I suppose for a long time."

She continued to sit with her cheek leaning against the back of the chair, her eyes directed outward through the windows. He asked reluctantly:

"Is there any trouble?"

"Yes, there is trouble."

"Can you tell me what it is?"

"No, I cannot tell you what it is. I cannot tell any one what it is."

"Is there anything I can do?"

"No, there is nothing you can do. There is nothing any one can do."

Silence followed for some time. He smiled at her sadly:

"Shall I tell you what the trouble is?"

"You do not know what it is. I believe I wish you did know. But I cannot tell you."

"Is it not Rowan?"

She waited awhile without change of posture and answered at length without change of tone:

"Yes, it is Rowan."

The stillness of the room became intense and prolonged; the rustling of the leaves about the window sounded like noise.

"Are you not going to marry him, Isabel?"

"No, I am not going to marry him. I am never going to marry him."

She stretched out her hand helplessly to him. He would not take it and it fell to her side: at that moment he did not dare. But of what use is it to have kept faith with high ideals through trying years if they do not reward us at last with strength in the crises of character? No doubt they rewarded him now: later he reached down and took her hand and held it tenderly.

"You must not go away. You must be reconciled, to him. Otherwise it will sadden your whole summer. And it will sadden his."

"Sadden, the whole summer," she repeated, "a summer? It will sadden a life. If there is eternity, it will sadden eternity."

"Is it so serious?"

"Yes, it is as serious as anything, could be."

After a while she sat up wearily and turned her face to him for the first time.

"Cannot you help me?" she asked. "I do not believe I can bear this. I do not believe I can bear it."

Perhaps it is the doctors who hear that tone oftenest—little wonder that they are men so often with sad or with calloused faces.

"What can I do?"

"I do not know what you can do. But cannot you do something? You were the only person in the world that I could go to. I did not think I could ever come to you; but I had to come. Help me."

He perceived that commonplace counsel would be better than no counsel at all.

"Isabel," he asked, "are you suffering because you have wronged Rowan or because you think he has wronged you?"

"No, no, no," she cried, covering her face with her hands, "I have not wronged him! I have not wronged any one! He has wronged me!"

"Did he ever wrong you before?"

"No, he never wronged me before. But this covers everything—the whole past."

"Have you ever had any great trouble before, Isabel?"

"No, I have never had any great trouble before. At times in my life I may have thought I had, but now I know."

"You do not need to be told that sooner or later all of us have troubles that we think we cannot bear."

She shook her head wearily: "It does not do any good to think of that! It does not help me in the least!"

"But it does help if there is any one to whom we can tell our troubles."

"I cannot tell mine."

"Cannot you tell me?"

"No, I believe I wish you knew, but I could not tell you. No, I do not even wish you to know."

"Have you seen Kate?"

She covered her face with her hands again: "No, no, no," she cried, "not Kate!" Then she looked up at him with eyes suddenly kindling: "Have you

79

heard what Kate's life has been since her marriage?"

"We have all heard, I suppose."

"She has never spoken a word against him—not even to me from whom she never had a secret. How could I go to her about Rowan? Even if she had confided in me, I could not tell her this."

"If you are going away, change of scene will help you to forget it."

"No, it will help me to remember."

"There is prayer, Isabel."

"I know there is prayer. But prayer does not do any good. It has nothing to do with this."

"Enter as soon as possible into the pleasures of the people you are to visit."

"I cannot! I do not wish for pleasure,"

"Isabel," he said at last, "forgive him."

"I cannot forgive him."

"Have you tried?"

"No, I cannot try. If I forgave him, it would only be a change in me: it would not change him: it would not undo what he has done."

"Do you know the necessity of self-sacrifice?"

"But how can I sacrifice what is best in me without lowering myself? Is it a virtue in a woman to throw away what she holds to be as highest?"

"Remember," he said, returning to the point, "that, if you forgive him, you become changed yourself. You no longer see what he has done as you see it now. That is the beauty of forgiveness: it enables us better to understand those whom we have forgiven. Perhaps it will enable you to put yourself in his place."

She put her hands to her eyes with a shudder: "You do not know what you are saying," she cried, and rose.

"Then trust it all to time," he said finally, "that is best! Time alone solves so much. Wait! Do not act! Think and feel as little as possible. Give time its merciful chance. I'll come to see you."

They had moved toward the door. She drew off her glove which she was putting on and laid her hand once more in his.

"Time can change nothing. I have decided."

As she was going down the steps to the carriage, she turned and came back.

"Do not come to see me! I shall come to you to say good-by. It is better for you not to come to the house just now. I might not be able to see you."

Isabel had the carriage driven to the Osborns'.

The house was situated in a pleasant street of delightful residences. It had been newly built on an old foundation as a bridal present to Kate from her father. She had furnished it with a young wife's pride and delight and she had lined it throughout with thoughts of incommunicable tenderness about the life history just beginning. Now, people driving past (and there were few in town who did not know) looked at it as already a prison and a doom.

Kate was sitting in the hall with some work in her lap. Seeing Isabel she sprang up and met her at the door, greeting her as though she herself were the happiest of wives.

"Do you know how long it has been since you were here?" she exclaimed chidingly. "I had not realized how soon young married people can be forgotten and pushed aside."

"Forget you, dearest! I have never thought of you so much as since I was here last."

"Ah," thought Kate to herself, "she has heard. She has begun to feel sorry for me and has begun to stay away as people avoid the unhappy."

But the two friends, each smiling into the other's eyes, their arms around each other, passed into the parlors.

"Now that you are here at last, I shall keep you," said Kate, rising from the seat they had taken. "I will send the carriage home. George cannot be here to lunch and we shall have it all to ourselves as we used to when we were girls together."

"No," exclaimed Isabel, drawing her down into the seat again, "I cannot stay. I had only a few moments and drove by just to speak to you, just to tell you how much I love you."

Kate's face changed and she dropped her eyes. "Is so little of me so much nowadays?" she asked, feeling as though the friendship of a lifetime were indeed beginning to fail her along with other things.

"No, no, no," cried Isabel. "I wish we could never be separated."

She rose quickly and went over to the piano and began to turn over the music. "It seems so long since I heard any music. What has become of it? Has it all gone out of life? I feel as though there were none any more."

Kate came over and looked at one piece of music after another irresolutely.

"I have not touched the piano for weeks."

She sat down and her fingers wandered forcedly through a few chords. Isabel stepped quickly to her side and laid restraining hands softly upon hers: "No; not to-day."

Kate rose with averted face: "No; not any music to-day!"

The friends returned to their seat, on which Kate left her work.
She took it up and for a few moments Isabel watched her in silence.

"When did you see Rowan?"

"You know he lives in the country," replied Isabel, with an air of defensive gayety.

"And does he never come to town?"

"How should I know?"

Kate took this seriously and her head sank lower over her work: "Ah," she thought to herself, "she will not confide in me any longer. She keeps her secrets from me—me who shared them all my life."

"What is it you are making?"

Isabel stretched out her hand, but Kate with a cry threw her breast downward upon her work. With laughter they struggled over it; Kate released it and Isabel rising held it up before her. Then she allowed it to drop to the floor.

"Isabel!" exclaimed Kate, her face grown cold and hard. She stooped with dignity and picked up the garment.

"Oh, forgive me," implored Isabel, throwing her arms around her neck. "I did not know what I was doing!" and she buried her face on the young wife's shoulder. "I was thinking of myself: I cannot tell you why!"

Kate released herself gently. Her face remained grave. She had felt the first wound of motherhood: it could not be healed at once. The friends could not look at each other. Isabel began to draw on her gloves and Kate did not seek to keep her longer.

"I must go. Dear friend, have you forgiven me? I cannot tell you what was in my heart. Some day you will understand. Try to forgive till you do understand."

Kate's mouth trembled: "Isabel, why are you so changed toward me?"

"Ah, I have not changed toward you! I shall never change toward you!"

"Are you too happy to care for me any longer?"

"Ah, Kate, I am not too happy for anything. Some day you will understand."

She leaned far out and waved her hand as she drove away, and then she threw herself back into the carriage. "Dear injured friend! Brave loyal woman'" she cried, "the men we loved have ruined both our lives; and we who never had a secret from each other meet and part as hypocrites to shield them. Drive home," she said to the driver. "If any one motions to stop, pay no attention. Drive fast."

Mrs. Osborn watched the carriage out of sight and then walked slowly back to her work. She folded the soft white fabric over the cushions and then laid her cheek against it and gave it its first christening—the christening of tears.

IX

The court-house clock in the centre of the town clanged the hour of ten—hammered it out lavishly and cheerily as a lusty blacksmith strikes with prodigal arm his customary anvil. Another clock in a dignified church tower also struck ten, but with far greater solemnity, as though reminding the town clock that time is not to be measured out to man as a mere matter of business, but intoned savingly and warningly as the chief commodity of salvation. Then another clock: in a more attenuated cobwebbed steeple also struck ten, reaffirming the gloomy view of its resounding brother and insisting that the town clock had treated the subject with sinful levity.

Nevertheless the town clock seemed to have the best of the argument on this particular day; for the sun was shining, cool, breezes were blowing, and the streets were thronged with people intent on making bargains. Possibly the most appalling idea in most men's notions of eternity is the dread that there will be no more bargaining there.

A bird's-eye view of the little town as it lay outspread on its high fertile plateau, surrounded by green woods and waving fields, would have revealed near one edge of it a large verdurous spot which looked like an overrun oasis. This oasis was enclosed by a high fence on the inside of which ran a hedge of lilacs, privet, and osage orange. Somewhere in it was an old one-story manor house of rambling ells and verandas. Elsewhere was a little summer-house, rose-covered; still elsewhere an arbor vine-hung; at various other places secluded nooks with seats, where the bushes could hide you and not hear you —a virtue quite above anything human. Marguerite lived in this labyrinth.

As the dissenting clocks finished striking, had you been standing outside the fence near a little side gate used by grocers' and bakers' carts, you might have seen Marguerite herself. There came a soft push against the gate from within; and as it swung part of the way open, you might have observed that the push was delivered by the toe of a little foot. A second push sent it still farther. Then there was a pause and then it flew open and stayed open. At first there appeared what looked like an inverted snowy flagstaff but turned out to be a long, closed white parasol; then Marguerite herself appeared, bending her head low under the privet leaves and holding her skirts close in, so that they might not be touched by the whitewash on each edge. Once outside, she straightened herself up with the lithe grace of a young willow, released her skirts, and balancing herself on the point of her parasol, closed the gate with her toe: she was too dainty to touch it.

The sun shone hot and Marguerite quickly raised her parasol. It made you think of some silken white myriad-fluted mushroom of the dark May woods; and Marguerite did not so much seem to have come out of the house as out of the garden—to have slept there on its green moss with the new moon on her eyelids—indeed to have been born there, in some wise compounded of violets and hyacinths; and as the finishing touch to have had squeezed into her nature a few drops of wildwood spritishness.

She started toward the town with a movement somewhat like that of a tall thin lily stalk swayed by zephyrs—with a lilt, a cadence, an ever changing rhythm of joy: plain walking on the solid earth was not for her. At friendly houses along the way she peeped into open windows, calling to friends; she stooped over baby carriages on the sidewalk, noting but not measuring their mysteries; she bowed to the right and to the left at passing carriages; and people leaned far out to bow and smile at her. Her passage through the town was somewhat like that of a butterfly crossing a field.

"Will he be there?" she asked. "I did not tell him I was coming, but he heard me say I should be there at half-past ten o'clock. It is his duty to notice my least remark."

When she reached her destination, the old town library, she mounted the lowest step and glanced rather guiltily up and down the street. Three ladies were going up and two men were going down: no one was coming toward Marguerite.

"Now, why is he not here? He shall be punished for this."

She paced slowly backward and forward yet a little while. Then she started resolutely in the direction of a street where most of the law offices were situated. Turning a corner, she came full upon Judge, Morris.

"Ah, good morning, good morning," he cried, putting his gold-headed cane under his arm and holding out both hands. "Where did you sleep last night? On rose leaves?"

"I was in grandmother's bed when I left off," said Marguerite, looking up at the rim of her hat.

"And where were you when you began again?"

"Still in grandmother's bed. I think I must have been there all the time. I know all about your old Blackstone and all that kind of thing," she continued, glancing at a yellow book under his arm and speaking with a threat as though he had adjudged her ignorant.

"Ah, then you will make a good lawyer's wife."

"I supposed I'd make a good wife of any kind. Are you coming to my ball?"

"Well, you know I am too old to make engagements far ahead. But I expect to be there. If I am not, my ghost shall attend."

"How shall I recognize it? Does it dance? I don't want to mistake it for Barbee."

"Barbee shall not come if I can keep him at home."

"And why, please?"

"I am afraid he is falling in love with you."

"But why shouldn't he?"

"I don't wish my nephew to be flirted."

"But how do you know I'd flirt him?"

"Ah, I knew your mother when she was young and your grandmother when she was young: you're all alike."

"We, are so glad we are," said Marguerite, as she danced away from him under her parasol.

Farther down the street she met Professor Hardage.

"I know all about your old Odyssey—your old Horace and all those things," she said threateningly. "I am not as ignorant as you think."

"I wish Horace had known you."

"Would it have been nice?"

"He might have written an ode *Ad Margaritam* instead of *Ad Lalagem.*"

"Then I might have been able to read it," she said. "In school I couldn't read the other one. But you mustn't think that I did not read a great deal of Latin. The professor used to say that I read my Latin b-e-a-u-t-i-f-u-l-l-y, but that I didn't get much English out of it. I told him I got as much English out of it as the Romans did, and that they certainly ought to have known what it was meant for."

"That must have taught him a lesson!"

"Oh, he said I'd do: I was called the girl who read Latin perfectly, regardless of English. And, then, I won a prize for an essay on the three most important things that the United States has contributed to the civilizations of the Old World. I said they were tobacco, wild turkeys and idle curiosity. Of course every one knew about tobacco and turkeys; but wasn't it clever of me to think of idle curiosity? Now, wasn't it? I made a long list of things and then I selected these from my list."

"I'd like to know what the other things were!"

"Oh, I've forgotten now! But they were very important at the time. Are you coming to my ball?"

"I hope to come."

"And is Miss Anna coming?"

"Miss Anna is coming. She is coming as a man; and she is going to bring a lady."

"How is she going to dress as a man?" said Marguerite, as she danced away from him under her parasol.

She strolled slowly on until she reached the street of justice and the jail; turning into this, she passed up the side opposite the law offices. Her parasol rested far back on one shoulder; to any lateral observer there could have been no mistake regarding the face in front of it. She passed through a group of firemen sitting in their shirtsleeves in front of the engine-house, disappeared around the corner, and went to a confectioner's. Presently she reentered the street, and this time walked along the side where the law offices were grouped. She disappeared around the corner and entered a dry-goods store. A few moments later she reentered the street for the third and last time. Just as she passed a certain law office, she dropped her packages. No one came out to pick them up. Marguerite did this herself—very slowly. Still no one appeared. She gave three sharp little raps on the woodwork of the door.

From the rear office a red head was thrust suddenly out like a surprised woodpecker's. Barbee hurried to the entrance and looked up the street. He saw a good many people. He looked down the street and noticed a parasol moving away.

"I supposed you were in the courthouse," she said, glancing at him with surprise. "Haven't you any cases?"

"One," he answered, "a case of life and death."

"You need not walk against me, Barbee; I am not a vine to need propping. And you need not walk with me. I am quite used to walking alone: my nurse taught me years ago."

"But now you have to learn *not* to walk alone, Marguerite."

"It will be very difficult."

"It will be easy when the right man steps forward: am I the right man?"

"I am going to the library. Good morning."

"So am I going to the library."

"Aren't all your authorities in your office?"

"All except one."

They turned into the quiet shady street: they were not the first to do this.

When they reached the steps, Marguerite sank down.

"Why do I get so tired when I walk with you, Barbee? You exhaust me *very* rapidly."

He sat down not very near her, but soon edged a little closer.

Marguerite leaned over and looked intently at his big, thin ear.

"What a lovely red your ear is, seen against a clear sky. It would make a beautiful lamp-shade."

"You may have both of them—and all the fixtures—solid brass—an antique some day."

He edged a little closer.

Marguerite coughed and pointed across the street: "Aren't those trees beautiful?"

"Oh, don't talk to me about trees! What do I care about *wood*! You're the tree that I want to dig up, and take home, and plant, and live under, and be buried by."

"That's a great deal—all in one sentence."

"Are you never going to love me a little, Marguerite?"

"How can I tell?"

"Don't torture me."

"What am I doing?"

"You are not doing anything, that's the trouble. The other night I was sure you loved me."

"I didn't say so."

"But you looked it."

"Then I looked all wrong: I shall change my looks."

"Will you name the day?"

"What day?"

"*The* day."

"I'll name them all: Monday, Tuesday—"

"Ah, Lord—"

"Barbee, I'm going to sing you a love song—an old, old, old love song. Did you ever hear one?"

"I have been hearing mine for some time."

"This goes back to grandmother's time. But it's the man's song: you ought to be singing it to me."

"I shall continue to sing my own."

Marguerite began to sing close to Barbee's ear:

"I'll give to you a paper of pins,
If that's the way that love begins,
If you will marry me, me, me,
If you will marry me."

"Pins!" said Barbee; "why, that old-time minstrel must have been singing when pins were just invented. You can have—"

Marguerite quieted him with a finger on his elbow:

"I'll give to you a dress of red,
Bound all around with golden thread,
If you will marry me, me, me,
If you will marry me."

"How about a dress not simply bound with golden thread but made of it, made of nothing else! and then hung all over with golden ornaments and the heaviest golden utensils?"

Marguerite sang on:

"I'll give to you a coach and six,
Every horse as black as pitch,
If you will marry me, me, me,
If you will marry me."

"I'll make it two coaches and twelve white ponies."

Marguerite sang on, this time very tenderly:

"I'll give to you the key of my heart,
That we may love and never part,

If you will marry me, me, me,
If you will marry me."

"No man can give anything better," said Barbee, moving closer (as close as possible) and looking questioningly full into Marguerite's eyes.

Marguerite glanced up and down the street. The moment was opportune, the disposition of the universe seemed kind. The big parasol slipped a little lower.

"Marguerite… Please, Marguerite… *Marguerite.*"

The parasol was suddenly pulled down low and remained very still a moment: then a quiver ran round the fringe. It was still again, and there was another quiver. It swayed to and fro and round and round, and then stood very, very still indeed, and there was a violent quiver.

Then Marguerite ran into the library as out of a sudden shower; and Barbee with long slow strides returned to his office.

"Anna," said Professor Hardage, laying his book across his knee as they sat that afternoon in the shady side porch, "I saw Marguerite this morning and she sent her compliments. They were very pretty compliments. I sometimes wonder where Marguerite came from—out of what lands she has wandered."

"Well, now that you have stopped reading," said Miss Anna, laying down her work and smoothing her brow (she never spoke to him until he did stop—perfect woman), "that Is what I have been waiting to talk to you about: do you wish to go with Harriet to Marguerite's ball?"

"I most certainly do not wish to go with Harriet to Marguerite's ball," he said, laughing, "I am going with you."

"Well, you most certainly are not going with me: I am going with Harriet."

"Anna!"

"If I do not, who will? Now what I want you to do is to pay Harriet some attention after I arrive with her. I shall take her into supper, because if you took her in, she would never get any. But suppose that after supper you strolled carelessly up to us—you know how men do—and asked her to take a turn with you."

"What kind of a turn in Heaven's name?"

"Well, suppose you took her out into the yard—to one of those little rustic seats of Marguerite's—and sat there with her for half an hour—in the darkest place you could possibly find. And I want you to try to hold her hand."

"Why, Anna, what on earth—"

"Now don't you suppose Harriet would let you do it," she said indignantly. "But what I want her to have is the pleasure of refusing: it would be such a triumph. It would make her happy for days: it might lengthen her life a little."

"What effect do you suppose it would have on mine?"

His face softened as he mused on the kind of woman his sister was.

"Now don't you try to do anything else," she added severely. "I don't like your expression."

He laughed outright: "What do you suppose I'd do?"

"I don't suppose you'd do anything; but don't you do it!"

Miss Anna's invitation to Harriet had been written some days before.

She had sent down to the book-store for ten cents' worth of tinted note paper and to the drugstore for some of Harriet's favorite sachet powder. Then she put a few sheets of the paper in a dinner plate and sprinkled the powder over them and set the plate where the powder could perfume the paper but not the house. Miss Anna was averse to all odor-bearing things natural or artificial. The perfect triumph of her nose was to perceive absolutely nothing. The only trial to her in cooking was the fact that so often she could not make things taste good without making them smell good.

In the course of time, bending over a sheet of this note paper, with an expression of high nasal disapproval. Miss Anna had written the following note:

"A. Hardage, Esq., presents the compliments of the season to Miss Crane and begs the pleasure of her company to the ball. The aforesaid Hardage, on account of long intimacy with the specified Crane, hopes that she (Crane) will not object to riding alone at night in a one-horse rockaway with no side curtains. Crane to be hugged on the way if Hardage so desires—and Hardage certainly will desire. Hardage and Crane to dance at the ball together while their strength lasts."

Having posted this letter, Miss Anna went off to her orphan and foundling asylum where she was virgin mother to the motherless, drawing the mantle of her spotless life around little waifs straying into the world from hidden paths of shame.

X

It was past one o'clock on the night of the ball.

When dew and twilight had fallen on the green labyrinths of Marguerite's yard, the faintest, slenderest moon might have been seen bending over toward the spot out of drapery of violet cloud. It descended through the secluded windows of Marguerite's room and attended her while she dressed, weaving about her and leaving with her the fragrance of its divine youth passing away. Then it withdrew, having appointed a million stars for torches.

Matching the stars were globe-like lamps, all of one color, all of one shape, which Marguerite had had swung amid the interlaced greenery of trees and vines: as lanterns around the gray bark huts of slow-winged owls; as sun-tanned grapes under the arches of the vine-covered summer-house; as love's lighthouses above the reefs of tumbling rose-bushes: all to illumine the paths which led to nooks and seats. For the night would be very warm; and then Marguerite—but was she the only one?

The three Marguerites,—grandmother, mother, and daughter,—standing side by side and dressed each like each as nearly as was fitting, had awaited their guests. Three high-born fragile natures, solitary each on the stem of its generation; not made for blasts and rudeness. They had received their guests with the graciousness of sincere souls and not without antique distinction; for in their veins flowed blood which had helped to make manners gentle in France centuries ago.

The eldest Marguerite introduced some of her aged friends, who had ventured forth to witness the launching of the frail life-boat, to the youngest; the youngest Marguerite introduced some of hers to the eldest; the Marguerite linked between made some of hers known to her mother and to her child.

Mrs. Conyers arrived early, leaning on the arm of her grandson, Victor Fielding. To-night she was ennobled with jewels—the old family jewels of her last husband's family, not of her own.

When the three Marguerites beheld her, a shadow fell on their faces. The change was like the assumption of a mask behind which they could efface themselves as ladies and receive as hostesses. While she lingered, they forebore even to exchange glances lest feelings injurious to a guest should be thus revealed: so pure in them was the strain of courtesy that went with proffered hospitality. (They were not of the kind who invite you to their houses and having you thus in their power try to pierce you with little insults which they would never dare offer openly in the street: verbal Borgias at their own tables and firesides.) The moment she left them, the three faces became effulgent again.

A little later, strolling across the rooms toward them alone, came Judge Morris, a sprig of wet heliotrope in his button-hole, plucked from one of Marguerite's plants. The paraffin starch on his shirt front and collar and cuffs gave to them the appearance and consistency of celluloid—it being the intention of his old laundress to make him indeed the stiffest and most highly polished gentleman of his high world. His noble face as always a sermon on kindness, sincerity, and peace; yet having this contradiction, that the happier it seemed, the sadder it was to look at: as though all his virtues only framed his great wrong; so that the more clearly you beheld the bright frame, the more deeply you felt the dark picture.

As soon as they discovered him, the Marguerites with a common impulse linked their arms endearingly. Six little white feet came regimentally forward; each of six little white hands made individual forward movements to be the first to lie within his palm; six velvet eyes softened and glistened.

Miss Anna came with Harriet; Professor Hardage came alone; Barbee—burgeoning Alcibiades of the ballroom—came with Self-Confidence. He strolled indifferently toward the eldest Marguerite, from whom he passed superiorly to the central one; by that time the third had vanished.

Isabel came with the Osborns: George soon to be taken secretly home by Rowan; Kate (who had forced herself to accompany him despite her bereavement), lacerated but giving no sign even to Isabel, who relieved the situation by attaching herself momentarily to her hostesses.

"Mamma," protested Marguerite, with indignant eyes, "do you wish Isabel to stand here and eclipse your daughter? Station her on the far side of grandmother, and let the men pass this way first!"

The Merediths were late. As they advanced to pay their respects, Isabel maintained her composure. An observer, who had been told to watch, might have noticed that when Rowan held out his hand, she did not place hers in it; and that while she did not turn her face away from his face, her eyes never met his eyes. She stood a little apart from the receiving group at the moment and spoke to him quickly and awkwardly:

"As soon as you can, will you come and walk with me through the parlors? Please do not pay me any more attention. When the evening is nearly over, will you find me and take me to some place where we may not be interrupted? I will explain."

Without waiting for his assent, she left him, and returned with a laugh to the side of Marguerite, who was shaking a finger threateningly at her.

It was now past one o'clock: guests were already leaving.

When Rowan went for Isabel, she was sitting with Professor Hardage. They were not talking; and her eyes had a look of strained expectancy. As soon as she saw him, she rose and held out her hand to Professor Hardage; then without speaking and still without looking at him, she placed the tips of her fingers on the elbow of his sleeve. As they walked away, she renewed her request in a low voice: "Take me where we shall be undisturbed."

They left the rooms. It was an interval between the dances: the verandas were crowded. They passed out into the yard. Along the cool paths, college boys and college girls strolled by in couples, not caring who listened to their words and with that laughter of youth, the whole meaning of which is never realized save by those who hear it after they have lost it. Older couples sat here and there in quiet nooks—with talk not meant to be heard and with occasional laughter so different.

They moved on, seeking greater privacy. Marguerite's lamps were burnt out— brief flames as measured by human passion. But overhead burnt the million torches of the stars. How brief all human passion measured by that long, long light!

He stopped at last:

"Here?"

She placed herself as far as possible from him.

The seat was at the terminus of a path in the wildest part of Marguerite's garden. Overhead against the trunk of a tree a solitary lantern was flickering fitfully. It soon went out. The dazzling lights of the ballroom, glimmering through boughs and vines, shot a few rays into their faces. Music, languorous, torturing the heart, swelled and died on the air, mingled with the murmurings of eager voices. Close around them in the darkness was the heavy fragrance of perishing blossoms—earth dials of yesterday; close around them the clean sweetness of fresh ones—breath of the coming morn. It was an hour when the heart, surrounded by what can live no more and by what never before has lived, grows faint and sick with yearnings for its own past and forlorn with the inevitableness of change—the cruelty of all change.

For a while silence lasted. He waited for her to speak; she tried repeatedly to do so. At length with apparent fear that he might misunderstand, she interposed an agitated command:

"Do not say anything."

A few minutes later she began to speak to him, still struggling for her self-control.

"I do not forget that to-night I have been acting a part, and that I have asked you to act a part with me. I have walked with you and I have talked with you, and I am with you now to create an impression that is false; to pretend before those who see us that nothing is changed. I do not forget that I have been doing this thing which is unworthy of me. But it is the first time—try not to believe it to be my character. I am compelled to tell you that it is one of the humiliations you have forced upon me."

"I have understood this," he said hastily, breaking the silence she had imposed upon him.

"Then let it pass," she cried nervously. "It is enough that I have been obliged to observe my own hypocrisies, and that I have asked you to countenance and to conceal them."

He offered no response. And in a little while she went on:

"I ought to tell you one thing more. Last week I made all my arrangements to go away at once, for the summer, for a long time. I did not expect to see you again. Two or three times I started to the station. I have stayed until now because it seemed best after all to speak to you once more. This is my reason for being here to-night; and it is the only apology I can offer to myself or to you for what I am doing."

There was a sad and bitter vehemence in her words; she quivered with passion.

"Isabel," he said more urgently, "there is nothing I am not prepared to tell you."

When she spoke again, it was with difficulty and everything seemed to hang upon her question:

"Does any one else know?"

His reply was immediate:

"No one else knows."

"Have you every reason to believe this?"

"I have every reason to believe this."

"You kept your secret well," she said with mournful irony. "You reserved it for the one person whom it could most injure: my privilege is too great!"

"It is true," he said.

She turned and looked at him. She felt the depth of conviction with which he spoke, yet it hurt her. She liked his dignity and his self-control, and would not have had them less; yet she gathered fresh bitterness from the fact that he did not lose them. But to her each moment disclosed its new and uncontrollable emotions; as words came, her mind quickly filled again with the things she could not say. She now went on:

"I am forced to ask these questions, although I have no right to ask them and certainly I have no wish. I have wanted to know whether I could carry out the plan that has seemed to me best for each of us. If others shared your secret, I could not do this. I am going away—I am going in the morning. I shall remain away a long time. Since we have been seen together here to-night as usual, no one suspects now that for us everything has become nothing. While I am away, no one can have the means of finding this out. Before I return, there will be changes—there may be many changes. If we meet with indifference then, it will be thought that we have become indifferent, one of us, or both of us: I suppose it will be thought to be you. There will be comment, comment that will be hard to stand; but this will be the quietest way to end everything —as far as anything can ever be ended."

"Whatever you wish! I leave it all to you."

She did not pause to heed his words:

"This will spare me the linking of my name with yours any further just now; it will spare me all that I should suffer if the matter which estranges us should be discovered and be discussed. It will save me hereafter, perhaps, from being pointed out as a woman who so trusted and was so deceived. It may shield my life altogether from some notoriety: I could be grateful for that!"

She was thinking of her family name, and of the many proud eyes that were turned upon her in the present and out of the past. There was a sting for her in the remembrance and the sting passed into her concluding words:

"I do not forget that when I ask you to do all this, I, who am not given to practising deception, am asking you to go on practising yours. I am urging you to shirk the consequences of your wrong-doing—to enjoy in the world an untarnished name after you have tarnished your life. Do not think I forget that! Still I beg you to do as I say. This is another of the humiliations you have led me to: that although I am separated from you by all that once united us, I must remain partner with you in the concealment of a thing that would ruin you if it were known."

She turned to him as though she experienced full relief through her hard and cruel words:

"Do I understand, then, that this is to be buried away by you—and by me—from the knowledge of the world?"

"No one else has any right to know it. I have told you that."

"Then that is all!"

She gave a quick dismissal to the subject, so putting an end to the interview.

She started to rise from her seat; but impulses, new at the instant, checked her: all the past checked her, all that she was herself and all that he had been to her.

Perhaps what at each moment had angered her most was the fact that she was speaking, not he. She knew him to be of the blood of silent men and to have inherited their silence. This very trait of his had rendered association with him so endearing. Love had been so divinely apart from speech, either his or her own: most intimate for having been most mute. But she knew also that he was capable of speech, full and strong and quick enough upon occasion; and her heart had cried out that in a lifetime this was the one hour when he should not have given way to her or allowed her to say a word—when he should have borne her down with uncontrollable pleading.

It was her own work that confronted her and she did not recognize it. She had exhausted resources to convince him of her determination to cast him off at once; to render it plain that further parley would to her be further insult. She had made him feel this on the night of his confession; in the note of direct repulse she sent him by the hand of a servant in her own house the following afternoon; by returning to him everything that he had ever given her; by her refusal to acknowledge his presence this evening beyond laying upon him a command; and by every word that she had just spoken. And in all this she had thought only of what she suffered, not of what he must be suffering.

Perhaps some late instantaneous recognition of this flashed upon her as she started to leave him—as she looked at him sitting there, his face turned toward her in stoical acceptance of his fate. There was something in the controlled strength of it that touched her newly. She may have realized that if he had not been silent, if he had argued, defended himself, pleaded, she would have risen and walked back to the house without a word. It turned her nature toward him a little, that he placed too high a value upon her dismissal of him not to believe it irrevocable.

Yet it hurt her: she was but one woman in the world; could the thought of this have made it easier for him to let her go away now without a protest?

The air of the summer night grew unbearable for sweetness about her. The faint music of the ballroom had no pity for her. There young eyes found joy in answering eyes, passed on and found joy in others and in others. Palm met palm and then palms as soft and then palms yet softer. Some minutes before, the laughter of Marguerite in the shrubbery quite close by had startled Isabel. She had distinguished a voice. Now Marguerite's laughter reached her again —and there was a different voice with hers. Change! change! one put away, the place so perfectly filled by another.

A white moth of the night wandered into Rowan's face searching its features; then it flitted over to her and searched hers, its wings fanning and clinging to her lips; and then it passed on, pursuing amid mistakes and inconstancies its life-quest lasting through a few darknesses.

Fear suddenly reached down into her heart and drew up one question; and she asked that question in a voice low and cold and guarded:

"Sometime, when you ask another woman to marry you, will you think it your duty to tell her?"

"I will never ask any other woman."

"I did not inquire for your intention; I asked what you would believe to be your duty."

"It will never become my duty. But if it should, I would never marry without being true to the woman; and to be true is to tell the truth."

"You mean that you would tell her?"

"I mean that I would tell her."

After a little silence she stirred in her seat and spoke, all her anger gone:

"I am going to ask you, if you ever do, not to tell her as you have told me— after it is too late. If you cannot find some way of letting her know the truth before she loves you, then do not tell her afterward, when you have won her life away from her. If there is deception at all, then it is not worse to go on deceiving her than it was to begin to deceive her. Tell her, if you must, while she is indifferent and will not care, not after she has given herself to you and will then have to give you up. But what can you, a man, know what it means to a woman to tell her this! How can you know, how can you ever, ever know!"

She covered her face with her hands and her voice broke with tears.

"Isabel—"

"You have no right to call me by my name, and I have no right to hear it, as though nothing were changed between us."

"I have not changed."

"How could you tell me! Why did you ever tell me!" she cried abruptly, grief breaking her down.

"There was a time when I did not expect to tell you. I expected to do as other men do."

"Ah, you would have deceived me!" she exclaimed, turning upon him with fresh suffering. "You would have taken advantage of my ignorance and have married me and never have let me know! And you would have called that deception love and you would have called yourself a true man!"

"But I did not do this! It was yourself who helped me to see that the beginning of morality is to stop lying and deception."

"But if you had this on your conscience already, what right had you ever to come near me?"

"I had come to love you!"

"Did your love of me give you the right to win mine?"

"It gave me the temptation."

"And what did you expect when you determined to tell me this? What did you suppose such a confession would mean to me? Did you imagine that while it was still fresh on your lips, I would smile in your face and tell you it made no difference? Was I to hear you speak of one whose youth and innocence you took away through her frailties, and then step joyously into her place? Was this the unfeeling, the degraded soul you thought to be mine? Would I have been worthy even of the poor love you could give me, if I had done that?"

"I expected you to marry me! I expected you to forgive. I have this at least to remember: I lost you honestly when I could have won you falsely."

"Ah, you have no right to seek any happiness in what is all sadness to me! And all the sadness, the ruin of everything, comes from your wrong-doing."

"Remember that my wrong-doing did not begin with me. I bear my share: it is enough: I will bear no more."

A long silence followed. She spoke at last, checking her tears:

"And so this is the end of my dream! This is what life has brought me to! And what have I done to deserve it? To leave home, to shun friends, to dread scandal, to be misjudged, to bear the burden of your secret and share with you its shame, to see my years stretch out before me with no love in them, no ambitions, no ties—this is what life has brought me, and what have I done to deserve it?"

As her tears ceased, her eyes seemed to be looking into a future that lacked the relief of tears. As though she were already passed far on into it and were looking back to this moment, she went on, speaking very slowly and sadly:

"We shall not see each other again in a long time, and whenever we do, we shall be nothing to each other and we shall never speak of this. There is one thing I wish to tell you. Some day you may have false thoughts of me. You may think that I had no deep feeling, no constancy, no mercy, no forgiveness; that it was easy to give you up, because I never loved you. I shall have enough to bear and I cannot bear that. So I want to tell you that you will never know what my love for you was. A woman cannot speak till she has the right; and before you gave me the right, you took it away. For some little happiness it may bring me hereafter let me tell you that you were everything to me, everything! If I had taught myself to make allowances for you, if I had seen things to forgive in you, what you told me would have been only one thing more and I might have forgiven. But all that I saw in you I loved. Rowan, and I believed that I saw everything. Remember this, if false thoughts of me ever come to you! I expect to live a long time: the memory of my love of you will be the sorrow that will keep me alive."

After a few moments of silent struggle she moved nearer.

"Do not touch me," she said; "remember that what love makes dear, it makes sacred."

She put out a hand in the darkness and, closing her eyes over welling tears, passed it for long remembrance over his features: letting the palm lie close against his forehead with her fingers in his hair; afterward pressing it softly over his eyes and passing it around his neck. Then she took her hand away as though fearful of an impulse. Then she put her hand out again and laid her fingers across his lips. Then she took her hand away, and leaning over, laid her lips on his lips:

"Good-by!" she murmured against his face, "good-by! good-by! good-by!"

Mrs. Conyers had seen Rowan and Isabel together in the parlors early in the evening. She had seen them, late in the evening, quit the house. She had counted the minutes till they returned and she had marked their agitation as they parted. The closest association lasting from childhood until now had convinced her of the straightforwardness of Isabel's character; and the events of the night were naturally accepted by her as evidences of the renewal of relationship with Rowan, if not as yet of complete reconciliation.

She herself had encountered during the evening unexpected slights and repulses. Her hostesses had been cool, but she expected them to be cool: they did not like her nor she them. But Judge Morris had avoided her; the Hardages had avoided her; each member of the Meredith family had avoided her; Isabel had avoided her; even Harriet, when once she crossed the rooms to her, had with an incomprehensible flare of temper turned her back and sought refuge with Miss Anna. She was very angry.

But overbalancing the indignities of the evening was now this supreme joy of Isabel's return to what she believed to be Isabel's destiny. She sent her grandson home that she might have the drive with the girl alone. When Isabel, upon entering the carriage, her head and eyes closely muffled in her shawl, had withdrawn as far as possible into one corner and remained silent on the way, she refrained from intrusion, believing that she understood the emotions dominating her behavior.

The carriage drew up at the door. She got out quickly and passed to her room —with a motive of her own.

Isabel lingered. She ascended the steps without conscious will. At the top she missed her shawl: it had become entangled in the fringe of a window strap, had slipped from her bare shoulders as she set her foot on the pavement, and now lay in the track of the carriage wheels. As she picked it up, an owl flew viciously close to her face. What memories, what memories came back to her! With a shiver she went over to a frame-like opening in the foliage on one side of the veranda and stood looking toward the horizon where the moon had sunk on that other night—that first night of her sorrow. How long it was since then!

At any other time she would have dreaded the parting which must take place with her grandmother: now what a little matter it seemed!

As she tapped and opened the door, she put her hand quickly before her eyes, blinded by the flood of light which streamed out into the dark hall. Every gas-jet was turned on—around the walls, in the chandelier; and under the chandelier stood her grandmother, waiting, her eyes fixed expectantly on the door, her countenance softened with returning affection, the fire of triumph in her eyes.

She had unclasped from around her neck the diamond necklace of old family jewels, and held it in the pool of her rosy palms, as though it were a mass of clear separate raindrops rainbow-kindled. It was looped about the tips of her two upright thumbs; part of it had slipped through the palms and flashed like a pendent arc of light below.

The necklace was an heirloom; it had started to grow in England of old; it had grown through the generations of the family in the New World.

It had begun as a ring—given with the plighting of troth; it had become ear-rings; it had become a pendant; it had become a tiara; it had become part of a necklace; it had become a necklace—completed circlet of many hopes.

As Isabel entered Mrs. Conyers started forward, smiling, to clasp it around her neck as the expression of her love and pleasure; then she caught sight of Isabel's face, and with parted lips she stood still.

Isabel, white, listless, had sunk into the nearest chair, and now said, quietly and wearily, noticing nothing:

"Grandmother, do not get up to see me off in the morning. My trunk is packed; the others are already at the station. All my arrangements are made. I'll say good-by to you now," and she stood up.

Mrs. Conyers stood looking at her. Gradually a change passed over her face; her eyes grew dull, the eyelids narrowed upon the balls; the round jaws relaxed; and instead of the smile, hatred came mysteriously out and spread itself rapidly over her features: true horrible revelation. Her fingers tightened and loosened about the necklace until it was forced out through them, until it glided, crawled, as though it were alive and were being strangled and were writhing. She spoke with entire quietness:

"After all that I have seen to-night, are you not going to marry Rowan?"

Isabel stirred listlessly as with remembrance of a duty:

"I had forgotten, grandmother, that I owe you an explanation. I found, after all, that I should have to see Rowan again: there was a matter about which I was compelled to speak with him. That is all I meant by being with him to-night: everything now is ended between us."

"And you are going away without giving me the reason of all this?"

Isabel gathered her gloves and shawl together and said with simple distaste:

"Yes."

As she did so, Mrs. Conyers, suddenly beside herself with aimless rage, raised one arm and hurled the necklace against the opposite wall of the room. It leaped a tangled braid through the air and as it struck burst asunder, and the stones scattered and rattled along the floor and rolled far out on the carpet.

She turned and putting up a little white arm, which shook as though palsied, began to extinguish the lights. Isabel watched her a moment remorsefully:

"Good night, grandmother, and good-by. I am sorry to go away and leave you angry."

As she entered her room, gray light was already creeping in through the windows, left open to the summer night. She went mournfully to her trunk. The tray had been lifted out and placed upon a chair near by. The little tops to the divisions of the tray were all thrown back, and she could see that the last thing had been packed into its place. Her hand satchel was open on her bureau, and she could see the edge of a handkerchief and the little brown wicker neck of a cologne bottle. Beside the hand satchel were her purse, baggage checks, and travelling ticket: everything was in readiness. She looked at it all a long time:

"How can I go away? How can I, how can I?"

She went over to her bed. The sheet had been turned down, the pillow dented for her face. Beside the pillow was a tiny reading-stand and on this was a candle and a book—with thought of her old habit of reading after she had come home from pleasures like those of to-night—when they were pleasures. Beside the book her maid had set a little cut-glass vase of blossoms which had opened since she put them there—were just opening now.

"How can I read? How can I sleep?"

She crossed to a large window opening on the lawn in the rear of the house—and looked for the last time out at the gray old pines and dim blue, ever wintry firs. Beyond were house-tops and tree-tops of the town; and beyond these lay the country—stretching away to his home. Soon the morning light would be crimsoning the horizon before his window.

"How can I stay?" she said. "How can I bear to stay?"

She recalled her last words to him as they parted:

"Remember that you are forgotten!"

She recalled his reply:

"Forget that you are remembered!"

She sank down on the floor and crossed her arms on the window sill and buried her face on her arms. The white dawn approached, touched her, and passed, and she did not heed.

PART SECOND

The home of the Merediths lay in a region of fertile lands adapted alike to tillage and to pasturage. The immediate neighborhood was old, as civilization reckons age in the United States, and was well conserved, It held in high esteem its traditions of itself, approved its own customs, was proud of its prides: a characteristic community of country gentlemen at the side of each of whom a characteristic lady lived and had her peculiar being.

The ownership of the soil had long since passed into the hands of capable families—with this exception, that here and there between the borders of large estates little farms were to be found representing all that remained from slow processes of partition and absorption. These scant freeholds had thus their pathos, marking as they did the losing fight of successive holders against more fortunate, more powerful neighbors. Nothing in its way records more surely the clash and struggle and ranking of men than the boundaries of land. There you see extinction and survival, the perpetual going under of the weak, the perpetual overriding of the strong.

Two such fragmentary farms lay on opposite sides of the Meredith estate. One was the property of Ambrose Webb, a married but childless man who, thus exempt from necessity of raking the earth for swarming progeny, had sown nearly all his land in grass and rented it as pasturage: no crops of children, no crops of grain.

The other farm was of less importance. Had you ridden from the front door of the Merediths northward for nearly a mile, you would have reached the summit of a slope sweeping a wide horizon. Standing on this summit any one of these bright summer days, you could have seen at the foot of the slope, less than a quarter of a mile away on the steep opposite side, a rectangle of land covering some fifty acres. It lay crumpled into a rough depression in the landscape. A rivulet of clear water by virtue of indomitable crook and turn made its way across this valley; a woodland stood in one corner, nearly all its timber felled; there were a few patches of grain so small that they made you think of the variegated peasant strips of agricultural France; and a few lots smaller still around a stable. The buildings huddled confusedly into this valley seemed to have backed toward each other like a flock of sheep, encompassed by peril and making a last stand in futile defence of their right to exist at all.

What held the preeminence of castle in the collection of structures was a small brick house with one upper bedroom. The front entrance had no porch; and beneath the door, as stepping-stones of entrance, lay two circular slabs of wood resembling sausage blocks, one half superposed. Over the door was a trellis of gourd vines now profusely, blooming and bee-visited. Grouped around this castle in still lower feudal and vital dependence was a log cabin of one room and of many more gourd vines, an ice-house, a house for fowls, a stable, a rick for hay, and a sagging shed for farm implements.

If the appearance of the place suggested the struggles of a family on the verge of extinction, this idea was further borne out by what looked like its determination to stand a long final siege at least in the matter of rations, for it swarmed with life. In the quiet crystalline air from dawn till after sunset the sounds arising from it were the clamor of a sincere, outspoken multitude of what man calls the dumb creatures. Evidently some mind, full of energy and forethought, had made its appearance late in the history of these failing generations and had begun a fight to reverse failure and turn back the tide of aggression. As the first step in self-recovery this rugged island of poverty must be made self-sustaining. Therefore it had been made to teem with animal and vegetable plenty.

On one side of the house lay an orderly garden of vegetables and berry-bearing shrubs; the yard itself was in reality an orchard of fruit trees, some warmed by the very walls; under the shed there were beegums alive with the nectar builders; along the garden walks were frames for freighted grape-vines. The work of regeneration had been pushed beyond the limits of utilitarianism over into a certain crude domain of aesthetics. On one front window-sill what had been the annual Christmas box of raisins had been turned into a little hot-bed of flowering plants; and under the panes of glass a dense forest of them, sun-drawn, looked like a harvest field swept by a storm. On the opposite window ledge an empty drum of figs was now topped with hardy jump-up-johnnies. It bore some resemblance to an enormous yellow muffin stuffed with blueberries. In the garden big-headed peonies here and there fell over upon the young onions. The entire demesne lay white and green with tidiness under yellow sun and azure sky; for fences and outhouses, even the trunks of trees several feet up from the ground, glistened with whitewash. So that everywhere was seen the impress and guidance of a spirit evoking abundance, order, even beauty, out of what could so easily have been squalor and despondent wretchedness.

This was the home of Pansy Vaughan; and Pansy was the explanation of everything beautiful and fruitful, the peaceful Joan of Arc of that valley, seeing rapt visions of the glory of her people.

In the plain upper room of the plain brick house, on her hard white bed with her hard white thoughts, lay Pansy—sleepless throughout the night of Marguerite's ball. The youngest of the children slept beside her; two others lay in a trundle-bed across the room; and the three were getting out of sleep all that there is in it for tired, healthy children. In the room below, her father and the eldest boy were resting; and through the rafters of the flooring she could hear them both: her father a large, fluent, well-seasoned, self-comforting bassoon; and her brother a sappy, inexperienced bassoon trying to imitate it. Wakefulness was a novel state for Pansy herself, who was always tired when bedtime came and as full of wild vitality as one of her young guineas in the summer wheat; so that she sank into slumber as a rock sinks into the sea, descending till it reaches the unstirred bottom.

What kept her awake to-night was mortification that she had not been invited to the ball. She knew perfectly well that she was not entitled to an invitation, since the three Marguerites had never heard of her. She had never been to a fashionable party even in the country. But her engagement to Dent Meredith already linked her to him socially and she felt the tugging of those links: what were soon to become her rights had begun to be her rights already. Another little thing troubled her: she had no flower to send him for his button-hole, to accompany her note wishing him a pleasant evening. She could not bear to give him anything common; and Pansy believed that no one was needed to tell her what a common thing is.

For a third reason slumber refused to descend and weigh down her eyelids: on the morrow she was to call upon Dent's mother, and the thought of this call preoccupied her with terror. She was one of the bravest of souls; but the terror which shook her was the terror that shakes them all—terror lest they be not loved.

All her life she had looked with awe upward out of her valley toward that great house. Its lawns with stately clumps of evergreens, its many servants, its distant lights often seen twinkling in the windows at night, the tales that reached her of wonderful music and faery dancing; the flashing family carriages which had so often whirled past her on the turnpike with scornful footman and driver—all these recollections revisited her to-night. In the morning she was to cross the boundary of this inaccessible world as one who was to hold a high position in it.

How pictures came crowding back! One of the earliest recollections of childhood was hearing the scream of the Meredith peacocks as they drew their gorgeous plumage across the silent summer lawns; at home they had nothing better than fussing guineas. She had never come nearer to one of those proud birds than handling a set of tail feathers which Mrs. Meredith had presented to her mother for a family fly brush. Pansy had good reason to remember because she had often been required to stand beside the table and, one little bare foot set alternately on the other little bare foot, wield the brush over the dishes till arms and eyelids ached.

Another of those dim recollections was pressing her face against the window-panes when the first snow began to fall on the scraggy cedars in the yard; and as she began to sing softly to herself one of the ancient ditties of the children of the poor, "Old Woman, picking Geese," she would dream of the magical flowers which they told her bloomed all winter in a glass house at the Merediths' while there was ice on the pines outside. Big red roses and icicles separated only by a thin glass—she could hardly believe it; and she would cast her eye toward their own garden where a few black withered stalks marked the early death-beds of the pinks and jonquils.

But even in those young years Pansy had little time to look out of windows and to dream of anything. She must help, she must work; for she was the oldest of five children, and the others followed so closely that they pushed her out of her garments. A hardy, self-helpful child life, bravened by necessities, never undermined by luxuries. For very dolls Pansy used small dried gourds, taking the big round end of the gourd for the head of the doll and all the rest of the gourd for all the rest of the body.

One morning when she was fourteen, the other children were clinging with tears to her in a poor, darkened room—she to be little mother to them henceforth: they never clung in vain.

That same autumn when woods were turning red and wild grapes turning black and corn turning yellow, a cherished rockaway drawn by a venerated horse, that tried to for conversation on the highroad whenever he passed a neighbor's vehicle, rattled out on the turnpike with five children in it and headed for town: Pansy driving, taking herself and the rest to the public school. For years thereafter, through dark and bright days, she conveyed that nest of hungry fledglings back and forth over bitter and weary miles, getting their ravenous minds fed at one end of the route, and their ravenous bodies fed at the other. If the harness broke, Pansy got out with a string. If the horse dropped a shoe, or dropped himself, Pansy picked up what she could. In town she drove to the blacksmith shop and to all other shops whither business called her. Her friends were the blacksmith and the tollgate keeper, her teachers—all who knew her and they were few: she had no time for friendships. At home the only frequent visitor was Ambrose Webb, and Pansy did not care for Ambrose. The first time she remembered seeing him at dinner, she—a very little girl—had watched his throat with gloomy fascination. Afterward her mother told her he had an Adam's apple; and Pansy, working obscurely at some problem of theology, had secretly taken down the Bible and read the story of Adam and the fearful fruit. Ambrose became associated in her mind with the Fall of Man; she disliked the proximity.

No time for friendships. Besides the labors at school, there was the nightly care of her father on her return, the mending of his clothes; there was the lonely burning of her candle far into the night as she toiled over lessons. When she had learned all that could be taught her at the school, she left the younger children there and victoriously transferred herself for a finishing course to a seminary of the town, where she was now proceeding to graduate.

This was Pansy, child of plain, poor, farmer folk, immemorially dwelling close to the soil; unlettered, unambitious, long-lived, abounding in children, without physical beauty, but marking the track of their generations by a path lustrous with right-doing. For more than a hundred years on this spot the land had lessened around them; but the soil had worked upward into their veins, as into the stalks of plants, the trunks of trees; and that clean, thrilling sap of the earth, that vitality of the exhaustless mother which never goes for nothing, had produced one heavenly flower at last—shooting forth with irrepressible energy a soul unspoiled and morally sublime. When the top decays, as it always does in the lapse of time, whence shall come regeneration if not from below? It is the plain people who are the eternal breeding grounds of high destinies.

In the long economy of nature, this, perhaps, was the meaning and the mission of this lofty child who now lay sleepless, shaken to the core with thoughts of the splendid world over into which she was to journey to-morrow.

At ten o'clock next morning she set out.

It had been a question with her whether she should go straight across the fields and climb the fences, or walk around by the turnpike and open the gates. Her preference was for fields and fences, because that was the short and direct way, and Pansy was used to the short and direct way of getting to the end of her desires. But, as has been said, she had already fallen into the habit of considering what was due her and becoming to her as a young Mrs. Meredith; and it struck her that this lady would not climb field fences, at least by preference and with facility. Therefore she chose the highroad, gates, dust, and dignity.

It could scarcely be said that she was becomingly raimented. Pansy made her own dresses, and the dresses declared the handiwork of their maker. The one she wore this morning was chiefly characterized by a pair of sleeves designed by herself; from the elbow to the wrist there hung green pouches that looked like long pea-pods not well filled. Her only ornament was a large oval pin at her throat which had somewhat the relation to a cameo as that borne by Wedgwood china. It represented a white horse drinking at a white roadside well; beside the shoulder of the horse stood a white angel, many times taller, with an arm thrown caressingly around the horse's neck; while a stunted forest tree extended a solitary branch over the horse's tail.

She had been oppressed with dread that she should not arrive in time. No time had been set, no one knew that she was coming, and the forenoons were long. Nevertheless impatience consumed her to encounter Mrs. Meredith; and once on the way, inasmuch as Pansy usually walked as though she had been told to go for the doctor, but not to run, she was not long in arriving.

When she reached the top of the drive in front of the Meredith homestead, her face, naturally colorless, was a consistent red; and her heart, of whose existence she had never in her life been reminded, was beating audibly. Although she said to herself that it was bad manners, she shook out her handkerchief, which she had herself starched and ironed with much care; and gathering her skirts aside, first to the right and then to the left, dusted her shoes, lifting each a little into the air, and she pulled some grass from around the buttons. With the other half of her handkerchief she wiped her brow; but a fresh bead of perspiration instantly appeared; a few drops even stood on her dilated nostrils—raindrops on the eaves. Even had the day been cool she must have been warm, for she wore more layers of clothing than usual, having deposited some fresh strata in honor of her wealthy mother-in-law.

As Pansy stepped from behind the pines, with one long, quivering breath of final self-adjustment, she suddenly stood still, arrested by the vision of so glorious a hue and shape that, for the moment, everything else was forgotten. On the pavement just before her, as though to intercept her should she attempt to cross the Meredith threshold, stood a peacock, expanding to the utmost its great fan of pride and love. It confronted her with its high-born composure and insolent grace, all its jewelled feathers flashing in the sun; then with a little backward movement of its royal head and convulsion of its breast, it threw out its cry,—the cry she had heard in the distance through dreaming years,—warning all who heard that she was there, the intruder. Then lowering its tail and drawing its plumage in fastidiously against the body, it crossed her path in an evasive circle and disappeared behind the pines.

"Oh, Dent, why did you ever ask me to marry you!" thought Pansy, in a moment of soul failure.

Mrs. Meredith was sitting on the veranda and was partly concealed by a running rose. She was not expecting visitors; she had much to think of this morning, and she rose wonderingly and reluctantly as Pansy came forward: she did not know who it was, and she did not advance.

Pansy ascended the steps and paused, looking with wistful eyes at the great lady who was to be her mother, but who did not even greet her.

"Good morning, Mrs. Meredith," she said, in a shrill treble, holding herself somewhat in the attitude of a wooden soldier, "I suppose I shall have to introduce myself: it is Pansy."

The surprise faded from Mrs. Meredith's face, the reserve melted. With outstretched hands she advanced smiling.

"How do you do. Pansy," she said with motherly gentleness; "it is very kind of you to come and see me, and I am very glad to know you. Shall we go in where it is cooler?"

They entered the long hall. Near the door stood a marble bust: each wall was lined with portraits. She passed between Dent's ancestors into the large darkened parlors.

"Sit here, won't you?" said Mrs. Meredith, and she even pushed gently forward the most luxurious chair within her reach. To Pansy it seemed large enough to hold all the children. At home she was used to chairs that were not only small, but hard. Wherever the bottom of a chair seemed to be in that household, there it was—if it was anywhere. Actuated now by this lifelong faith in literal furniture, she sat down with the utmost determination where she was bid; but the bottom offered no resistance to her descending weight and she sank. She threw out her hands and her hat tilted over her eyes. It seemed to her that she was enclosed up to her neck in what might have been a large morocco bath-tub—which came to an end at her knees. She pushed back her hat, crimson.

"That was a surprise," she said, frankly admitting the fault, "but there'll never be another such."

"I am afraid you found it warm walking, Pansy," said Mrs. Meredith, opening her fan and handing it to her.

"Oh, no, Mrs. Meredith, I never fan!" said Pansy, declining breathlessly. "I have too much use for my hands. I'd rather suffer and do something else. Besides, you know I am used to walking in the sun. I am very fond of botany, and I am out of doors for hours at a time when I can find the chance."

Mrs. Meredith was delighted at the opportunity to make easy vague comment on a harmless subject.

"What a beautiful study it must be," she said with authority.

"Must be!" exclaimed Pansy; "why, Mrs. Meredith, don't you *know*? Don't you understand botany?"

111

Pansy had an idea that in Dent's home botany was as familiarly apprehended as peas and turnips in hers.

"I am afraid not," replied Mrs. Meredith, a little coolly. Her mission had been to adorn and people the earth, not to study it. And among persons of her acquaintance it was the prime duty of each not to lay bare the others' ignorance, but to make a little knowledge appear as great as possible. It was discomfiting to have Pansy charge upon what after all was only a vacant spot in her mind. She added, as defensively intimating that the subject had another dangerous side:

"When I was a girl, young ladies at school did not learn much botany; but they paid a great deal of attention to their manners."

"Why did not they learn it after they had left school and after they had learned manners?" inquired Pansy, with ruthless enthusiasm. "It is such a mistake to stop learning everything simply because you have stopped school. Don't you think so?"

"When a girl marries, my dear, she soon has other studies to take up. She has a house and husband. The girls of my day, I am afraid, gave up their botanies for their duties: it may be different now."

"No matter how many children I may have," said Pansy, positively, "I shall never—give—up—botany! Besides, you know, Mrs. Meredith, that we study botany only during the summer months, and I do hope—" she broke off suddenly.

Mrs. Meredith smoothed her dress nervously and sought to find her chair comfortable.

"Your mother named you Pansy," she remarked, taking a gloomy view of the present moment and of the whole future of this acquaintanceship.

That this should be the name of a woman was to her a mistake, a crime. Her sense of fitness demanded that names should be given to infants with reference to their adult characters and eventual positions in life. She liked her own name "Caroline"; and she liked "Margaret" and all such womanly, motherly, dignified, stately appellatives. As for "Pansy," it had been the name of one of her husband's shorthorns, a premium animal at the county fairs; the silver cup was on the sideboard in the dining room now.

"Yes, Mrs. Meredith," replied Pansy, "that was the name my mother gave me. I think she must have had a great love of flowers. She named me for the best she had. I hope I shall never forget that," and Pansy looked at Mrs. Meredith with a face of such gravity and pride that silence lasted in the parlors for a while.

Buried in Pansy's heart was one secret, one sorrow: that her mother had been poor. Her father wore his yoke ungalled; he loved rough work, drew his religion from privations, accepted hardship as the chastening that insures reward. But that her mother's hands should have been folded and have returned to universal clay without ever having fondled the finer things of life —this to Pansy was remembrance to start tears on the brightest day.

"I think she named you beautifully," said Mrs. Meredith, breaking that silence, "and I am glad you told me, Pansy." She lingered with quick approval on the name.

But she turned the conversation at once to less personal channels. The beauty of the country at this season seemed to offer her an inoffensive escape. She felt that she could handle it at least with tolerable discretion. She realized that she was not deep on the subject, but she did feel fluent.

"I suppose you take the same pride that we all do in such a beautiful country."

Sunlight instantly shone out on Pansy's face. Dent was a geologist; and since she conceived herself to be on trial before Mrs. Meredith this morning, it was of the first importance that she demonstrate her sympathy and intelligent appreciation of his field of work.

"Indeed I do feel the greatest pride in it, Mrs. Meredith," she replied. "I study it a great deal. But of course you know perfectly the whole formation of this region."

Mrs. Meredith coughed with frank discouragement.

"I do not know it," she admitted dryly. "I suppose I ought to know it, but I do not. I believe school-teachers understand these things. I am afraid I am a very ignorant woman. No one of my acquaintances is very learned. We are not used to scholarship."

"I know all the strata," said Pansy. "I tell the children stories of how the Mastodon once virtually lived in our stable, and that millions of years ago there were Pterodactyls under their bed."

"I think it a misfortune for a young woman to have much to say to children about Pterodactyls under their bed—is that the name? Such things never seem to have troubled Solomon, and I believe he was reputed wise." She did not care for the old-fashioned reference herself, but she thought it would affect Pansy.

"The children in the public schools know things that Solomon never heard of," said Pansy, contemptuously.

"I do not doubt it in the least, my dear. I believe it was not his knowledge that made him rather celebrated, but his wisdom. But I am not up in Solomon!" she admitted hastily, retreating from the subject in new dismay.

The time had arrived for Pansy to depart; but she reclined in her morocco alcove with somewhat the stiffness of a tilted bottle and somewhat the contour. She felt extreme dissatisfaction with her visit and reluctance to terminate it.

Her idea of the difference between people in society and other people was that it hinged ornamentally upon inexhaustible and scanty knowledge. If Mrs. Meredith was a social leader, and she herself had no social standing at all, it was mainly because that lady was publicly recognized as a learned woman, and the world had not yet found out that she herself was anything but ignorant. Being ignorant was to her mind the quintessence of being common; and as she had undertaken this morning to prove to Dent's mother that she was not common, she had only to prove that she was learned. For days she had prepared for this interview with that conception of its meaning. She had converted her mind into a kind of rapid-firing gun; she had condensed her knowledge into conversational cartridges. No sooner had she taken up a mental position before Mrs. Meredith than the parlors resounded with light, rapid detonations of information. That lady had but to release the poorest, most lifeless, little clay pigeon of a remark and Pansy shattered it in mid air and refixed suspicious eyes on the trap.

But the pigeons soon began to fly less frequently. And finally they gave out. And now she must take nearly all her cartridges home! Mrs. Meredith would think her ignorant, therefore she would think her common. If Pansy had only known what divine dulness, what ambrosial stupidity, often reclines on those Olympian heights called society!

As last she rose. Neither had mentioned Dent's name, though each had been thinking of him all the time. Not a word had been spoken to indicate the recognition of a relationship which one of them so desired and the other so dreaded. Pansy might merely have hurried over to ask Mrs. Meredith for the loan of an ice-cream freezer or for a setting of eggs. On the mother's part this silence was kindly meant: she did not think it right to take for granted what might never come to pass. Uppermost in her mind was the cruelty of accepting Pansy as her daughter-in-law this morning with the possibility of rejecting her afterward.

As Pansy walked reluctantly out into the hall, she stopped with a deep wish in her candid eyes.

"Oh, Mrs. Meredith, I should so much like to see the portrait of Dent's father: he has often spoken to me about It."

Mrs. Meredith led her away in silence to where the portrait hung, and the two stood looking at it side by side. She resisted a slight impulse to put her arm around the child. When they returned to the front of the house, Pansy turned:

"Do you think you will ever love me?"

The carriage was at the door. "You must not walk," said Mrs. Meredith, "the sun is too hot now."

As Pansy stepped into the carriage, she cast a suspicious glance at the cushions: Meredith upholstery was not to be trusted, and she seated herself warily.

Mrs. Meredith put her hand through the window: "You must come to see me soon again, Pansy. I am a poor visitor, but I shall try to call on you in a few days."

She went back to her seat on the veranda.

It has been said that her insight into goodness was her strength; she usually had a way of knowing at once, as regards the character of people, what she was ever to know at all. Her impressions of Pansy unrolled themselves disconnectedly:

"She makes mistakes, but she does not know how to do wrong. Guile is not in her. She is so innocent that she does not realize sometimes the peril of her own words. She is proud—a great deal prouder than Dent. To her, life means work and duty; more than that, it means love. She is ambitious, and ambition, in her case, would be indispensable. She did not claim Dent: I appreciate that. She is a perfectly brave girl, and it is cowardice that makes so many women hypocrites. She will improve—she improved while she was here. But oh, everything else! No figure, no beauty, no grace, no tact, no voice, no hands, no anything that is so much needed! Dent says there are cold bodies which he calls planets without atmosphere: he has found one to revolve about him. If she only had some clouds! A mist here and there, so that everything would not be so plain, so exposed, so terribly open! But neither has *he* any clouds, any mists, any atmosphere. And if she only would not so try to expose other people! If she had not so trampled upon me in my ignorance; and with such a sense of triumph! I was never so educated in my life by a visitor. The amount of information she imparted in half an hour—how many months it would have served the purpose of a well-bred woman! And her pride in her family— were there ever such little brothers and sisters outside a royal family! And her devotion to her father, and remembrance of her mother. I shall go to see her, and be received, I suppose, somewhere between the griddle and the churn."

As Pansy was driven home, feeling under herself for the first time the elasticity of a perfect carriage, she experimented with her posture. "This carriage is not to be sat in in the usual way," she said. And indeed it was not.

In the family rockaway there was constant need of muscular adjustment to different shocks at successive moments; here muscular surrender was required: a comfortable collapse—and there you were!

Trouble awaited her at home. Owing to preoccupation with her visit she had, before setting out, neglected much of her morning work. She had especially forgotten the hungry multitude of her dependants. The children, taking advantage of her absence, had fed only themselves. As a consequence, the trustful lives around the house had suffered a great wrong, and they were attempting to describe it to each other. The instant Pansy descended from the carriage the ducks, massed around the doorsteps, discovered her, and with frantic outcry and outstretched necks ran to find out what it all meant. The signal was taken up by other species and genera. In the stable lot the calves responded as the French horn end of the orchestra; and the youngest of her little brothers, who had climbed into a fruit tree as a lookout for her return, in scrambling hurriedly down, dropped to the earth with the boneless thud of an opossum.

Pansy walked straight up to her room, heeding nothing, leaving a wailing wake. She locked herself in. It was an hour before dinner and she needed all those moments for herself.

She sat on the edge of her bed and new light brought new wretchedness. It was not, after all, quantity of information that made the chief difference between herself and Dent's mother. The other things, all the other things—would she ever, ever acquire them! Finally the picture rose before her of how the footman had looked as he had held the carriage door open for her, and the ducks had sprawled over his feet; and she threw herself on the bed, hat and all, and burst out crying with rage and grief and mortification.

"She will think I am common," she moaned, "and I am not common! Why did I say such things? It is not my way of talking. Why did I criticise the way the portrait was hung? And she will think this is what I really am, and it is not what I am! She will think I do not even know how to sit in a chair, and she will tell Dent, and Dent will believe her, and what will become of me?"

"Pansy," said Dent next afternoon, as they were in the woods together, "you have won my mother's heart."

"Oh, Dent," she exclaimed, tears starting, "I was afraid she would not like me. How could she like me, knowing me no better?"

"She doesn't yet know that she likes you," he replied, with his honest thinking and his honest speech, "but I can see that she trusts you and respects you; and with my mother everything else follows in time."

"I was embarrassed. I did myself such injustice."

"It is something you never did any one else."

He had been at work in his quarry on the vestiges of creation; the quarry lay at an outcrop of that northern hill overlooking the valley in which she lived. Near by was a woodland, and she had come out for some work of her own in which he guided her. They lay on the grass now side by side.

"I am working on the plan of our house, Pansy. I expect to begin to build in the autumn. I have chosen this spot for the site. How do you like it?"

"I like it very well. For one reason, I can always see the old place from it."

"My father left his estate to be equally divided between Rowan and me. Of course he could not divide the house; that goes to Rowan: it is a good custom for this country as it was a good custom for our forefathers in England. But I get an equivalent and am to build for myself on this part of the land: my portion is over here. You see we have always been divided only by a few fences and they do not divide at all."

"The same plants grow on each side, Dent."

"There is one thing I have to tell you. If you are coming into our family, you ought to know it beforehand. There is a shadow over our house. It grows deeper every year and we do not know what it means. That is, my mother and I do not know. It is some secret in Rowan's life. He has never offered to tell us, and of course we have never asked him, and in fact mother and I have never even spoken to each other on the subject."

It was the first time she had even seen sadness in his eyes; and she impulsively clasped his hand. He returned the pressure and then their palms separated. No franker sign of their love had ever passed between them.

He went on very gravely: "Rowan was the most open nature I ever saw when he was a boy. I remember this now. I did not think of it then. I believe he was the happiest. You know we are all pantheists of some kind nowadays. I could never see much difference between a living thing that stands rooted in the earth like a tree and a living thing whose destiny it is to move the foot perpetually over the earth, as man. The union is as close in one case as in the other. Do you remember the blind man of the New Testament who saw men as trees walking? Rowan seemed to me, as I recall him now, to have risen out of the earth through my father and mother—a growth of wild nature, with the seasons in his face, with the blood of the planet rising into his veins as intimately as it pours into a spring oak or into an autumn grape-vine. I often heard Professor Hardage call him the earth-born. He never called any one else that. He was wild with happiness until he went to college. He came back all changed; and life has been uphill with him ever since. Lately things have grown worse. The other day I was working on the plan of our house; he came in and looked over my shoulder: 'Don't build, Dent,' he said, 'bring your wife here,' and he walked quickly out of the room. I knew what that meant: he has been unfortunate in his love affair and is ready to throw up the whole idea of marrying. This is our trouble, Pansy. It may explain anything that may have been lacking in my mother's treatment of you; she is not herself at all." He spoke with great tenderness and he looked disturbed.

"Can I do anything?" What had she been all her life but burden-bearer, sorrow-sharer?

"Nothing."

"If I ever can, will you tell me?"

"This is the only secret I have kept from you, Pansy. I am sure you have kept none from me. I believe that if I could read everything in you, I should find nothing I did not wish to know."

She did not reply for a while. Then she said solemnly: "I have one secret. There is something I try to hide from every human being and I always shall. It is not a bad secret, Dent. But I do not wish to tell you what it is, and I feel sure you will never ask me."

He turned his eyes to her clear with unshakable confidence: "I never will."

Pansy was thinking of her mother's poverty.

They sat awhile in silence.

He had pulled some stems of seeding grass and drew them slowly across his palm, pondering Life. Then he began to talk to her in the way that made them so much at home with one another.

"Pansy, men used to speak of the secrets of Nature: there is not the slightest evidence that Nature has a secret. They used to speak of the mysteries of the Creator. I am not one of those who claim to be authorities on the traits of the Creator. Some of my ancestors considered themselves such. But I do say that men are coming more and more to think of Him as having no mysteries. We have no evidence, as the old hymn declares, that He loves to move in a mysterious way. The entire openness of Nature and of the Creator—these are the new ways of thinking. They will be the only ways of thinking in the future unless civilization sinks again into darkness. What we call secrets and mysteries of the universe are the limitations of our powers and our knowledge. The little that we actually do know about Nature, how open it is, how unsecretive! There is nowhere a sign that the Creator wishes to hide from us even what is Life. If we ever discover what Life is, no doubt we shall then realize that it contained no mystery."

She loved to listen, feeling that he was drawing her to his way of thinking for the coming years.

"It was the folly and the crime of all ancient religions that their priesthoods veiled them; whenever the veil was rent, like the veil of Isis, it was not God that men found behind it: it was nothing. The religions of the future will have no veils. As far as they can set before their worshippers truth at all, it will be truth as open as the day. The Great Teacher in the New Testament—what an eternal lesson on light itself: that is the beauty of his Gospel. And his Apostles —where do you find him saying to them, 'Preach my word to all men as the secrets of a priesthood and the mysteries of the Father'?

"It is the tragedy of man alone that he has his secrets. No doubt the time will come when I shall have mine and when I shall have to hide things from you, Pansy, as Rowan has his and hides things from us. Life is full of things that we cannot tell because they would injure us; and of things that we cannot tell because they would injure others. But surely we should all like to live in a time when a man's private life will be his only life."

After a silence he came back to her with a quiet laugh: "Here I am talking about the future of the human race, and we have never agreed upon our marriage ceremony! What a lover!"

"I want the most beautiful ceremony in the world."

"The ceremony of your church?" he asked with great respect, though wincing.

"My church has no ceremony: every minister in it has his own; and rather than have one of them write mine, I think I should rather write it myself: shouldn't you?"

"I think I should," he said, laughing.

He drew a little book out of his breast pocket: "Perhaps you will like this: a great many people have been married by it."

"I want the same ceremony that is used for kings and queens, for the greatest and the best people of the earth. I will marry you by no other!"

"A good many of them have used this," and he read to her the ceremony of his church.

When he finished neither spoke.

It was a clear summer afternoon. Under them was the strength of rocks; around them the noiseless growth of needful things; above them the upward-drawing light: two working children of the New World, two pieces of Nature's quietism.

II

It was the second morning after Marguerite's ball.

Marguerite, to herself a girl no longer, lay in the middle of a great, fragrant, drowsy bed of carved walnut, once her grandmother's. She had been dreaming; she had just awakened. The sun, long since risen above the trees of the yard, was slanting through the leaves and roses that formed an outside lattice to her window-blinds.

These blinds were very old. They had been her grandmother's when she was Marguerite's age; and one day, not long before this, Marguerite, pillaging the attic, had found them and brought them down, with adoring eyes, and put them up before her own windows. They were of thin muslin, and on them were painted scenes representing the River of Life, with hills and castles, valleys and streams, in a long series; at the end there was a faint vision of a crystal dome in the air—the Celestial City—nearly washed away. You looked at these scenes through the arches of a ruined castle. A young man (on one blind) has just said farewell to his parents on the steps of the castle and is rowing away down the River of Life. At the prow of his boat is the figurehead of a winged woman holding an hour-glass.

Marguerite lay on her side, sleepily contemplating the whole scene between her thick, bosky lashes. She liked everything but the winged woman holding the hour-glass. Had she been that woman, she would have dropped the hour-glass into the blue, burying water, and have reached up her hand for the young man to draw her into the boat with him. And she would have taken off her wings and cast them away upon the hurrying river. To have been alone with him, no hour-glass, no wings, rowing away on Life's long voyage, past castles and valleys, and never ending woods and streams! As to the Celestial City, she would have liked her blinds better if the rains of her grandmother's youth had washed it away altogether. It was not the desirable end of such a journey: she did not care to land *there*.

Marguerite slipped drowsily over to the edge of the bed in order to be nearer the blinds; and she began to study what was left of the face of the young man just starting on his adventures from the house of his fathers. Who was he? Of whom did he cause her to think? She sat up in bed and propped her face in the palms of her hands—the April face with its October eyes—and lapsed into what had been her dreams of the night. The laces of her nightgown dropped from her wrists to her elbows; the masses of her hair, like sunlit autumn maize, fell down over her neck and shoulders into the purity of the bed.

Until the evening of her party the world had been to Marguerite something that arranged all her happiness and never interfered with it. Only soundness and loveliness of nature, inborn, undestroyable, could have withstood such luxury, indulgence, surfeit as she had always known.

On that night which was designed to end for her the life of childhood, she had, for the first time, beheld the symbol of the world's diviner beauty—a cross. All her guests had individually greeted her as though each were happier in her happiness. Except one—he did not care. He had spoken to her upon entering with the manner of one who wished himself elsewhere, he alone brought no tribute to her of any kind, in his eyes, by his smile, through the pressure of his hand.

The slight wounded her at the moment; she had not expected to have a guest to whom she would be nothing and to whom it would seem no unkindness to let her know this. The slight left its trail of pain as the evening wore on and he did not come near her. Several times, while standing close to him, she had looked her surprise, had shadowed her face with coldness for him to see. For the first time in her life she felt herself rejected, suffered the fascination of that pain. Afterward she had intentionally pressed so close to him in the throng of her guests that her arm brushed his sleeve. At last she had disengaged herself from all others and had even gone to him with the inquiries of a hostess; and he had forced himself to smile at her and had forgotten her while he spoke to her—as though she were a child. All her nature was exquisitely loosened that night, and quivering; it was not a time to be so wounded and to forget.

She did not forget as she sat in her room after all had gone. She took the kindnesses and caresses, the congratulations and triumphs, of those full-fruited hours, pressed them together and derived merely one clear drop of bitterness—the languorous poison of one haunting desire. It followed her into her sleep and through the next day; and not until night came again and she had passed through the gateway of dreams was she happy: for in those dreams it was he who was setting out from the house of his fathers on a voyage down the River of Life; and he had paused and turned and called her to come to him and be with him always.

Marguerite lifted her face from her palms, as she finished her revery. She slipped to the floor out of the big walnut bed, and crossing to the blinds laid her fingers on the young man's shoulder. It was the movement with which one says: "I have come."

With a sigh she drew one of the blinds aside and looked out upon the leaves and roses of her yard and at the dazzling sunlight. Within a few feet of her a bird was singing. "How can you?" she said. "If you loved, you would be silent. Your wings would droop. You could neither sing nor fly." She turned dreamily back into her room and wandered over to a little table on which her violin lay in its box. She lifted the top and thrummed the strings. "How could I ever have loved you?"

She dressed absent-mindedly. How should she spend the forenoon? Some of her friends would be coming to talk over the party; there would be callers; there was the summer-house, her hammock, her phaeton; there were nooks and seats, cool, fragrant; there were her mother and grandmother to prattle to and caress. "No," she said, "not any of them. One person only. I must see *him*."

She thought of the places where she could probably see him if he should be in town that day. There was only one—the library. Often, when there, she had seen him pass in and out. He had no need to come for books or periodicals, all these he could have at home; but she had heard the librarian and him at work; over the files of old papers containing accounts of early agricultural affairs and the first cattle-shows of the state. She resolved to go to the library: what desire had she ever known that she had not gratified?

When Marguerite, about eleven o'clock, approached the library a little fearfully, she saw Barbee pacing to and fro on the sidewalk before the steps. She felt inclined to turn back; he was the last person she cared to meet this morning. Play with him had suddenly ended as a picnic in a spring grove is interrupted by a tempest.

"I ought to tell him at once," she said; and she went forward.

He came to meet her—with a countenance dissatisfied and reproachful. It struck her that his thin large ears looked yellowish instead of red and that his freckles had apparently spread and thickened. She asked herself why she had never before realized how boyish he was.

"Marguerite," he said at once, as though the matter were to be taken firmly in hand, "you treated me shabbily the night of your party. It was unworthy of you. And I will not stand it. You ought not be such a child!"

Her breath was taken away. She blanched and her eyes dilated as she looked at him: the lash of words had never been laid on her.

"Are you calling me to account?" she asked. "Then I shall call you to an account. When you came up to speak to grandmother and to mamma and me, you spoke to us as though you were an indifferent suitor of mine—as though I were a suitor of yours. As soon as you were gone, mamma said to me: 'What have you been doing, Marguerite, that he should think you are in love with him—that he should treat us as though we all wished to catch him?'"

"That was a mistake of your mother's. But after what had passed between us —"

"No matter what had passed between us, I do not think that a *man* would virtually tell a girl's mother on her: a boy might."

He grew ashen; and he took his hand out of his pockets and straightened himself from his slouchy lounging posture, and stood before her, his head in the air on his long neck like a young stag affronted and enraged.

"It is true, I have sometimes been too much like a boy with you," he said. "Have you made it possible for me to be anything else?"

"Then I'll make it possible for you now: to begin, I am too old to be called to account for my actions—except by those who have the right."

"You mean, that I have no right—after what has passed—"

"Nothing has passed between us!"

"Marguerite," he said, "do you mean that you do not love me?"

"Can you not see?"

She was standing on the steps above him. The many-fluted parasol with its long silken fringes rested on one shoulder. Her face in the dazzling sunlight, under her hat, had lost its gayety. Her eyes rested upon his with perfect quietness.

"I do not believe that you yourself know whether you love me," he said, laughing pitifully. His big mouth twitched and his love had come back into his eyes quickly enough.

"Let me tell you how I know," she said, with more kindness. "If I loved you, I could not stand here and speak of it to you in this way. I could not tell you you are not a man. Everything in me would go down before you. You could do with my life what you pleased. No one in comparison with you would mean anything to me—not even mamma. As long as I was with you, I should never wish to sleep; if you were away from me, I should never wish to waken. If you were poor, if you were in trouble, you would be all the dearer to me—if you only loved me, only loved me!"

Who is it that can mark down the moment when we ceased to be children? Gazing backward in after years, we sometimes attempt dimly to fix the time. "It probably occurred on that day," we declare; "it may have taken place during that night. It coincided with that hardship, or with that mastery of life." But a child can suffer and can triumph as a man or a woman, yet remain a child. Like man and woman it can hate, envy, malign, cheat, lie, tyrannize; or bless, cheer, defend, drop its pitying tears, pour out its heroic spirit. Love alone among the passions parts the two eternities of a lifetime. The instant it is born, the child which was its parent is dead.

As Marguerite suddenly ceased speaking, frightened by the secret import of her own words, her skin, which had the satinlike fineness and sheen of white poppy leaves, became dyed from brow to breast with a surging flame of rose. She turned partly away from Barbee, and she waited for him to go.

He looked at her a moment with torment in his eyes; then, lifting his hat without a word, he turned and walked proudly down the street toward his office.

Marguerite did not send a glance after him. What can make us so cruel to those who vainly love us as our vain love of some one else? What do we care for their suffering? We see it in their faces, hear it in their speech, feel it as the tragedy of their lives. But we turn away from them unmoved and cry out at the heartlessness of those whom our own faces and words and sorrow do not touch.

She lowered her parasol, and pressing her palm against one cheek and then the other, to force back the betraying blood, hurried agitated and elated into the library. A new kind of excitement filled her: she had confessed her secret, had proved her fidelity to him she loved by turning off the playmate of childhood. Who does not know the relief of confessing to some one who does not understand?

The interior of the library was an immense rectangular room. Book shelves projected from each side toward the middle, forming alcoves. Seated in one of these alcoves, you could be seen only by persons who should chance to pass. The library was never crowded and it was nearly empty now. Marguerite lingered to speak with the librarian, meantime looking carefully around the room; and then moved on toward the shelves where she remembered having once seen a certain book of which she was now thinking. It had not interested her then; she had heard it spoken of since, but it had not interested her since. Only to-day something new within herself drew her toward it.

No one was in the alcove she entered. After a while she found her book and seated herself in a nook of the walls with her face turned in the one direction from which she could be discovered by any one passing. While she read, she wished to watch: might he not pass?

It was a very old volume, thumbed by generations of readers. Pages were gone, the halves of pages worn away or tattered. It was printed in an old style of uncertain spelling so that the period of its authorship could in this way be but doubtfully indicated. Ostensibly it came down from the ruder, plainer speech of old English times, which may have found leisure for such "A Booke of Folly."

Marguerite's eyes settled first on the complete title: "Lady Bluefields' First Principles of Courting for Ye Use of Ye Ladies; but Plainly Set Down for Ye Good of Ye Beginners."

"I am not a beginner," thought Marguerite, who had been in love three days; and she began to read:

"Now of all artes ye most ancient is ye lovely arte of courting. It is ye earliest form of ye chase. It is older than hawking or hunting ye wilde bore. It is older than ye flint age or ye stone aye, being as old as ye bones in ye man his body and in ye woman her body. It began in ye Garden of Eden and is as old as ye old devil himself."

Marguerite laughed: she thought Lady Bluefields delightful.

"Now ye only purpose in all God His world of ye arte of courting is to create love where love is not, or to make it grow where it has begun. But whether ye wish to create love or to blow ye little coal into ye big blaze, ye principles are ye same; for ye bellows that will fan nothing into something will easily roast ye spark into ye roaring fire; and ye grander ye fire, ye grander ye arte."

Marguerite laughed again. Then she stopped reading and tested the passage in the light of her experience. A bellows and—nothing to begin. Then something. Then a spark. Then a name. She returned to the book with the conclusion that Lady Bluefields was a woman of experience.

"This little booke will not contain any but ye first principles: if is enough for ye stingy price ye pay. But ye woman who buys ye first principles and fails, must then get ye larger work on ye Last Principles of Courting, with ye true account of ye mysteries which set ye principles to going: it is ye infallible guide to ye irresistible love. Ye pay more for ye Big Booke, and God knows it is worth ye price: it is written for ye women who are ye difficult cases—ye floating derelicts in ye ocean of love, ye hidden snags, terror of ye seafaring men."

This did not so much interest Marguerite. She skipped two or three pages which seemed to go unnecessarily into the subject of derelicts and snags. "I am not quite sure as to what a derelict is: I do not think I am one; out certainly I am not a snag."

"Now ye only reason for ye lovely arts of courtinge is ye purpose to marry. If ye do not expect to marry, positively ye must not court: flirting is ye dishonest arte. Courting is ye honest arte; if ye woman knows in ye woman her heart that she will not make ye man a good wife, let her not try to Cage ye man: let her keep ye cat or cage ye canary: that is enough for her."

"I shall dispose of my canary at once. It goes to Miss Harriet Crane."

"Now of all men there is one ye woman must not court: ye married man. Positively ye must not court such a man. If he wishes to court ye, ye must make resistance to him with all ye soul; if you wish to court him, ye must resist yourself. If he is a married man and happy, let him alone. If he is married and unhappy, let him bear his lot and beat his wife."

Marguerite's eyes flashed. "It is well the writer did not live in this age," she thought.

"Ye men to court are three kinds: first ye swain; second ye old bachelor; third ye widower. Ye old bachelor is like ye green chimney of ye new house—hard to kindle. But ye widower is like ye familiar fireplace. Ye must court according to ye kind. Ye bachelor and ye widower are treated in ye big booke."

"The swain is left," said Marguerite. "How and when is the swain to be courted?"

"Now ye beauty of ye swain is that ye can court him at all seasons of ye year. Ye female bird will signal for ye mate only when ye woods are green; but even ye old maid can go to ye icy spinnet and drum wildly in ye dead of winter with ye aching fingers and ye swain mate will sometimes come to her out of ye cold."

Marguerite was beginning to think that nearly every one treated in Lady Bluefields' book was too advanced in years: it was too charitable to the problems of spinsters. "Where do the young come in?" she asked impatiently.

"Ye must not court ye young swain with ye food or ye wine. That is for ye old bachelors and ye widowers to whom ye food and wine are dear, but ye woman who gives them not dear enough. Ye woman gives them meat and drink and they give ye woman hope: it is ye bargain: let each be content with what each gets. But if ye swain be bashful and ye know that he cannot speak ye word that he has tried to speak, a glass of ye wine will sometimes give him that missing word. Ye wine passes ye word to him and he passes ye word to you: and ye keep it! When ye man is soaked with wine he does not know what he loves nor cares: he will hug ye iron post in ye street or ye sack of feathers in ye man his bed and talk to it as though nothing else were dear to him in all ye world. It is not ye love that makes him do this; it is ye wine and ye man his own devilish nature. No; ye must marry with wine, but ye must court with water. Ye love that will not begin with water will not last with wine."

This did not go to the heart of the matter. Marguerite turned over several pages.

"In ye arte of courting, it is often ye woman her eyes that settle ye man his fate, But if ye woman her eyes are not beautiful, she must not court with them but with other members of ye woman her body. Ye greatest use of ye ugly eyes is to see but not be seen. If ye try to court with ye ugly eyes, ye scare ye man away or make him to feel sick; and ye will be sorry. Ye eyes must be beautiful and ye eyes must have some mystery. They must not be like ye windows of ye house in summer when ye curtains are taken down and ye shutters are taken off. As ye man stands outside he must want to see all that is within, but he must not be able. What ye man loves ye woman for is ye mystery in her; if ye woman contain no mystery, let her marry if she must; but not aspire to court. (This is enough for ye stingy price ye pay: if ye had paid more money, ye would have received more instruction.)"

Marguerite thought it very little instruction for any money. She felt disappointed and provoked. She passed on to "Clothes." "What can she teach me on that subject?" she thought.

"When ye court with ye clothes, ye must not lift ye dress above ye ankle bone."

"Then I know what kind of ankle bone *she* had," said Marguerite, bitter for revenge on Lady Bluefields.

"Ye clothes play a greate part in ye arte of courtinge."

Marguerite turned the leaf; but she found that the other pages on the theme were too thumbed and faint to be legible.

She looked into the subject of "Hands": learning where the palms should be turned up and when turned down; the meaning of a crooked forefinger, and of full moons rising on the horizons of the finger nails; why women with freckled hands should court bachelors. Also how the feet, if of such and such sizes and configurations, must be kept as *"ye two dead secrets."* Similarly how dimples must be born and not made—with a caution against *"ye dimple under ye nose"* (reference to "Big Booke"—well worth the money, etc.).

When she reached the subject of the kiss, Marguerite thought guiltily of the library steps.

"Ye kiss is ye last and ye greatest act in all ye lovely arte of courtinge. Ye eyes, ye hair, ye feet, ye dimple, ye whole trunk, are of no account if they do not lead up to ye kiss. There are two kinds of ye kiss: ye kiss that ye give and ye kiss that ye take. Ye kiss that ye take is ye one ye want. Ye woman often wishes to give ye man one but cannot; and ye man often wishes to take one (or more) from ye woman but cannot; and between her not being able to give and his not being able to take, there is suffering enough in this ill-begotten and ill-

sorted world. Ye greatest enemy of ye kiss that ye earth has ever known is ye sun; ye greatest friend is ye night.

"Ye most cases where ye woman can take ye kiss are put down in ye 'Big Booke.'

"When ye man lies sick in ye hospital and ye woman bends over him and he is too weak to raise his head, she can let her head fall down on his; it is only the law of gravitation. But not while she is giving him ye physick. If ye woman is riding in ye carriage and ye horses run away; and ye man she loves is standing in ye bushes and rushes out and seizes ye horses but is dragged, when he lies in ye road in ye swoon, ye woman can send ye driver around behind ye carriage and kiss him then—as she always does in ye women their novels but never does in ye life. There is one time when any woman can freely kiss ye man she loves: in ye dreame. It is ye safest way, and ye best. No one knows; and it does not disappoint as it often does disappoint when ye are awake.

"Lastly when ye beautiful swain that ye woman loved is dead, she way go into ye room where he lies white and cold and kiss him then: but she waited too long."

Marguerite let the book fall as though an arrow had pierced her. At the same time she heard the librarian approaching. She quickly restored the volume to its place and drew out another book. The librarian entered the alcove, smiled at Marguerite, peeped over her shoulder into the book she was reading, searched for another, and took it away. When she disappeared, Marguerite rose and looked; Lady Bluefields was gone.

She could not banish those heart-breaking words: "*When ye beautiful swain that ye woman loved is dead.*" The longing of the past days, the sadness, the languor that was ecstasy and pain, swept back over her as she sat listening now, hoping for another footstep. Would he not come? She did not ask to speak with him. If she might only see him, only feel him near for a few moments.

She quitted the library slowly at last, trying to escape notice; and passed up the street with an unconscious slight drooping of that aerial figure. When she reached her yard, the tree-tops within were swaying and showing the pale gray under-surfaces of their leaves. A storm was coming. She turned at the gate, her hat in her hand, and looked toward the cloud with red lightnings darting from it: a still white figure confronting that noonday darkness of the skies.

"Grandmother never loved but once," she said. "Mamma never loved but once: it is our fate."

III

"Anna," said Professor Hardage that same morning, coming out of his library into the side porch where Miss Anna, sitting in a green chair and wearing a pink apron and holding a yellow bowl with a blue border, was seeding scarlet cherries for a brown roll, "see what somebody has sent *me*." He held up a many-colored bouquet tied with a brilliant ribbon; to the ribbon was pinned an old-fashioned card.

"Ah, now, that is what comes of your being at the ball," said Miss Anna, delighted and brimming with pride. "Somebody fell in love with you. I told you you looked handsome that night," and she beckoned impatiently for the bouquet.

He surrendered it with a dubious look. She did not consider the little tumulus of Flora, but devoured the name of the builder. Her face turned crimson; and leaning over to one side, she dropped the bouquet into the basket for cherry seed. Then she continued her dutiful pastime, her head bent so low that he could see nothing but the part dividing the soft brown hair of her fine head.

He sat down and laughed at her: "I knew you'd get me into trouble."

It was some moments before she asked in a guilty voice: "What did you *do*?"

"What did you tell me to do?"

"I asked you to be kind to Harriet," she murmured mournfully.

"You told me to take her out into the darkest place I could find and to sit there with her and hold her hand."

"I did not tell you to hold her hand. I told you to *try* to hold her hand."

"Well! I built better than you knew: give me my flowers."

"What did you do?" she asked again, in a voice that admitted the worst.

"How do I know? I was thinking of something else! But here comes Harriet," he said, quickly standing up and gazing down the street.

"Go in," said Miss Anna, "I want to see Harriet alone."

"*You* go in. The porch isn't dark; but I'll stay here with her!"

"Please."

When he had gone, Miss Anna leaned over and lifting the bouquet from the sticking cherry seed tossed it into the yard—tossed it *far*.

Harriet came out into the porch looking wonderfully fresh. "How do you do, Anna?" she said with an accent of new cordiality, established cordiality.

The accent struck Miss Anna's ear as the voice of the bouquet. She had at once discovered also that Harriet was beautifully dressed—even to the point of wearing her best gloves.

"Oh, good morning, Harriet," she replied, giving the yellow bowl an unnecessary shake and speaking quite incidentally as though the visit were not of the slightest consequence. She did not invite Harriet to be seated. Harriet seated herself.

"Aren't you well, Anna?" she inquired with blank surprise.

"I am always well."

"Is any one ill, Anna?"

"Not to my knowledge."

Harriet knew Miss Anna to have the sweetest nature of all women. She realized that she herself was often a care to her friend. A certain impulse inspired her now to give assurance that she had not come this morning to weigh her down with more troubles.

"Do you know, Anna, I never felt so well! Marguerite's ball really brought me out. I have turned over a new leaf of destiny and I am going out more after this. What right has a woman to give up life so soon? I shall go out more, and I shall read more, and be a different woman, and cease worrying you. Aren't women reading history now? But then they are doing everything. Still that is no reason why I should not read a little, because my mind is really a blank on the subject of the antiquities. Of course I can get the ancient Hebrews out of the Bible; but I ought to know more about the Greeks and Romans. Now oughtn't I?"

"You don't want to know anything about the Greeks and the Romans, Harriet," said Miss Anna. "Content yourself with the earliest Hebrews. You have gotten along very well without the Greeks and the Romans—for—a—long—time."

Harriet understood at last; there was no mistaking now. She was a very delicate instrument and much used to being rudely played upon. Her friend's reception of her to-day had been so unaccountable that at one moment she had suspected that her appearance might be at fault. Harriet had known women to turn cold at the sight of a new gown; and it had really become a life principle not to dress even as well as she could, because she needed the kindness that flows out so copiously from new clothes to old clothes. But it was embarrassment that caused her now to say rather aimlessly:

"I believe I feel overdressed. What possessed me?"

"Don't overdress again," enjoined Miss Anna in stern confidence. "Never try to change yourself in anyway. I like you better as you are—a—great—deal—better."

"Then you shall have me as you like me, Anna dear," replied Harriet, faithfully and earnestly, with a faltering voice; and she looked out into the yard with a return of an expression very old and very weary. Fortunately she was short-sighted and was thus unable to see her bouquet which made such a burning blot on the green grass, with the ribbon trailing beside it and the card still holding on as though determined to see the strange adventure through to the end.

"Good-by, Anna," she said, rising tremblingly, though at the beginning of her visit.

"Oh, good-by, Harriet," replied Miss Anna, giving a cheerful shake to the yellow bowl.

As Harriet walked slowly down the street, a more courageously dressed woman than she had been for years, her chin quivered and she shook with sobs heroically choked back.

Miss Anna went into the library and sat down near the door. Her face which had been very white was scarlet again: "What was it you did—tell me quickly. I cannot stand it."

He came over and taking her cheeks between his palms turned her face up and looked down into her eyes. But she shut them quickly. "What do you suppose I did? Harriet and I sat for half an hour in another room. I don't remember what I did; but it could not have been anything very bad: others were all around us."

She opened her eyes and pushed him away harshly: "I have wounded Harriet in her most sensitive spot; and then I insulted her after I wounded her," and she went upstairs.

Later he found the bouquet on his library table with the card stuck in the top. The flowers stayed there freshly watered till the petals strewed his table: they were not even dusted away.

As for Harriet herself, the wound of the morning must have penetrated till it struck some deep flint in her composition; for she came back the next day in high spirits and severely underdressed—in what might be called toilet reduced to its lowest terms, like a common fraction. She had restored herself to the footing of an undervalued intercourse. At the sight of her Miss Anna sprang up, kissed her all over the face, was atoningly cordial with her arms, tried in every way to say: "See, Harriet, I bare my heart! Behold the dagger of remorse!"

Harriet saw; and she walked up and took the dagger by the handle and twisted it to the right and to the left and drove it in deeper and was glad.

"How do you like this dress, Anna?" she inquired with the sweetest solicitude. "Ah, there is no one like a friend to bring you to your senses! You were right. I am too old to change, too old to dress, too old even to read: thank you, Anna, as always."

Many a wound of friendship heals, but the wounder and the wounded are never the same to each other afterward. So that the two comrades were ill at ease and welcomed a diversion in the form of a visitor. It happened to be the day of the week when Miss Anna received her supply of dairy products from the farm of Ambrose Webb. He came round to the side entrance now with two shining tin buckets and two lustreless eyes.

The old maids stood on the edge of the porch with their arms wrapped around each other, and talked to him with nervous gayety. He looked up with a face of dumb yearning at one and then at the other, almost impartially.

"Aren't you well, Mr. Webb?" inquired Miss Anna, bending over toward him with a healing smile.

"Certainly I am well," he replied resentfully. "There is nothing the matter with me. I am a sound man."

"But you were certainly groaning," insisted Miss Anna, "for I heard you; and you must have been groaning about *something*."

He dropped his eyes, palpably crestfallen, and scraped the bricks with one foot.

Harriet nudged Miss Anna not to press the point and threw herself gallantly into the breach of silence.

"I am coming out to see you sometime, Mr. Webb," she said threateningly; "I want to find out whether you are taking good care of my calf. Is she growing?"

"Calves always grow till they stop," said Ambrose, axiomatically.

"How high is she?"

He held his hand up over an imaginary back.

"Why, that is *high*! When she stops growing, Anna, I am going to sell her, sell her by the pound. She is my beef trust. Now don't forget, Mr. Webb, that I am coming out some day."

"I'll be there," he said, and he gave her a peculiar look.

"You know, Anna," said Harriet, when they were alone again, "that his wife treats him shamefully. I have heard mother talking about it. She says his wife is the kind of woman that fills a house as straw fills a barn: you can see it through every crack. That accounts for his heavy expression, and for his dull eyes, and for the groaning. They say that most of the time he sits on the fences when it is clear, and goes into the stable when it rains."

"Why, I'll have to be kinder to him than ever," said Miss Anna. "But how do you happen to have a calf, Harriet?" she added, struck by the practical fact.

"It was the gift of my darling mother, my dear, the only present she has made me that I can remember. It was an orphan, and you wouldn't have it in your asylum, and my mother was in a peculiar mood, I suppose. She amused herself with the idea of making me such a present. But Anna, watch that calf, and see if thereby does not hang a tale. I am sure, in some mysterious way, my destiny is bound up with it. Calves do have destinies, don't they, Anna?"

"Oh, don't ask *me*, Harriet! Inquire of their Creator; or try the market-house."

It was at the end of this visit that Harriet as usual imparted to Miss Anna the freshest information regarding affairs at home: that Isabel had gone to spend the summer with friends at the seashore, and was to linger with other friends in the mountains during autumn; that her mother had changed her own plans, and was to keep the house open, and had written for the Fieldings—Victor's mother and brothers and sisters—to come and help fill the house; that everything was to be very gay.

"I cannot fathom what is under it all," said Harriet, with her hand on the side gate at leaving. "But I know that mother and Isabel have quarrelled. I believe mother has transferred her affections—and perhaps her property. She has rewritten her will since Isabel went away. What have I to do, Anna, but interest myself in other people's affairs? I have none of my own. And she never calls Isabel's name, but pets Victor from morning till night. And her expression sometimes! I tell you, Anna, that when I see it, if I were a bird and could fly, gunshot could not catch me. I see a summer before me! If there is ever a chance of my doing *anything*, don't be shocked if I do it;" and in Harriet's eyes there were two mysterious sparks of hope—two little rising suns.

"What did she mean?" pondered Miss Anna.

IV

"Barbee," said Judge Morris one morning a fortnight later, "what has become of Marguerite? One night not long ago you complained of her as an obstacle in the path of your career: does she still annoy you with her attentions? You could sue out a writ of habeas corpus in your own behalf if she persists. I'd take the case. I believe you asked me to mark your demeanor on the evening of that party. I tried to mark it; but I did not discover a great deal of demeanor to mark."

The two were sitting in the front office. The Judge, with nothing to do, was facing the street, his snow-white cambric handkerchief thrown across one knee, his hands grasping the arms of his chair, the newspaper behind his heels, his straw hat and cane on the floor at his side, and beside them the bulldog—his nose thrust against the hat.

Barbee was leaning over his desk with his fingers plunged in his hair and his eyes fixed on the law book before him—unopened. He turned and remarked with dry candor:

"Marguerite has dropped me."

"If she has, it's a blessed thing."

"There was more depth to her than I thought."

"There always is. Wait until you get older."

"I shall have to work and climb to win her."

"You might look up meantime the twentieth verse of the twenty-ninth chapter of Genesis."

Barbee rose and took down a Bible from among the law books: it had been one of the Judge's authorities, a great stand-by for reference and eloquence in his old days of pleading. He sat down and read the verse and laid the volume aside with the mere comment: "All this time I have been thinking her too much of a child; I find that she has been thinking the same of me."

"Then she has been a sound thinker."

"The result is she has wandered away after some one else. I know the man; and I know that he is after some one else. Why do people desire the impossible person? If I had been a Greek sculptor and had been commissioned to design as my masterwork the world's Frieze of Love, it should have been one long array of marble shapes, each in pursuit of some one fleeing. But some day Marguerite will be found sitting pensive on a stone —pursuing no longer; and when I appear upon the scene, having overtaken her at last, she will sigh, but she will give me her hand and go with me: and I'll have to stand it. That is the worst of it. I shall have to stand it—that she preferred the other man."

The Judge did not care to hear Barbee on American themes with Greek imagery. He yawned and struggled to his feet with difficulty. "I'll take a stroll," he said; "it is all I can take."

Barbee sprang forward and picked up for him his hat and cane. The dog, by what seemed the slow action of a mental jackscrew, elevated his cylinder to the tops of his legs; and presently the two stiff old bodies turned the corner of the street, one slanting, one prone: one dotting the bricks with his three legs, the other with his four.

Formerly the man and the brute had gone each his own way, meeting only at meal time and at irregular hours of the night in the Judge's chambers. The Judge had his stories regarding the origin of their intimacy. He varied these somewhat according to the sensibilities of the persons to whom they were related—and there were not many habitues of the sidewalks who did not hear them sooner or later. "No one could disentangle fact and fiction and affection in them.

"Some years ago," he said one day to Professor Hardage, "I was a good deal gayer than I am now and so was he. We cemented a friendship in a certain way, no matter what: that is a story I'm not going to tell. And he came to live with me on that footing of friendship. Of course he was greatly interested in the life of his own species at that time; he loved part of it, he hated part; but he was no friend to either. By and by he grew older. Age removed a good deal of his vanity, and I suppose it forced him to part with some portion of his self-esteem. But I was growing older myself and no doubt getting physically a little helpless. I suppose I made senile noises when I dressed and undressed, expressive of my decorative labors. This may have been the reason; possibly not; but at any rate about this time he conceived it his duty to give up his friendship as an equal and to enter my employ as a servant. He became my valet—without wages—and I changed his name to 'Brown.'

"Of course you don't think this true; well, then, don't think it true. But you have never seen him of winter mornings get up before I do and try to keep me out of the bath-tub. He'll station himself at the bath-room door; and as I approach he will look at me with an air of saying; 'Now don't climb into that cold water! Stand on the edge of it and lap it if you wish! But don't get into it. Drink it, man, don't wallow in it.' He waits until I finish, and then he speaks his mind plainly again: 'Now see how wet you are! And to-morrow you will do the same thing.' And he will stalk away, suspicious of the grade of my intelligence.

"He helps me to dress and undress. You'd know this if you studied his face when I struggle to brush the dust off of my back and shoulders: the mortification, the sense of injustice done him, in his having been made a quadruped. When I stoop over to take off my shoes, if I do it without any noise and he lies anywhere near, very well; but if I am noisy about it, he always comes and takes a seat before me and assists. Then he makes his same speech: 'What a shame that you should have to do this for yourself, when I am here to do it for you, but have no hands.'

"You know his portrait in my sitting room. When it was brought home and he discovered it on the wall, he looked at it from different angles, and then came across to me with a wound and a grievance: 'Why have you put that thing there? How can you, who have me, tolerate such a looking object as that? See the meanness in his face! See how used up he is and how sick of life! See what a history is written all over him—his crimes and disgraces! And you can care for him when you have *me*, your Brown.' After I am dead, I expect him to publish a memorial volume entitled 'Reminiscences of the late Judge Ravenel Morris, By his former Friend, afterward his Valet, *Taurus-Canis*.'"

The long drowsing days of summer had come. Business was almost suspended; heat made energy impossible. Court was not in session, farmers were busy with crops. From early morning to late afternoon the streets were well-nigh deserted.

Ravenel Morris found life more active for him during this idlest season of his native town. Having no business to prefer, people were left more at leisure to talk with him; more acquaintances sat fanning on their doorsteps and bade him good night as he passed homeward. There were festivals in the park; and he could rest on one of the benches and listen to the band playing tunes. He had the common human heart in its love of tunes. When tunes stopped, music stopped for him. If anything were played in which there was no traceable melody, when the instruments encountered a tumult of chords and dissonances, he would exclaim though with regretful toleration:

"What are they trying to do now? What is it all about? Why can't music be simple and sweet? Do noise and confusion make it better or greater?"

One night Barbee had him serenaded. He gave the musicians instruction as to the tunes, how they were to be played, in what succession, at what hour of the night. The melodists grouped themselves in the middle of the street, and the Judge came out on a little veranda under one of his doors and stood there, a great silver-haired figure, looking down. The moonlight shone upon him. He remained for a while motionless, wrapped loosely in what looked like a white toga. Then with a slight gesture of the hand full of mournful dignity he withdrew.

It was during these days that Barbee, who always watched over him with a most reverent worship and affection, made a discovery. The Judge was breaking; that brave life was beginning to sink and totter toward its fall and dissolution. There were moments when the cheerfulness, which had never failed him in the midst of trial, failed him now when there was none; when the ancient springs of strength ceased to run and he was discovered to be feeble. Sometimes he no longer read his morning newspaper; he would sit for long periods in the front door of his office, looking out into the street and caring not who passed, not even returning salutations: what was the use of saluting the human race impartially? Or going into the rear office, he would reread pages and chapters of what at different times in his life had been his favorite books: "Rabelais" and "The Decameron" when he was young; "Don Quixote" later, and "Faust"; "Clarissa" and "Tom Jones" now and then; and Shakespeare always; and those poems of Burns that tell sad truths; and the account of the man in Thackeray who went through so much that was large and at the end of life was brought down to so much that was low. He seemed more and more to feel the need of grasping through books the hand of erring humanity. And from day to day his conversations with Barbee began to take more the form of counsels about life and duty, about the ideals and mistakes and virtues and weaknesses in men. He had a good deal to say about the ethics of character in the court room and in the street.

One afternoon Barbee very thoughtfully asked him a question: "Uncle, I have wanted to know why you always defended and never prosecuted. The State is supposed to stand for justice, and the State is the accuser; in always defending the accused and so in working against the State, have you not always worked against justice?"

The Judge sat with his face turned away and spoke as he sat—very gravely and quietly: "I always defended because the State can punish only the accused, and the accused is never the only criminal. In every crime there are three criminals. The first criminal is the Origin of Evil. I don't know what the Origin of Evil is, or who he is; but if I could have dragged the Origin of Evil into the court room, I should have been glad to try to have it hanged, or have him hanged. I should have liked to argue the greatest of all possible criminal cases: the case of the Common People vs. the Devil—so nominated. The second criminal is all that coworked with the accused as involved in his nature, in his temptation, and in his act. If I could have arraigned all the other men and women who have been forerunners or copartners of the accused as furthering influences in the line of his offence, I should gladly have prosecuted them for their share of the guilt. But most of the living who are accessory can no more be discovered and summoned than can the dead who also were accessory. You have left the third criminal; and the State is forced to single him out and let the full punishment fall upon him alone. Thus it does not punish the guilty—it punishes the last of the guilty. It does not even punish him for his share of the guilt: it can never know what that share is. This is merely a feeling of mine, I do not uphold it. Of course I often declined to defend also."

They returned to this subject another afternoon as the two sat together a few days later:

"There was sometimes another reason why I felt unwilling to prosecute: I refer to cases in which I might be taking advantage of the inability of a fellow-creature to establish his own innocence. I want you to remember this —nothing that I have ever said to you is of more importance: a good many years ago I was in Paris. One afternoon I was walking through the most famous streets in the company of a French scholar and journalist, a deep student of the genius of French civilization. As we passed along, he pointed out various buildings with reference to the history that had been made and unmade within them. At one point he stopped and pointed to a certain structure with a high wall in front of it and to a hole in that wall. 'Do you know what that is?' he asked. He told me. Any person can drop a letter into that box, containing any kind of accusation against any other person; it is received by the authorities and it becomes their duty to act upon its contents. Do you know what that means? Can you for a moment realize what is involved? A man's enemy, even his so-called religious enemy, any assassin, any slanderer, any liar, even the mercenary who agrees to hire out his honor itself for the wages of a slave, can deposit an anonymous accusation against any one whom he hates or wishes to ruin; and it becomes the duty of the authorities to respect his communication as much as though it came before a court of highest equity. An innocent man may thus become an object of suspicion, may be watched, followed, arrested and thrown into prison, disgraced, ruined in his business, ruined in his family; and if in the end he is released, he is never even told what he has been charged with, has no power of facing his accuser, of bringing him to justice, of recovering damages from the State. While he himself is kept in close confinement, his enemy may manufacture evidence which he alone would be able to disprove; and the chance is never given him to disprove it."

The Judge turned and looked at Barbee in simple silence.

Barbee sprang to his feet: "It is a damned shame!" he cried. "Damn the French! damn such a civilization."

"Why damn the French code? In our own country the same thing goes on, not as part of our system of jurisprudence, but as part of our system of—well, we'll say—morals. In this country any man's secret personal enemy, his so-called religious enemy for instance, may fabricate any accusation against him. He does not drop it into the dark crevice of a dead wall, but into the blacker hole of a living ear. A perfectly innocent man by such anonymous or untraceable slander can be as grossly injured in reputation, in business, in his family, out of a prison in this country as in a prison in France. Slander may circulate about him and he will never even know what it is, never be confronted by his accuser, never have power of redress.

"Now what I wish you to remember is this: that in the very nature of the case a man is often unable to prove his innocence. All over the world useful careers come to nothing and lives are wrecked, because men may be ignorantly or malignantly accused of things of which they cannot stand up and prove that they are innocent. Never forget that it is impossible for a man finally to demonstrate his possession of a single great virtue. A man cannot so prove his bravery. He cannot so prove his honesty or his benevolence or his sobriety or his chastity, or anything else. As to courage, all that he can prove is that in a given case or in all tested cases he was not a coward. As to honesty, all that he can prove is that in any alleged instance he was not a thief. A man cannot even directly prove his health, mental or physical: all that he can prove is that he shows no unmistakable evidences of disease. But an enemy may secretly circulate the charge that these evidences exist; and all the evidences to the contrary that the man himself may furnish will never disperse that impression. It is so for every great virtue. His final possession of a single virtue can be proved by no man.

"This was another reason why I was sometimes unwilling to prosecute a fellow-creature; it might be a case in which he alone would actually know whether he were innocent, but his simple word would not be taken, and his simple word would be the only proof that he could give. I ask you, as you care for my memory, never to take advantage of the truth that the man before you, as the accused, may in the nature of things be unable to prove his innocence. Some day you are going to be a judge. Remember you are always a judge; and remember that a greater Judge than you will ever be gave you the rule: 'Judge as you would be judged.' The great root of the matter is this: that all human conduct is judged; but a very small part of human conduct is ever brought to trial."

He had many visitors at his office during these idle summer days. He belonged to a generation of men who loved conversation—when they conversed. All the lawyers dropped in. The report of his failing strength brought these and many others.

He saw a great deal of Professor Hardage. One morning as the two met, he said with more feeling than he usually allowed himself to show: "Hardage, I am a lonesome old man; don't you want me to come and see you every Sunday evening? I always try to get home by ten o'clock, so that you couldn't get tired of me; and as I never fall asleep before that time, you wouldn't have to put me to bed. I want to hear you talk, Hardage. My time is limited; and you have no right to shut out from me so much that you know—your learning, your wisdom, yourself. And I know a few things that I have picked up in a lifetime. Surely we ought to have something to say to each other."

But when he came, Professor Hardage was glad to let him find relief in his monologues—fragments of self-revelation. This last phase of their friendship had this added significance: that the Judge no longer spent his Sunday evenings with Mrs. Conyers. The last social link binding him to womankind had been broken. It was a final loosening and he felt it, felt the desolation in which it left him. His cup of life had indeed been drained, and he turned away from the dregs.

One afternoon Professor Hardage found him sitting with his familiar Shakespeare on his knees. As he looked up, he stretched out his hand in eager welcome and said: "Listen once more;" and he read the great kindling speech of King Henry to his English yeomen on the eve of battle.

He laid the book aside.

"Of course you have noticed how Shakespeare likes this word 'mettle,' how he likes the *thing*. The word can be seen from afar over the vast territory of his plays like the same battle-flag set up in different parts of a field. It is conspicuous in the heroic English plays, and in the Roman and in the Greek; it waves alike over comedy and tragedy as a rallying signal to human nature. I imagine I can see his face as he writes of the mettle of children—the mettle of a boy—the quick mettle of a schoolboy—a lad of mettle—the mettle of a gentleman—the mettle of the sex—the mettle of a woman, Lady Macbeth—the mettle of a king—the mettle of a speech—even the mettle of a rascal—mettle in death. I love to think of him, a man who had known trouble, writing the words: 'The insuppressive mettle of our spirits.'

"But this particular phrase—the mettle of the pasture—belongs rather to our century than to his, more to Darwin than to the theatre of that time. What most men are thinking of now, if they think at all, is of our earth, a small grass-grown planet hung in space. And, unaccountably making his appearance on it, is man, a pasturing animal, deriving his mettle from his pasture. The old question comes newly up to us: Is anything ever added to him? Is anything ever lost to him? Evolution—is it anything more than change? Civilizations—are they anything but different arrangements of the elements of man's nature with reference to the preeminence of some elements and the subsidence of others?

"Suppose you take the great passions: what new one has been added, what old one has been lost? Take all the passions you find in Greek literature, in the Roman. Have you not seen them reappear in American life in your own generation? I believe I have met them in my office. You may think I have not seen Paris and Helen, but I have. And I have seen Orestes and Agamemnon and Clytemnestra and Oedipus. Do you suppose I have not met Tarquin and Virginia and Lucretia and Shylock—to come down to nearer times—and seen Lear and studied Macbeth in the flesh? I knew Juliet once, and behind locked doors I have talked with Romeo. They are all here in any American commonwealth at the close of our century: the great tragedies are numbered —the oldest are the newest. So that sometimes I fix my eyes only on the old. I see merely the planet with its middle green belt of pasture and its poles of snow and ice; and wandering over that green belt for a little while man the pasturing animal—with the mystery of his ever being there and the mystery of his dust—with nothing ever added to him, nothing ever lost out of him—his only power being but the power to vary the uses of his powers.

"Then there is the other side, the side of the new. I like to think of the marvels that the pasturing animal has accomplished in our own country. He has had new thoughts, he has done things never seen elsewhere or before. But after all the question remains, what is our characteristic mettle? What is the mettle of the American? He has had new ideas; but has he developed a new virtue or carried any old virtue forward to characteristic development? Has he added to the civilizations of Europe the spectacle of a single virtue transcendently exercised? We are not braver than other brave people, we are not more polite, we are not more honest or more truthful or more sincere or kind. I wish to God that some virtue, say the virtue of truthfulness, could be known throughout the world as the unfailing mark of the American—the mettle of his pasture. Not to lie in business, not to lie in love, not to lie in religion—to be honest with one's fellow-men, with women, with God—suppose the rest of mankind would agree that this virtue constituted the characteristic of the American! That would be fame for ages.

"I believe that we shall sometime become celebrated for preeminence in some virtue. Why, I have known young fellows in my office that

I have believed unmatched for some fine trait or noble quality.
You have met them in your classes."

He broke off abruptly and remained silent for a while.

"Have you seen Rowan lately?" he asked, with frank uneasiness: and receiving the reply which he dreaded, he soon afterward arose and passed brokenly down the street.

For some weeks now he had been missing Rowan; and this was the second cause of his restlessness and increasing loneliness. The failure of Rowan's love affair was a blow to him: it had so linked him to the life of the young— was the last link. And since then he had looked for Rowan in vain; he had waited for him of mornings at his office, had searched for him on the streets, scanning all young men on horseback or in buggies; had tried to find him in the library, at the livery stable, at the bank where he was a depositor and director. There was no ground for actual uneasiness concerning Rowan's health, for Rowan's neighbors assured him in response to his inquiries that he was well and at work on the farm.

"If he is in trouble, why does he not come and tell me? Am I not worth coming to see? Has he not yet understood what he is to me? But how can he know, how can the young ever know how the old love them? And the old are too proud to tell." He wrote letters and tore them up.

As we stand on the rear platform of a train and see the mountains away from which we are rushing rise and impend as if to overwhelm us, so in moving farther from his past very rapidly now, it seemed to follow him as a landscape growing always nearer and clearer. His mind dwelt more on the years when hatred had so ruined him, costing him the only woman he had ever asked to be his wife, costing him a fuller life, greater honors, children to leave behind.

He was sitting alone in his rear office the middle of one afternoon, alone among his books. He had outspread before him several that are full of youth. Barbee was away, the street was very quiet. No one dropped in—perhaps all were tired of hearing him talk. It was not yet the hour for Professor Hardage to walk in. A watering-cart creaked slowly past the door and the gush of the drops of water sounded like a shower and the smell of the dust was strong. Far away in some direction were heard the cries of school children at play in the street. A bell was tolling; a green fly, entering through the rear door, sang loud on the dusty window-panes and then flew out and alighted on a plant of nightshade springing up rank at the doorstep.

He was not reading and his thoughts were the same old thoughts. At length on the quiet air, coming nearer, were heard the easy roll of wheels and the slow measured step of carriage horses. The sound caught his ear and he listened with quick eagerness. Then he rose trembling and waited. The carriage had stopped at the door; a moment later there was a soft low knock on the lintel and Mrs. Meredith entered. He met her but she said: "May I go in there?" and entered the private office.

She brought with her such grace and sweetness of full womanly years that as she seated herself opposite him and lifted her veil away from the purity of her face, it was like the revelation of a shrine and the office became as a place of worship. She lifted the veil from the dignity and seclusion of her life. She did not speak at once but looked about her. Many years had passed since she had entered that office, for it had long ago seemed best to each of them that they should never meet. He had gone back to his seat at the desk with the opened books lying about him as though he had been searching one after another for the lost fountain of youth. He sat there looking at her, his white hair falling over his leonine head and neck, over his clear mournful eyes. The sweetness of his face, the kindness of it, the shy, embarrassed, almost guilty look on it from the old pain of being misunderstood—the terrible pathos of it all, she saw these; but whatever her emotions, she was not a woman to betray them at such a moment, in such a place.

"I do not come on business," she said. "All the business seems to have been attended to; life seems very easy, too easy: I have so little to do. But I am here, Ravenel, and I suppose I must try to say what brought me."

She waited for some time, unable to speak.

"Ravenel," she said at length, "I cannot go on any longer without telling you that my great sorrow in life has been the wrong I did you."

He closed his eyes quickly and stretched out his hand against her, as though to shut out the vision of things that rose before him—as though to stop words that would unman him.

"But I was a young girl! And what does a young girl understand about her duty in things like that? I know it changed your whole life; you will never know what it has meant in mine."

"Caroline," he said, and he looked at her with brimming eyes, "if you had married me, I'd have been a great man. I was not great enough to be great without you. The single road led the wrong way—to the wrong things!"

"I know," she said, "I know it all. And I know that tears do not efface mistakes, and that our prayers do not atone for our wrongs."

She suddenly dropped her veil and rose,

"Do not come out to help me," she said as he struggled up also.

He did not wish to go, and he held out his hand and she folded her soft pure hands about it; then her large noble figure moved to the side of his and through her veil—her love and sorrow hidden from him—she lifted her face and kissed him.

V

And during these days when Judge Morris was speaking his mind about old tragedies that never change, and new virtues—about scandal and guilt and innocence—it was during these days that the scandal started and spread and did its work on the boy he loved—and no one had told him.

The summer was drawing to an end. During the last days of it Kate wrote to Isabel:

"I could not have believed, dearest friend, that so long a time would pass without my writing. Since you went away it has been eternity. And many things have occurred which no one foresaw or imagined. I cannot tell you how often I have resisted the impulse to write. Perhaps I should resist now; but there are some matters which you ought to understand; and I do not believe that any one else has told you or will tell you. If I, your closest friend, have shrunk, how could any one else be expected to perform the duty?

"A week or two after you left I understood why you went away mysteriously, and why during that last visit to me you were unlike yourself. I did not know then that your gayety was assumed, and that you were broken-hearted beneath your brave disguises. But I remember your saying that some day I should know. The whole truth has come out as to why you broke your engagement with Rowan, and why you left home. You can form no idea what a sensation the news produced. For a while nothing else was talked of, and I am glad for your sake that you were not here.

"I say the truth came out; but even now the town is full of different stories, and different people believe different things. But every friend of yours feels perfectly sure that Rowan was unworthy of you, and that you did right in discarding him. It is safe to say that he has few friends left among yours. He seldom comes to town, and I hear that he works on the farm like a common hand as he should. One day not long after you left I met him on the street. He was coming straight up to speak to me as usual. But I had the pleasure of staring him in the eyes and of walking deliberately past him as though he were a stranger—except that I gave him one explaining look. I shall never speak to him.

"His mother has the greatest sympathy of every one. They say that no one has told her the truth: how could any one tell her such things about her own son? Of course she must know that you dropped him and that we have all dropped him. They say that she is greatly saddened and that her health seems to be giving way.

"I do not know whether you have heard the other sensation regarding the Meredith family. You refused Rowan; and now Dent is going to marry a common girl in the neighborhood. Of course Dent Meredith was always noted for being a quiet little bookworm, near-sighted, and without any knowledge of girls. So it doesn't seem very unnatural for him to have collected the first specimen that he came across as he walked about over the country. This marriage which is to take place in the autumn is the second shock to his mother.

"You will want to hear of other people. And this reminds me that a few of your friends have turned against you and insist that these stories about Rowan are false, and even accuse you of starting them. This brings me to Marguerite.

"Soon after her ball she had typhoid fever. In her delirium of whom do you suppose she incessantly and pitifully talked? Every one had supposed that she and Barbee were sweethearts—and had been for years. But Barbee's name was never on her lips. It was all Rowan, Rowan, Rowan. Poor child, she chided him for being so cold to her; and she talked to him about the river of life and about his starting on the long voyage from the house of his fathers; and begged to be taken with him, and said that in their family the women never loved but once. When she grew convalescent, there was a consultation of the grandmother and the mother and the doctors: one passion now seemed to constitute all that was left of Marguerite's life; and that was like a flame burning her strength away.

"They did as the doctor said had to be done. Mrs. Meredith had been very kind during her illness, had often been to the house. They kept from her of course all knowledge of what Marguerite had disclosed in her delirium. So when Marguerite by imperceptible degrees grew stronger, Mrs. Meredith begged that she might be moved out to the country for the change and the coolness and the quiet; and the doctors availed themselves of this plan as a solution of their difficulty—to lessen Marguerite's consuming desire by gratifying it. So she and her mother went out to the Merediths'. The change proved beneficial. I have not been driving myself, although the summer has been so long and hot; and during the afternoons I have so longed to see the cool green lanes with the sun setting over the fields. But of course people drive a great deal and they often meet Mrs. Meredith with Marguerite in the carriage beside her. At first it was Marguerite's mother and Marguerite. Then it was Mrs. Meredith and Marguerite; and now it is Rowan and Marguerite. They drive alone and she sits with her face turned toward him—in open idolatry. She is to stay out there until she is quite well. How curiously things work around! If he ever proposes, scandal will make no difference to Marguerite.

"How my letter wanders! But so do my thoughts wander. If you only knew, while I write these things, how I am really thinking of other things. But I must go on in my round-about way. What I started out to say was that when the scandals, I mean the truth, spread over the town about Rowan, the three Marguerites stood by him. You could never have believed that the child had such fire and strength and devotion in her nature. I called on them one day and was coldly treated simply because I am your closest friend. Marguerite pointedly expressed her opinion of a woman who deserts a man because he has his faults. Think of this child's sitting in moral condemnation upon you!

"The Hardages also—of course you have no stancher friends than they are— have stood up stubbornly for Rowan. Professor Hardage became very active in trying to bring the truth out of what he believes to be gossip and misunderstanding. And Miss Anna has also remained loyal to him, and in her sunny, common-sense way flouts the idea of there being any truth in these reports.

"I must not forget to tell you that Judge Morris now spends his Sunday evenings with Professor Hardage. No one has told him: they have spared him. Of course every one knows that he was once engaged to Rowan's mother and that scandal broke the engagement and separated them for life. Only in his case it was long afterward found out that the tales were not true.

"I have forgotten Barbee. He and Marguerite had quarrelled before her illness —no one knows why, unless she was already under the influence of her fatal infatuation for Rowan. Barbee has gone to work. A few weeks ago he won his first serious case in court and attracted attention. They say his speech was so full of dignity and unnecessary rage that some one declared he was simply trying to recover his self-esteem for Marguerite's having called him trivial and not yet altogether grown up.

"Of course you must have had letters of your own, telling you of the arrival of the Fieldings—Victor's mother and sisters; and the house is continually gay with suppers and parties.

"How my letter wanders! It is a sick letter, Isabel, a dead letter. I must not close without going back to the Merediths once more. People have been driving out to see the little farm and the curious little house of Dent Meredith's bride elect—a girl called Pansy Something. It lies near enough to the turnpike to be in full view—too full view. They say it is like a poultry farm and that the bride is a kind of American goose girl: it will be a marriage between geology and the geese. The geese will have the best of it.

"Dearest friend, what shall I tell you of my own life—of my nights, of the mornings when I wake, of these long, lonesome, summerafternoons?

Nothing, nothing, nothing, nothing! I should rather write to you how, my thoughts go back to the years of our girlhood together when we were so happy, Isabel, so happy, so happy! What ideals we formed as to our marriages and our futures!

"**KATE.**

"P.S.—I meant to tell you that of course I shall do everything in my power to break up the old friendship between George and Rowan. Indeed, I have already done it."

VI

This letter brought Isabel home at once through three days of continuous travel. From the station she had herself driven straight to Mrs. Osborn's house, and she held the letter in her hand as she went.

Her visit lasted for some time and it was not pleasant. When Mrs. Osborn hastened down, surprised at Isabel's return and prepared to greet her with the old warmth, her greeting was repelled and she herself recoiled, hurt and disposed to demand an explanation.

"Isabel," she said reproachfully, "is this the way you come back to me?"

Isabel did not heed but spoke: "As soon as I received this letter, I determined to come home. I wished to know at once what these things are that are being said about Rowan. What are they?"

Mrs. Osborn hesitated: "I should rather not tell you."

"But you must tell me: my name has been brought into this, and I must know."

While she listened her eyes flashed and when she spoke her voice trembled with excitement and anger. "These things are not true," she said. "Only Rowan and I know what passed between us. I told no one, he told no one, and it is no one's right to know. A great wrong has been done him and a great wrong has been done me; and I shall stay here until these wrongs are righted."

"And is it your feeling that you must begin with me?" said Mrs. Osborn, bitterly.

"Yes, Kate; you should not have believed these things. You remember our once saying to each other that we would try never to believe slander or speak slander or think slander? It is unworthy of you to have done so now."

"Do you realize to whom you are speaking, and that what I have done has been through friendship for you?"

Isabel shook her head resolvedly. "Your friendship for me cannot exact of you that you should be untrue to yourself and false to others. You say that you refuse to speak to Rowan on the street. You say that you have broken up the friendship between Mr. Osborn and him. Rowan is the truest friend Mr. Osborn has ever had; you know this. But in breaking off that friendship, you have done more than you have realized: you have ended my friendship with you."

"And this is gratitude for my devotion to you and my willingness to fight your battles!" said Mrs. Osborn, rising.

"You cannot fight my battles without fighting Rowan's. My wish to marry him or not to marry him is one thing; my willingness to see him ruined is another."

Isabel drove home. She rang the bell as though she were a stranger. When her maid met her at the door, overjoyed at her return, she asked for her grandmother and passed at once into her parlors. As she did so, Mrs. Conyers came through the hall, dressed to go out. At the sound of Isabel's voice, she, who having once taken hold of a thing never let it go, dropped her parasol; and as she stooped to pick it up, the blood rushed to her face.

"I wish to speak to you," said Isabel, coming quickly out into the hall as though to prevent her grandmother's exit. Her voice was low and full of shame and indignation.

"I am at your service for a little while," said Mrs. Conyers, carelessly; "later I am compelled to go out." She entered the parlors, followed by Isabel, and, seating herself in the nearest chair, finished buttoning her glove.

Isabel sat silent a moment, shocked by her reception. She had not realized that she was no longer the idol of that household and of its central mind; and we are all loath to give up faith in our being loved still, where we have been loved ever. She was not aware that since she had left home she had been disinherited. She would not have cared had she known; but she was now facing what was involved in the disinheritance—dislike; and in the beginning of dislike there was the ending of the old awe with which the grandmother had once regarded the grandchild.

But she came quickly back to the grave matter uppermost in her mind. "Grandmother," she said, "I received a few days ago a letter from Kate Osborn. In it she told me that there were stories in circulation about Rowan. I have come home to find out what these stories are. On the way from the station I stopped at Mrs. Osborn's, and she told me. Grandmother, this is your work."

Mrs. Conyers pushed down the thumb of her glove.

"Have I denied it? But why do you attempt to deny that it is also your work?"

Isabel sat regarding her with speechless, deepening horror. She was not prepared for this revelation. Mrs. Conyers did not wait, but pressed on with a certain debonair enjoyment of her advantage.

"You refused to recognize my right to understand a matter that affected me and affected other members of the family as well as yourself. You showed no regard for the love I had cherished for you many a year. You put me aside as though I had no claim upon your confidence—I believe you said I was not worthy of it; but my memory is failing—perhaps I wrong you."

"It is *true!*" said Isabel, with triumphant joy in reaffirming it on present grounds. "It is *true!*"

"Very well," said Mrs. Conyers, "we shall let that pass. It was of consequence then; it is of no consequence now: these little personal matters are very trivial. But there was a serious matter that you left on my hands; the world always demands an explanation of what it is compelled to see and cannot understand. If no explanation is given, it creates an explanation. It was my duty to see that it did not create an explanation in this case. Whatever it may have been that took place between you and Rowan, I did not intend that the responsibility should rest upon you, even though you may have been willing that it should rest there. You discarded Rowan; I was compelled to prevent people from thinking that Rowan discarded you. Your reason for discarding him you refused to confide to me; I was compelled therefore to decide for myself what it probably was. Ordinarily when a man is dropped by a girl under such circumstances, it is for this," she tapped the tips of her fingers one by one as she went on, "or for this, or for this, or for this; you can supply the omitted words—nearly any one can—the world always does. You see, it becomes interesting. As I had not your authority for stating which one of these was the real reason, I was compelled to leave people at liberty to choose for themselves. I could only say that I myself did not know; but that certainly it was for some one of these reasons, or two of them, or for all of them."

"You have tried to ruin him!" Isabel cried, white with suffering.

"On the contrary, I received my whole idea of this from you. Nothing that I said to others about him was quite so bad as what you said to me; for you knew the real reason of your discarding him, and the reason was so bad—or so good—that you could not even confide it to me, your natural confidant. You remember saying that we must drop him from the list of our acquaintances, must not receive him at the house, or recognize him in society, or speak, to him in public. I protested that this would be very unjust to him, and that he might ask me at least the grounds for so insulting him; you assured me that he would never dare ask. And now you affect to be displeased with me for believing what you said, and trying to defend you from criticism, and trying to protect the good name of the family."

"Ah," cried Isabel, "you can give fair reasons for foul deeds. You always could. We often do, we women. The blacker our conduct, the better the names with which we cover it. If you would only glory openly in what you have done and stand by it! Not a word of what you have said is true, as you have said it. When I left home not a human being but yourself knew that there had been trouble between Rowan and me. It need never have become public, had you let the matter be as I asked you to do, and as you solemnly promised that you would. It is you who have deliberately made the trouble and scattered the gossip and spread the scandal. Why do you not avow that your motive was revenge, and that your passion was not justice, but malice. Ah, you are too deep a woman to try to seem so shallow!"

"Can I be of any further service to you?" said Mrs. Conyers with perfect politeness, rising. "I am sorry that the hour of my engagement has come. Are you to be in town long?"

"I shall be here until I have undone what you have done," cried Isabel, rising also and shaking with rage. "The decencies of life compel me to shield you still, and for that reason I shall stay in this house. I am not obliged to ask this as a privilege; it is my right."

"Then I shall have the pleasure of seeing you often."

Isabel went up to her room as usual and summoned her maid, and ordered her carriage to be ready in half an hour.

Half an hour later she came down and drove to the Hardages'. She showed no pleasure in seeing him again, and he no surprise in seeing her.

"I have been expecting you," he said; "I thought you would be brought back by all this."

"Then you have heard what they are saying about Rowan?"

"I suppose we have all heard," he replied, looking at her sorrowfully.

"You have not believed these things?"

"I have denied them as far as I could. I should have denied that anything had occurred; but you remember I could not do that after what you told me. You said something had occurred."

"Yes, I know," she said. "But you now have my authority at least to say that these things are not true. What I planned for the best has been misused and turned against him and against me. Have you seen him?"

"He has been in town, but I have not seen him."

"Then you must see him at once. Tell me one thing: have you heard it said that I am responsible for the circulation of these stories?"

"Yes."

"Do you suppose he has heard that? And could he believe it? Yet might he not believe it? But how could he, how could he!"

"You must come here and stay with us. Anna will want you." He could not tell her his reason for understanding that she would not wish to stay at home.

"No, I should like to come; but it is better for me to stay at home. But I wish Rowan to come to see me here. Judge Morris—has he done nothing?"

"He does not know. No one has told him."

Her expression showed that she did not understand.

"Years ago, when he was about Rowan's age, scandals like these were circulated about him. We know how much his life is wrapped up In Rowan. He has not been well this summer: we spared him."

"But you must tell him at once. Say that I beg him to write to Rowan to come to see him. I want Rowan to tell him everything—and to tell you everything."

All the next day Judge Morris stayed in his rooms. The end of life seemed suddenly to have been bent around until it touched the beginning. At last he understood.

"It was *she* then," he said. "I always suspected her; but I had no proof of her guilt; and if she had not been guilty, she could never have proved her innocence. And now for years she has smiled at me, clasped my hands, whispered into my ear, laughed in my eyes, seemed to be everything to me that was true. Well, she has been everything that is false. And now she has fallen upon the son of the woman whom she tore from me. And the vultures of scandal are tearing at his heart. And he will never be able to prove his innocence!"

He stayed in his rooms all that day. Rowan, in answer to his summons, had said that he should come about the middle of the afternoon; and it was near the middle of the afternoon now. As he counted the minutes, Judge Morris was unable to shut out from his mind the gloomier possibilities of the case.

"There is some truth behind all this," he said. "She broke her engagement with him,—at least, she severed all relations with him; and she would not do that without grave reason." He was compelled to believe that she must have learned from Rowan himself the things that had compelled her painful course. Why had Rowan never confided these things to him? His mind, while remaining the mind of a friend, almost the mind of a father toward a son, became also the mind of a lawyer, a criminal lawyer, with the old, fixed, human bloodhound passion for the scent of crime and the footsteps of guilt.

It was with both attitudes that he himself answered Rowan's ring; he opened the door half warmly and half coldly. In former years when working up his great cases involving life and death, it had been an occasional custom of his to receive his clients, if they were socially his friends, not in his private office, but in his rooms; it was part of his nature to show them at such crises his unshaken trust in their characters. He received Rowan in his rooms now. It was a clear day; the rooms had large windows; and the light streaming in took from them all the comfort which they acquired under gaslight: the carpets were faded, the rugs were worn out and lay in the wrong places. It was seen to be a desolate place for a desolated life.

"How are you, Rowan?" he said, speaking as though he had seen him the day before, and taking no note of changes in his appearance. Without further words he led the way into his sitting room and seated himself in his leather chair.

"Will you smoke?"

They had often smoked as they sat thus when business was before them, or if no business, questions to be intimately discussed about life and character and good and bad. Rowan did not heed the invitation, and the Judge lighted a cigar for himself. He was a long time in lighting it, and burned two or three matches at the end of it after it was lighted, keeping a cloud of smoke before his eyes and keeping his eyes closed. When the smoke rose and he lay back in his chair, he looked across at the young man with the eyes of an old lawyer who had drawn the truth out of the breast of many a criminal by no other command than their manly light. Rowan sat before him without an effort at composure. There was something about him that suggested a young officer out of uniform, come home with a browned face to try to get himself court-martialled. He spoke first:

"I have had Isabel's letter, and I have come to tell you."

"I need not say to you, tell me the whole truth."

"No, you need not say that to me. I should have told you long ago, if it had been a duty. But it was not a duty. You had not the right to know; there was no reason why you should know. This was a matter which concerned only the woman whom I was to marry." His manner had the firm and quiet courtesy that was his birthright.

A little after dark, Rowan emerged into the street. His carriage was waiting for him and he entered it and went home. Some minutes later, Judge Morris came down and walked to the Hardages'. He rang and asked for Professor Hardage and waited for him on the door-step. When Professor Hardage appeared, he said to him very solemnly: "Get your hat."

The two men walked away, the Judge directing their course toward the edge of the town. "Let us get to a quiet place," he said, "where we can talk without being overheard." It was a pleasant summer night and the moon was shining, and they stepped off the sidewalk and took the middle of the pike. The Judge spoke at last, looking straight ahead.

"He had a child, and when he asked Isabel to marry him he told her."

They walked on for a while without anything further being said. When Professor Hardage spoke, his tone was reflective:

"It was this that made it impossible for her to marry him. Her love for him was everything to her; he destroyed himself for her when he destroyed himself as an ideal. Did he tell you the story?"

"Told everything."

By and by the Judge resumed: "It was a student's love affair, and he would have married her. She said that if she married him, there would never be any happiness for her in life; she was not in his social class, and, moreover, their marriage would never be understood as anything but a refuge from their shame, and neither of them would be able to deny this. She disappeared sometime after the birth of the child. More than a year later, maybe it was two years, he received a letter from her stating that she was married to a man in her own class and that her husband suspected nothing, and that she expected to live a faithful wife to him and be the mother of his children. The child had been adopted, the traces of its parentage had been wiped out, those who had adopted it could do more for its life and honor than he could. She begged him not to try to find her or ruin her by communicating the past to her husband. That's about all."

"The old tragedy—old except to them."

"Old enough. Were we not speaking the other day of how the old tragedies are the new ones? I get something new out of this; you get the old. What strikes me about it is that the man has declined to shirk—that he has felt called upon not to injure any other life by his silence. I wish I had a right to call it the mettle of a young American, his truthfulness. As he put the case to me, what he got out of it was this: Here was a girl deceiving her husband about her past —otherwise he would never have married her. As the world values such things, what it expected of Rowan was that he should go off and marry a girl and conceal his past. He said that he would not lie to a classmate in college, he would not cheat a professor; was it any better silently to lie to and cheat the woman that he loved and expected to make the mother of his children? Whatever he might have done with any one else, there was something in the nature of the girl whom he did come to love that made it impossible: she drove untruthfulness out of him as health drives away disease. He saved his honor with her, but he lost her."

"She saved her honor through giving up him. But it is high ground, it is a sad hilltop, that each has climbed to."

"Hardage, we can climb so high that we freeze."

They turned back. The Judge spoke again with a certain sad pride:

"I like their mettle, it is Shakespearean mettle, it is American mettle. We lie in business, and we lie in religion, and we lie to women. Perhaps if a man stopped lying to a woman, by and by he might begin to stop lying for money, and at last stop lying with his Maker. But this boy, what can you and I do for him? We can never tell the truth about this; and as we can try to clear him, unless we ourselves lie, we shall leave him the victim of a flock of lies."

Isabel remained at home a week.

During her first meeting with Rowan, she effaced all evidences that there had ever been a love affair between them. They resumed their social relations temporarily and for a definite purpose—this was what she made him understand at the outset and to the end. All that she said to him, all that she did, had no further significance than her general interest in his welfare and her determination to silence the scandal for which she herself was in a way innocently responsible. Their old life without reference to it was assumed to be ended; and she put all her interest into what she assumed to be his new life; this she spoke of as a certainty, keeping herself out of it as related to it in any way. She forced him to talk about his work, his plans, his ambitions; made him feel always not only that she did not wish to see him suffer, but that she expected to see him succeed.

They were seen walking together and driving together. He demurred, but she insisted. "I will not accept such a sacrifice," he said, but she overruled him by her reply: "It is not a sacrifice; it is a vindication of myself, that you cannot oppose." But he knew that there was more in it than what she called vindication of herself; there was the fighting friendship of a comrade.

During these days, Isabel met cold faces. She found herself a fresh target for criticism, a further source of misunderstanding. And there was fresh suffering, too, which no one could have foreseen. Late one twilight when she and Rowan were driving, they passed Marguerite driving also, she being still a guest at the Merediths', and getting well. Each carriage was driving slowly, and the road was not wide, and the wheels almost locked, and there was time enough for everything to be seen. And the next day, Marguerite went home from the Merediths' and passed into a second long illness.

The day came for Isabel to leave—she was going away to remain a long time, a year, two years. They had had their last drive and twilight was falling when they returned to the Hardages'. She was standing on the steps as she gave him both her hands.

"Good-by," she said, in the voice of one who had finished her work. "I hardly know what to say—I have said everything. Perhaps I ought to tell you my last feeling is, that you will make life a success, that nothing will pull you down. I suppose that the life of each of us, if it is worth while, is not made up of one great effort and of one failure or of one success, but of many efforts, many failures, partial successes. But I am afraid we all try at first to realize our dreams. Good-by!"

"Marry me," he said, tightening his grasp on her hands and speaking as though he had the right.

She stepped quickly back from him. She felt a shock, a delicate wound, and she said with a proud tear: "I did not think you would so misjudge me in all that I have been trying to do."

She went quickly in.

VII

It was a morning in the middle of October when Dent and Pansy were married.

The night before had been cool and clear after a rain and a long-speared frost had fallen. Even before the sun lifted itself above the white land, a full red rose of the sky behind the rotting barn, those early abroad foresaw what the day would be. Nature had taken personal interest in this union of her two children, who worshipped her in their work and guarded her laws in their characters, and had arranged that she herself should be present in bridal livery.

The two prim little evergreens which grew one on each side of the door-step waited at respectful attention like heavily powdered festal lackeys. The scraggy aged cedars of the yard stood about in green velvet and brocade incrusted with gems. The doorsteps themselves were softly piled with the white flowers of the frost, and the bricks of the pavement strewn with multitudinous shells and stars of dew and air. Every poor stub of grass, so economically cropped by the geese, wore something to make it shine. In the back yard a clothes-line stretched between a damson and a peach tree, and on it hung forgotten some of Pansy's father's underclothes; but Nature did what she could to make the toiler's raiment look like diamonded banners, flung bravely to the breeze in honor of his new son-in-law. Everything—the duck troughs, the roof of the stable, the cart shafts, the dry-goods box used as a kennel—had ugliness hidden away under that prodigal revelling ermine of decoration. The sun itself had not long risen before Nature even drew over that a bridal veil of silver mist, so that the whole earth was left wrapped in whiteness that became holiness.

Pansy had said that she desired a quiet wedding, so that she herself had shut up the ducks that they might not get to Mrs. Meredith. And then she had made the rounds and fed everything; and now a certain lethargy and stupor of food quieted all creatures and gave to the valley the dignity of a vocal solitude.

The botanist bride was not in the least abashed during the ceremony. Nor proud: Mrs. Meredith more gratefully noticed this. And she watched closely and discovered with relief that Pansy did not once glance at her with uneasiness or for approval. The mother looked at Dent with eyes growing dim. "She will never seem to be the wife of my son," she said, "but she will make her children look like his children."

And so it was all over and they were gone—slipped away through the hiding white mists without a doubt of themselves, without a doubt of each other, mating as naturally as the wild creatures who never know the problems of human selection, or the problems that civilization leaves to be settled after selection has been made.

Mrs. Meredith and Rowan and the clergyman were left with the father and the children, and with an unexampled wedding collation—one of Pansy's underived masterpieces. The clergyman frightened the younger children; they had never seen his like either with respect to his professional robes or his superhuman clerical voice—their imaginations balancing unsteadily between the impossibility of his being a man in a nightgown and the impossibility of his being a woman with a mustache.

After his departure their fright and apprehensions settled on Mrs. Meredith. They ranged themselves on chairs side by side against a wall, and sat confronting her like a class in the public school fated to be examined in deadly branches. None moved except when she spoke, and then all writhed together but each in a different way; the most comforting word from her produced a family spasm with individual proclivities. Rowan tried to talk with the father about crops: they were frankly embarrassed. What can a young man with two thousand acres of the best land say to an old man with fifty of the poorest?

The mother and son drove home in silence. She drew one of his hands into her lap and held it with close pressure. They did not look at each other.

As the carriage rolled easily over the curved driveway, through the noble forest trees they caught glimpses of the house now standing clear in afternoon sunshine. Each had the same thought of how empty it waited there without Dent—henceforth less than a son, yet how much more; more than brother, but how much less. How a brief ceremony can bind separated lives and tear bound ones apart!

"Rowan," she said, as they walked slowly from the carriage to the porch, she having clasped his arm more intimately, "there is something I have wanted to do and have been trying to do for a long time. It must not be put off any longer. We must go over the house this afternoon. There are a great many things that I wish to show you and speak to you about—things that have to be divided between you and Dent."

"Not to-day! not to-day!" he cried, turning to her with quick appeal. But she shook her head slowly, with brave cheerfulness.

"Yes; to-day. Now; and then we shall be over with it. Wait for me here." She passed down the long hall to her bedroom, and as she disappeared he rushed into the parlors and threw himself on a couch with his hands before his face;

then he sprang up and came out into the hall again and waited with a quiet face.

When she returned, smiling, she brought with her a large bunch of keys, and she took his arm dependently as they went up the wide staircase. She led him to the upper bedrooms first—in earlier years so crowded and gay with guests, but unused during later ones. The shutters were closed, and the afternoon sun shot yellow shafts against floors and walls. There was a perfume of lavender, of rose leaves.

"Somewhere in one of these closets there is a roll of linen." She opened one after another, looking into each. "No; it is not here. Then it must be in there. Yes; here it is. This linen was spun and woven from flax grown on your great-great-grandfather's land. Look at it! It is beautifully made. Each generation of the family has inherited part and left the rest for generations yet to come. Half of it is yours, half is Dent's. When it has been divided until there is no longer enough to divide, that will be the last of the home-made linen of the old time. It was a good time, Rowan; it produced masterful men and masterful women, not mannish women. Perhaps the golden age of our nation will some day prove to have been the period of the home-spun Americans."

As they passed on she spoke to him with an increasing, almost unnatural gayety. He had a new appreciation of what her charm must have been when she was a girl. The rooms were full of memories to her; many of the articles that she caressed with her fingers, and lingered over with reluctant eyes, connected themselves with days and nights of revelry and the joy of living; also with prides and deeds which ennobled her recollection.

"You and Dent know that your father divided equally all that he had. But everything in the house is mine, and I have made no will and shall not make any. What is mine belongs to you two alike. Still, I have made a list of things that I think he would rather have, and a list of things for you—merely because I wish to give something to each of you directly."

In a room on a lower floor she unlocked a closet, the walls of which were lined with shelves. She peeped in; then she withdrew her head and started to lock the door again; but she changed her mind and laughed.

"Do you know what these things are?" She touched a large box, and he carried it over to the bed and she lifted the top off, exposing the contents. "Did you ever see anything so *black*? This was the clerical robe in which one of your ancestors used to read his sermons. He is the one who wrote the treatise on 'God Properly and Unproperly Understood.' He was the great seminarian in your father's family—the portrait in the hall, you know. I shall not decide whether you or Dent must inherit this; decide for yourselves; I imagine you will end it in the quarrel. How black it is, and what black sermons flew out of it—ravens, instead of white doves, of the Holy Spirit. He was the friend of Jonathan Edwards." She made a wry face as he put the box back into the closet; and she laughed again as she locked it in.

"Here are some things from my side of the family." And she drew open a long drawer and spoke with proud reticence. They stood looking down at part of the uniform of an officer of the Revolution. She lifted one corner of it and disclosed a sword beneath. She lifted another corner of the coat and exposed a roll of parchment. "I suppose I should have had this parchment framed and hung up downstairs, so that it would be the first thing seen by any one entering the front door; and this sword should have been suspended over the fireplace, or have been exposed under a glass case in the parlors; and the uniform should have been fitted on a tailor's manikin; and we should have lectured to our guests on our worship of our ancestors—in the new American way, in the Chino-American way. But I'm afraid we go to the other extreme, Rowan; perhaps we are proud of the fact that we are not boastful. Instead of concerning ourselves with those who shed glory on us, we have concerned ourselves with the question whether we are shedding glory on them. Still, I wonder whether our ancestors may not possibly be offended that we say so little about them!"

She led him up and down halls and from floor to floor.

"Of course you know this room—the nursery. Here is where you began to be a bad boy; and you began before you can remember. Did you never see these things before? They were your first soldiers—I have left them to Dent. And here are some of Dent's things that I have left to you. For one thing, his castanets. His father and I never knew why he cried for castanets. He said that Dent by all the laws of spiritual inheritance from his side should be wanting the timbrel and harp—Biblical influence, you understand; but that my influence interfered and turned timbrel and harp into castanets. Do you remember the day when you ran away with Dent and took him to a prize fight? After that you wanted boxing-gloves, and Dent was crazy for a sponge. You fought him, and he sponged you. Here is the sponge; I do not know where the gloves are. And here are some things that belong to both of you; they are mine; they go with me." She laid her hand on a little box wrapped and tied, then quickly shut the closet.

In a room especially fragrant with lavender she opened a press in the wall and turned her face away from him for a moment.

"This is my bridal dress. This was my bridal veil; it has been the bridal veil of girls in my family for a good many generations. These were my slippers; you see I had a large foot; but it was well shaped—it was a woman's foot. That was my vanity—not to have a little foot. I leave these things to you both. I hope each of you may have a daughter to wear the dress and the veil." For the first time she dashed some tears from her eyes. "I look to my sons for sons and daughters."

It was near sunset when they stood again at the foot of the staircase. She was white and tired, but her spirit refused to be conquered.

"I think I shall lie down now," she said, "so I shall say good night to you here, Rowan. Fix the tray for me yourself, pour me out some tea, and butter me a roll." They stood looking into each other's eyes. She saw things in his which caused her suddenly to draw his forehead over and press her lips to one and then to the other, again and again.

The sun streamed through the windows, level and red, lighting up the darkened hall, lighting up the head and shoulders of his mother.

An hour later he sat at the head of his table alone—a table arranged for two instead of three. At the back of his chair waited the aged servitor of the household, gray-haired, discreet, knowing many things about earlier days on which rested the seal of incorruptible silence. A younger servant performed the duties.

He sat at the head of his table and excused the absence of his mother and forced himself with the pride and dignity of his race to give no sign of what had passed that day. His mother's maid entered, bringing him in a crystal vase a dark red flower for his coat. She had always given him that same dark red flower after he had turned into manhood. "It is your kind," she said; "I understand."

He arranged the tray for her, pouring out her tea, buttering the rolls. Then he forced himself to eat his supper as usual. From old candlesticks on the table a silver radiance was shed on the massive silver, on the gem-like glass. Candelabra on the mantelpiece and the sideboard lighted up the browned oak of the walls.

He left the table at last, giving and hearing a good night. The servants efficiently ended their duties and put out the lights. In the front hall lamps were left burning; there were lamps and candles in the library. He went off to a room on the ground floor in one ell of the house; it was his sitting room, smoking room, the lounging place of his friends. In one corner stood a large desk, holding old family papers; here also were articles that he himself had lately been engaged on—topics relating to scientific agriculture, soils, and stock-raising. It was the road by which some of the country gentlemen who had been his forefathers passed into a larger life of practical affairs—going into the Legislature of the state or into the Senate; and he had thought of this as a future for himself. For an hour or two he looked through family papers.

Then he put them aside and squarely faced the meaning of the day. His thoughts traversed the whole track of Dent's life—one straight track upward. No deviations, no pitfalls there, no rising and falling. And now early marriage and safety from so many problems; with work and honors and wifely love and children: work and rest and duty to the end. Dent had called him into his room that morning after he was dressed for his wedding and had started to thank him for his love and care and guardianship and then had broken down and they had locked their arms around each other, trying not to say what could not be said.

He lived again through that long afternoon with his mother. What had the whole day been to her and how she had risen to meet with nobility all its sadnesses! Her smile lived before him; and her eyes, shining with increasing brightness as she dwelt upon things that meant fading sunlight: she fondling the playthings of his infancy, keeping some of them to be folded away with her at last; touching her bridal dress and speaking her reliance on her sons for sons and daughters; at the close of the long trying day standing at the foot of the staircase white with weariness and pain, but so brave, so sweet, so unconquerable. He knew that she was not sleeping now, that she was thinking of him, that she had borne everything and would bear everything not only because it was due to herself, but because it was due to him.

He turned out the lights and sat at a window opening upon the night. The voices of the land came in to him, the voices of the vanished life of its strong men.

He remembered the kind of day it was when he first saw through its autumn trees the scattered buildings of his university. What impressions it had made upon him as it awaited him there, gray with stateliness, hoary with its honors, pervaded with the very breath and spirit of his country. He recalled his meeting with his professors, the choosing of his studies, the selection of a place in which to live. Then had followed what had been the great spectacle and experience of his life—the assembling of picked young men, all eager like greyhounds at the slips to show what was in them, of what stuff they were made, what strength and hardihood and robust virtues, and gifts and grace for manly intercourse. He had been caught up and swept off his feet by that influence. Looking back as he did to that great plateau which was his home, for the first time he had felt that he was not only a youth of an American commonwealth, but a youth of his whole country. They were all American youths there, as opposed to English youths and German youths and Russian youths. There flamed up in him the fierce passion, which he believed to be burning in them all, to show his mettle—the mettle of his state, the mettle of his nation. To him, newly come into this camp of young men, it lay around the walls of the university like a white spiritual host, chosen youths to be made into chosen men. And he remembered how little he then knew that about this white host hung the red host of those camp-followers, who beleaguer in outer darkness every army of men.

Then had followed warfare, double warfare: the ardent attack on work and study; athletic play, good fellowship, visits late at night to the chambers of new friends—chambers rich in furniture and pictures, friends richer in old names and fine manners and beautiful boyish gallant ways; his club and his secret society, and the whole bewildering maddening enchantment of student life, where work and duty and lights and wine and poverty and want and flesh and spirit strive together each for its own. At this point he put these memories away, locked them from himself in their long silence.

Near midnight he made his way quietly back into the main hall. He turned out the lamps and lighted his bedroom candle and started toward the stairway, holding it in front of him a little above his head, a low-moving star through the gloom. As he passed between two portraits, he paused with sudden impulse and, going over to one, held his candle up before the face and studied it once more. A man, black-browed, black-robed, black-bearded, looked down into his eyes as one who had authority to speak. He looked far down upon his offspring, and he said to him: "You may be one of those who through the flesh are chosen to be damned. But if He chooses to damn you, then be damned, but do not question His mercy or His justice: it is not for you to alter the fixed and the eternal."

He crossed with his candle to the opposite wall and held it up before another face: a man full of red blood out to the skin; full-lipped, red-lipped; audacious about the forehead and brows, and beautiful over his thick careless hair through which a girl's fingers seemed lately to have wandered. He looked level out at his offspring as though he still stood throbbing on the earth and he spoke to him: "I am not alive to speak to you with my voice, but I have spoken to you through my blood. When the cup of life is filled, drain it deep. Why does nature fill it if not to have you empty it?"

He blew his candle out in the eyes of that passionate face, and holding it in his hand, a smoking torch, walked slowly backward and forward in the darkness of the hall with only a little pale moonlight struggling in through a window here and there.

Then with a second impulse he went over and stood close to the dark image who had descended into him through the mysteries of nature. "You," he said, "who helped to make me what I am, you had the conscience and not the temptation. And you," he said, turning to the hidden face across the hall,

166

"who helped to make me what I am, you had the temptation and not the conscience. What does either of you know of me who had both?

"And what do I know about either of you," he went on, taking up again the lonely vigil of his walk and questioning; "you who preached against the Scarlet Woman, how do I know you were not the scarlet man? I may have derived both from you—both conscience and sin—without hypocrisy. All those years during which your face was hardening, your one sincere prayer to God may have been that He would send you to your appointed place before you were found out by men on earth. And you with your fresh red face, you may have lain down beside the wife of your youth, and have lived with her all your years, as chaste as she."

He resumed his walk, back and forth, back and forth; and his thoughts changed:

"What right have I to question them, or judge them, or bring them forward in my life as being responsible for my nature? If I roll back the responsibility to them, had they not fathers? and had not their fathers fathers? and if a man rolls back his deeds upon those who are his past, then where will responsibility be found at all, and of what poor cowardly stuff is each of us?"

How silent the night was, how silent the great house! Only his slow footsteps sounded there like the beating of a heavy heart resolved not to fail.

At last they died away from the front of the house, passing inward down a long hallway and growing more muffled; then the sound of them ceased altogether: he stood noiselessly before his mother's door.

He stood there, listening if he might hear in the intense stillness a sleeper's breathing. "Disappointed mother," he said as silently as a spirit might speak to a spirit.

Then he came back and slowly began to mount the staircase.

"Is it then wrong for a man to do right? Is it ever right to do wrong?" he said finally. "Should I have had my fling and never have cared and never have spoken? Is there a true place for deception in the world? May our hypocrisy with each other be a virtue? If you have done evil, shall you live the whited sepulchre? Ah, Isabel, how easily I could have deceived you! Does a woman care what a man may have done, if he be not found out? Is not her highest ideal for him a profitable reputation, not a spotless character? No, I will not wrong you by these thoughts. It was you who said to me that you once loved all that you saw in me, and believed that you saw everything. All that you asked of me was truthfulness that had no sorrow."

He reached the top of the stairs and began to feel his way toward his room.

"To have one chance in life, in eternity, for a white name, and to lose it!"

VIII

Autumn and winter had passed. Another spring was nearly gone. One Monday morning of that May, the month of new growths and of old growths with new starting-points on them, Ambrose Webb was walking to and fro across the fresh oilcloth in his short hall; the front door and the back door stood wide open, as though to indicate the receptivity of his nature in opposite directions; all the windows were wide open, as though to bring out of doors into his house: he was much more used to the former; during married life the open had been more friendly than the interior. But he was now also master of the interior and had been for nearly a year.

Some men succeed best as partial automata, as dogs for instance that can be highly trained to pull little domestic carts. Ambrose had grown used to pulling his cart: he had expected to pull it for the rest of his days; and now the cart had suddenly broken down behind him and he was left standing in the middle of the long life-road. But liberty was too large a destiny for a mind of that order; the rod of empire does not fit such hands; it was intolerable to Ambrose that he was in a world where he could do as he pleased.

On this courageous Monday, therefore,—whatsoever he was to do during the week he always decided on Mondays,—after months of irresolution he finally determined to make a second dash for slavery. But he meant to be canny; this time he would choose a woman who, if she ruled him, would not misrule him; what he could stand was a sovereign, not a despot, and he believed that he had found this exceptionally gifted and exceptionally moderated being: it was Miss Anna Hardage.

From the day of Miss Anna's discovery that Ambrose had a dominating consort, she had been, she had declared she should be, much kinder to him. When his wife died, Miss Anna had been kinder still. Affliction present, affliction past, her sympathy had not failed him.

He had fallen into the habit of lingering a little whenever he took his dairy products around to the side porch. Every true man yearns for the eyes of some woman; and Ambrose developed the feeling that he should like to live with Miss Anna's. He had no gift for judging human conduct except by common human standards; and so at bottom he believed that Miss Anna in her own way had been telling him that if the time ever came, she could be counted on to do the right thing by him.

So Ambrose paced the sticky oilcloth this morning as a man who has reached the hill of decision. He had bought him a new buggy and new harness.

Hitched to the one and wearing the other was his favorite roan mare with a Roman nose and a white eye, now dozing at the stiles in the front yard. He had curried her and had combed her mane and tail and had had her newly shod, and altogether she may have felt too comfortable to keep awake. He himself seemed to have received a coating of the same varnish as his buggy. Had you pinned a young beetle in the back of his coat or on either leg of his trousers, as a mere study in shades of blackness, it must have been lost to view at the distance of a few yards through sheer harmony with its background. Under his Adam's apple there was a green tie—the bough to the fruit. His eyes sparkled as though they had lately been reset and polished by a jeweller.

What now delayed and excited him at this last moment before setting out was uncertainty as to the offering he should bear Miss Anna. Fundamental instincts vaguely warned him that love's altar must be approached with gifts. He knew that some brought fortune, some warlike deeds, some fame, some the beauty of their strength and youth. He had none of these to offer; but he was a plain farmer, and he could give her what he had so often sold her—a pound of butter.

He had awaited the result of the morning churning; but the butter had tasted of turnips, and Ambrose did not think that the taste of turnips represented the flavor of his emotion. Nevertheless, there was one thing that she preferred even to butter; he would ensnare her in her own weakness, catch her in her own net: he would take her a jar of cream.

Miss Anna was in her usual high spirits that morning. She was trying a new recipe for some dinner comfort for Professor Hardage, when her old cook, who also answered the doorbell, returned to the kitchen with word that Mr. Webb was in the parlor.

"Why, I paid him for his milk," exclaimed Miss Anna, without ceasing to beat and stir. "And what is he doing in the parlor? Why didn't he come around to the side door? I'll be back in a moment." She took off her apron from an old habit of doing so whenever she entered the parlor.

She gave her dairyman the customary hearty greeting, hurried back to get him a glass of water, inquired dispassionately about grass, inundated him with a bounteous overflow of her impersonal humanity. But he did not state his business, and she grew impatient to return to her confection.

"Do I owe you for anything, Mr. Webb?" she suddenly asked, groping for some clew to this lengthening labyrinthine visit.

He rose and going to the piano raked heavily off of the top of it a glass jar and brought it over to her and resumed his seat with a speaking countenance.

"Cream!" cried Miss Anna, delighted, running her practised eye downward along the bottle to discover where the contents usually began to get blue: it was yellow to the bottom. "How much is it? I'm afraid we are too poor to buy so much cream all at once."

"It has no price; it is above price."

"How much is it, Mr. Webb?" she insisted with impatience.

"It is a free gift."

"Oh, what a beautiful present!" exclaimed Miss Anna, holding it up to the light admiringly. "How can I ever thank you."

"Don't thank me: you could have the dairy! You could have the cows, the farm."

"O dear, no!" cried Miss Anna, "that would be altogether too much! One bottle goes far beyond all that I ever hoped for."

"I wish ail women were like you."

"O dear, no! that would not do at all! I am an old maid, and women must marry, must, must! What would become of the world?"

"You need not be an old maid unless you wish."

"Now, I had never thought of that!" observed Miss Anna, in a very peculiar tone. "But we'll not talk about myself; let us talk about yourself. You are looking extremely well—now aren't you?"

"No one has a better right. It is due you to let you know this. There's good timber in me yet."

"Due *me*! I am not interested in timber."

"Anna," he said, throwing his arms around one of his knees, "our hour has come—we need not wait any longer."

"Wait for *what*?" inquired Miss Anna, bending toward him with the scrutiny of a near-sighted person trying to make out some looming horror.

"Our marriage."

Miss Anna rose as by an inward explosion.

"Go, *buzzard*!"

He kept his seat and stared at her with a dropped jaw. Habit was powerful in him; and there was something in her anger, in that complete sweeping of him out other way, that recalled the domestic usages of former years and brought to his lips an involuntary time-worn expression:

"I meant nothing offensive."

"I do not know what you meant, and I do not care: go!"

He rose and stood before her, and with a flash of sincere anger he spoke his honest mind: "It was you who put the notion in my head. You encouraged me, encouraged me systematically; and now you are pretending. You are a bad woman."

"I think I am a bad woman after what has happened to me this morning," said Miss Anna, dazed and ready to break down.

He hesitated when he reached the door, smarting with his honest hurt; and he paused there and made a request.

"At least I hope that you will never mention this; it might injure me." He did not explain how, but he seemed to know.

"Do you suppose I'd tell my Maker if He did not already know it?"
She swept past him into the kitchen.

"As soon as you have done your work, go clean the parlor," she said to the cook. "Give it a good airing. And throw that cream away, throw the bottle away."

A few moments later she hurried with her bowl into the pantry; there she left it unfinished and crept noiselessly up the backstairs to her room.

That evening as Professor Hardage sat opposite to her, reading, while she was doing some needlework, he laid his book down with the idea of asking her some question. But he caught sight of her expression and studied it a few moments. It was so ludicrous a commingling of mortification and rage that he laughed outright.

"Why, Anna, what on earth is the matter?"

At the first sound of his voice she burst into hysterical sobs.

He came over and tried to draw her fingers away from her eyes.
"Tell me all about it."

She shook her head frantically.

"Yes, tell me," he urged. "Is there anything in all these years that you have not told me?"

"I cannot," she sobbed excitedly. "I am disgraced."

He laughed. "What has disgraced you?"

"A man."

"Good heavens!" he cried, "has somebody been making love to you?"

"Yes."

His face flushed. "Come," he said seriously, "what is the meaning of this, Anna?"

She told him.

"Why aren't you angry with him?" she complained, drying her eyes. "You sit there and don't say a word!"

"Do you expect me to be angry with any soul for loving you and wishing to be loved by you? He cast his mite into the treasury, Anna."

"I didn't mind the mite," she replied. "But he said I encouraged him, that I encouraged him *systematically*."

"Did you expect him to be a philosopher?"

"I did not expect him to be a—" She hesitated at the harsh word.

"I'm afraid you expected him to be a philosopher. Haven't you been kind to him?"

"Why, of course."

"Systematically kind?"

"Why, of course."

"Did you have any motive?"

"You know I had no motive—aren't you ashamed!"

"But did you expect him to be genius enough to understand that? Did you suppose that he could understand such a thing as kindness without a motive? Don't be harsh with him, Anna, don't be hard on him: he is an ordinary man and judged you by the ordinary standard. You broke your alabaster box at his feet, and he secretly suspected that you were working for something more valuable than the box of ointment. The world is full of people who are kind without a motive; but few of those to whom they are kind believe this."

Before Miss Anna fell asleep that night, she had resolved to tell Harriet. Every proposal of marriage is known at least to three people. The distinction in Miss Anna's conduct was not in telling, but in not telling until she had actually been asked.

Two mornings later Ambrose was again walking through his hall. There is one compensation for us all in the large miseries of life—we no longer feel the little ones. His experience in his suit for Miss Anna's hand already seemed a trifle to Ambrose, who had grown used to bearing worse things from womankind. Miss Anna was not the only woman in the world, he averred, by way of swift indemnification. Indeed, in the very act of deciding upon her, he had been thinking of some one else. The road of life had divided equally before him: he had chosen Miss Anna as a traveller chooses the right fork; the left fork remained and he was now preparing to follow that: it led to Miss Harriet Crane.

As Ambrose now paced his hallway, revolving certain details connected with his next venture and adventure, the noise of an approaching carriage fell upon his ear, and going to the front door he recognized the brougham of Mrs. Conyers. But it was Miss Harriet Crane who leaned forward at the window and bowed smilingly to him as he hurried out.

"How do you do, Mr. Webb?" she said, putting out her hand and shaking his cordially, at the same time giving him a glance of new-born interest. "You know I have been threatening to come out for a long time. I must owe you an enormous bill for pasturage," she picked up her purse as she spoke, "and I have come to pay my debts. And then I wish to see my calf," and she looked into his eyes very pleasantly.

"You don't owe me anything," replied Ambrose. "What is grass? What do I care for grass? My mind is set on other things."

He noticed gratefully how gentle and mild she looked; there was such a beautiful softness about her and he had had hardness enough. He liked her ringlets: they were a novelty; and there hung around her, in the interior of the carriage, a perfume that was unusual to his sense and that impressed him as a reminder of her high social position. But Ambrose reasoned that if a daughter of his neighbor could wed a Meredith, surely he ought to be able to marry a Crane.

"If you want to see the calf," he said, but very reluctantly, "I'll saddle my horse and we'll go over to the back pasture."

"Don't saddle your horse," objected Harriet, opening the carriage door and moving over to the far cushion, "ride with me."

He had never ridden in a brougham, and as he got in very nervously and awkwardly, he reversed his figure and tried to sit on the little front seat on which lay Harriet's handkerchief and parasol.

"Don't ride backwards, Mr. Webb," suggested Harriet. "Unless you are used to it, you are apt to have a headache," and she tapped the cushion beside her as an invitation to him. "Now tell me about my calf," she said after they were seated side by side.

As she introduced this subject, Ambrose suddenly looked out of the window. She caught sight of his uneasy profile.

"Now, don't tell me that there's any bad hews about it!" she cried. "It is the only pet I have."

"Miss Harriet," he said, turning his face farther away, "you forget how long your calf has been out here; it isn't a calf any longer: it has had a calf."

He spoke so sternly that Harriet, who all her life had winced before sternness, felt herself in some wise to be blamed. And coolness was settling down upon them when she desired only a melting and radiant warmth.

"Well," she objected apologetically, "isn't it customary? What's the trouble? What's the objection? This is a free country! Whatever is natural is right! Why are you so displeased?"

About the same hour the next Monday morning Ambrose was again pacing his hallway and thinking of Harriet. At least she was no tyrant: the image of her softness rose before him again. "I make no mistake this time."

His uncertainty at the present moment was concerned solely with the problem of what his offering should be in this case: under what image should love present itself? The right thought came to him by and by; and taking from his storeroom an ornamental basket with a top to it, he went out to his pigeon house and selected two blue squabs. They were tender and soft and round; without harshness, cruelty, or deception. Whatever they seemed to be, that they were; and all that they were was good.

But as Ambrose walked back to the house, he lifted the top of the basket and could but admit that they did look bare. Might they not, as a love token, be— unrefined? He crossed to a flower bed, and, pulling a few rose-geranium leaves, tucked them here and there about the youngsters.

It was not his intention to present these to Harriet in person: he had accompanied the cream—he would follow the birds; they should precede him twenty-four hours and the amative poison would have a chance to work.

During that forenoon his shining buggy drawn by his roan mare, herself symbolic of softness, drew up before the entrance of the Conyers homestead. Ambrose alighted; he lifted the top of the basket—all was well.

"These pets are for your Miss Harriet," he said to the maid who answered his ring.

As the maid took the basket through the hall after having watched him drive away, incredulous as to her senses, she met Mrs. Conyers, who had entered the hall from a rear veranda.

"Who rang?" she asked; "and what is that?"

The maid delivered her instructions. Mrs. Conyers took the basket and looked in.

"Have them broiled for my supper," she said with a little click of the teeth, and handing the basket to the maid, passed on into her bedroom.

Harriet had been spending the day away from home. She returned late. The maid met her at the front door and a few moments of conversation followed. She hurried into the supper room; Mrs. Conyers sat alone.

"Mother," exclaimed Harriet with horror, "have you *eaten* my squabs?"

Mrs. Conyers stabbed at a little pile of bones on the side plate. "This is what is left of them," she said, touching a napkin to her gustatory lips. "There are your leaves," she added, pointing to a little vase in front of Harriet's plate. "When is he going to send you some more? But tell him we have geraniums."

The next day Ambrose received a note:

"Dear Mr. Webb: I have been thinking how pleasant my visit to you was that morning. It has not been possible for me to get the carriage since or I should have been out to thank you for your beautiful present. The squabs appealed to me. A man who loves them must have tender feeling; and that is what all my life I have been saying: Give me a man with a heart! Sometime when you are in town, I may meet you on the street somewhere and then I can thank you more fully than I do now. I shall always cherish the memory of your kind deed. You must give me the chance to thank you very soon, or I shall fear that you do not care for my thanks. I take a walk about eleven o'clock.

"Sincerely yours,

"HARRIET CRANE."

Ambrose must have received the note. A few weeks later Miss Anna one morning received one herself delivered by a boy who had ridden in from the farm; the boy waited with a large basket while she read:

"Dearest Anna: It is a matter of very little importance to mention to you of course, but I am married. My husband and I were married at ———
yesterday afternoon. He met me at an appointed place and we drove quietly out of town. What I want you to do at once is, send me some clothes, for I left all the Conyers apparel where it belonged. Send me something of everything. And as soon as I am pinned in, I shall invite you out. Of course I shall now give orders for whatever I desire; and then I shall return to Mrs. Conyers the things I used on my bridal trip.

"This is a very hurried note, and of course I have not very much to say as yet about my new life. As for my husband, I can at least declare with perfect sincerity that he is mine. I have made one discovery already, Anna: he cannot be bent except where he has already been broken. I am discovering the broken places and shall govern him accordingly.

"Do try to marry, Anna! You have no idea how a married woman feels toward one of her sex who is single.

"I want you to be sure to stand at the windows about five o'clock this afternoon and see the Conyers' cows all come travelling home: they graze no more these heavenly pastures. It will be the first intimation that Mrs. Conyers receives that I am no longer the unredeemed daughter of her household. Her curiosity will, of course, bring her out here as fast as the horse can travel. But, oh, Anna, my day has come at last! At last she shall realize that I am strong, *strong*! I shall receive her with the front door locked and talk to her out of the window; and I expect to talk to her a long, *long* time. I shall have the flowers moved from the porch to keep them from freezing during that interview.

"As soon as I am settled, as one has so much more time in the country than in town, I may, after all, take up that course of reading: would you object?

"It's a wise saying that every new experience brings some new trouble: I longed for youth before I married; but to marry after you are old—that, Anna, is sorrow indeed.

"Your devoted friend,

"HARRIET CRANE WEBB.

"P.S. Don't send any but the *plainest* things; for I remember, noble friend, how it pains you to see me *overdressed*."

IX

It was raining steadily and the night was cold. Miss Anna came hurriedly down into the library soon after supper. She had on an old waterproof; and in one hand she carried a man's cotton umbrella—her own—and in the other a pair of rubbers. As she sat down and drew these over her coarse walking shoes, she talked in the cheery tone of one who has on hand some congenial business.

"I may get back late and I may not get back at all; it depends upon how the child is. But I wish it would not rain when poor little children are sick at night —it is the one thing that gives me the blues. And I wish infants could speak out and tell their symptoms. When I see grown people getting well as soon as they can minutely narrate to you all their ailments, my heart goes out to babies. Think how they would crow and gurgle, if they could only say what it is all about. But I don't see why people at large should not be licensed to bring in a bill when their friends insist upon describing their maladies to them: doctors do. But I must be going. Good night."

She rose and stamped her feet into the rubbers to make them fit securely; and then she came across to the lamp-lit table beside which he sat watching her fondly—his book dropped the while upon his lap. He grasped her large strong hand in his large strong hand; and she leaned her side against his shoulder and put her arm around his neck.

"You are getting younger, Anna," he said, looking up into her face and drawing her closer.

"Why not?" she answered with a voice of splendid joy. "Harriet is married; what troubles have I, then? And she patronizes—or matronizes—me and tyrannizes over Ambrose: so the world is really succeeding at last. But I wish her husband had not asked me *first*; that is her thorn."

"And the thorn will grow!"

"Now, don't sit up late!" she pleaded. "I turned your bed down and arranged the pillows wrong end out as you will have them; and I put out your favorite night-shirt—the one with the sleeves torn off above the elbows and the ravellings hanging down just as you require. Aren't you tired of books yet? Are you never going to get tired? And the same books! Why, I get fresh babies every few years—a complete change."

"How many generations of babies do you suppose there have been since this immortal infant was born?" he asked, laying his hand reverently over the book on his lap as if upon the head of a divine child.

"I don't know and I don't care," she replied. "I wish the immortal infant would let you alone." She stooped and kissed his brow, and wrung his hand silently, and went out into the storm. He heard her close the street door and heard the rusty click of her cotton umbrella as she raised it. Then he turned to the table at his elbow and kindled his deep-bowled pipe and drew over his legs the skirts of his long gown, coarse, austere, sombre.

He looked comfortable. A rainy night may depress a woman nursing a sick child that is not her own—a child already fighting for its feeble, unclaimed, repudiated life, in a world of weeping clouds; but such a night diffuses cheer when the raindrops are heard tapping the roof above beloved bookshelves, tapping the window-panes; when there is low music in the gutter on the back porch; when a student lamp, throwing its shadow over the ceiling and the walls, reserves its exclusive lustre for lustrous pages—pages over which men for centuries have gladly burnt out the oil of their brief lamps, their iron and bronze, their silver and gold and jewelled lamps—many-colored eyes of the nights of ages.

It was now middle September of another year and Professor Hardage had entered upon the work of another session. The interval had left no outward mark on him. The mind stays young a long time when nourished by a body such as his; and the body stays young a long time when mastered by such a mind. Day by day faithfully to do one's work and to be restless for no more; without bitterness to accept obscurity for ambition; to possess all vital passions and to govern them; to stand on the world's thoroughfare and see the young generations hurrying by, and to put into the hands of a youth here and there a light which will burn long after our own personal taper is extinguished; to look back upon the years already gone as not without usefulness and honor, and forward to what may remain as safe at least from failure or any form of shame, and thus for one's self to feel the humility of the part before the greatness of the whole of life, and yet the privileges and duties of the individual to the race—this brings blessedness if it does not always bring happiness, and it had brought both to him.

He sat at peace beside his lamp. The interval had brought changes to his towns-people. As he had walked home this afternoon, he had paused and looked across at some windows of the second story of a familiar corner. The green shutters, tightly closed, were gray with cobweb and with dust. One sagged from a loosened hinge and flapped in the rising autumn wind, showing inside a window sash also dust-covered and with a newspaper crammed through a broken pane. Where did Ravenel Morris live now? Did he live at all?

Accustomed as he was to look through the distances of human history, to traverse the areas of its religions and see how its great conflicting faiths have each claimed the unique name of revelation for itself, he could not anywhere discover what to him was clear proof either of the separate existence of the soul or of its immortal life hereafter. The security of that belief was denied him. He had wished for it, had tried to make it his. But while it never became a conviction, it remained a force. Under all that reason could affirm or could deny, there dwelt unaccountable confidence that the light of human life, leaping from headland to headland,—the long transmitted radiance of thought,—was not to go out with the inevitable physical extinction of the species on this planet. Somewhere in the universe he expected to meet his own, all whom he had loved, and to see this friend. Meantime, he accepted the fact of death in the world with that uncomplaining submission to nature which is in the strength and sanity of genius. As acquaintances left him, one after another, memory but kindled another lamp; hope but disclosed another white flower on its mysterious stem.

He sat at peace. The walls of the library showed their changes. There were valuable maps on Caesar's campaigns which had been sent him from Berlin; there were other maps from Athens; there was something from the city of Hannibal, and something from Tiber. Indeed, there were not many places in Isabel's wandering from which she had not sent home to him some proof that he was remembered. And always she sent letters which were more than maps or books, being in themselves charts to the movements of her spirit. They were regular; they were frank; they assured him how increasingly she needed his friendship. When she returned, she declared she would settle down to be near him for the rest of life. Few names were mentioned in these letters: never Rowan's; never Mrs. Osborn's—that lifelong friendship having been broken; and in truth since last March young Mrs. Osborn's eyes had been sealed to the reading of all letters. But beneath everything else, he could always trace the presence of one unspoken certainty—that she was passing through the deeps without herself knowing what height or what heath her feet would reach at last, there to abide.

As he had walked homeward this afternoon through the dust, something else had drawn his attention: he was passing the Conyers homestead, and already lights were beginning to twinkle in the many windows; there was to be a ball that night, and he thought of the unconquerable woman ruling within, apparently gaining still in vitality and youth. "Unjailed malefactors often attain great ages," he said to himself, as he turned away and thought of the lives she had helped to blight and shorten.

As the night advanced, he fell under the influence of his book, was drawn out of his poor house, away from his obscure town, his unknown college, quitted his country and his age, passing backward until there fell around him the glorious dawn of the race before the sunrise of written history: the immortal still trod the earth; the human soldier could look away from his earthly battle-field and see, standing on a mountain crest, the figure and the authority of his Divine Commander. Once more it was the flower-dyed plain, blood-dyed as well; the ships drawn up by the gray, the wrinkled sea; over on the other side, well-built Troy; and the crisis of the long struggle was coming. Hector, of the glancing plume, had come back to the city for the last time, mindful of his end.

He read once more through the old scene that is never old, and then put his book aside and sat thoughtful. "*I know not if the gods will not overthrow me... . I have very sore shame if, like a coward, I shrink away from battle; moreover mine own soul forbiddeth me... . Destiny ... no man hast escaped, be he coward or be he valiant, when once he hath been born.*"

His eyes had never rested on any spot in human history, however separated in time and place, where the force of those words did not seem to reign. Whatsoever the names under which men have conceived and worshipped their gods or their God, however much they have believed that it was these or it was He who overthrew them and made their destinies inescapable, after all, it is the high compulsion of the soul itself, the final mystery of personal choice, that sends us forth at last to our struggles and to our peace: "*mine own soul forbiddeth me*"—there for each is right and wrong, the eternal beauty of virtue.

He did not notice the sound of approaching wheels, and that the sound ceased at his door.

A moment later and Isabel with light footsteps stood before him. He sprang up with a cry and put his arms around her and held her.

"You shall never go away again."

"No, I am never going away again; I have come back to marry Rowan."

These were her first words to him as they sat face to face. And she quickly went on:

"How is he?"

He shook his head reproachfully at her: "When I saw him at least he seemed better than you seem."

"I knew he was not well—I have known it for a long time. But you saw him —in town—on the street—with his friends—attending to business?"

"Yes—in town—on the street—with his friends—attending to business."

"May I stay here? I ordered my luggage to be sent here."

"Your room is ready and has always been ready and waiting since the day you left. I think Anna has been putting fresh flowers in it all autumn. You will find some there to-night. She has insisted of late that you would soon be coming home."

An hour later she came down into the library again. She had removed the traces of travel, and she had travelled slowly and was not tired. All this enabled him to see how changed she was; and without looking older, how strangely oldened and grown how quiet of spirit. She had now indeed become sister for him to those images of beauty that were always haunting him— those far, dim images of the girlhood of her sex, with their faces turned away from the sun and their eyes looking downward, pensive in shadow, too freighted with thoughts of their brief fate and their immortality.

"I must have a long talk with you before I try to sleep. I must empty my heart to you once."

He knew that she needed the relief, and that what she asked of him during these hours would be silence.

"I have tried everything, and everything has failed. I have tried absence, but absence has not separated me from him. I have tried silence, but through the silence I have never ceased speaking to him. Nothing has really ever separated us; nothing ever can. It is more than will or purpose, it is my life. It is more than life to me, it is love."

She spoke very quietly, and at first she seemed unable to progress very far from the beginning. After every start, she soon came back to that one beginning.

"It is of no use to weigh the right and the wrong of it: I tried that at first, and I suppose that is why I made sad mistakes. You must not think that I am acting now from a sense of duty to him or to myself. Duty does not enter into my feeling: it is love; all that I am forbids me to do anything else."

But after a while she went back and bared before him in a way the history of her heart. "The morning after he told me, I went to church. I remember the lessons of the day and the hymns, and how I left the church before the sermon, because everything seemed to be on his side, and no one was on mine. He had done wrong and was guilty; and I had been wrong and was innocent; and the church comforted him and overlooked me; and I was angry and walked out of it.

"And do you remember the day I came to see you and you proposed everything to me, and I rejected everything? You told me to go away for a while, to throw myself into the pleasures of other people; you reminded me of prayer and of the duty of forgiveness; you told me to try to put myself in his place, and reminded me of self-sacrifice, and then said at last that I must leave it to time, which sooner or later settles everything. I rejected everything that you suggested. But I have accepted everything since, and have learned a lesson and a service from each: the meaning of prayer and of forgiveness and of self-sacrifice; and what the lapse of time can do to bring us to ourselves and show us what we wish. I say, I have lived through all these, and I have gotten something out of them all; but however much they may mean, they never constitute love; and it is my love that brings me back to him now."

Later on she recurred to the idea of self-sacrifice: much other deepest feeling seemed to gather about that.

"I am afraid that you do not realize what it means to a woman when a principle like this is involved. Can any man ever know? Does he dream what it means to us women to sacrifice ourselves as they often require us to do? I have been travelling in old lands—so old that the history of each goes back until we can follow it with our eyes no longer. But as far as we can see, we see this sorrow—the sorrow of women who have wished to be first in the love of the men they have loved. You, who read everything! Cannot you see them standing all through history, the sad figures of girls who have only asked for what they gave, love in its purity and its singleness—have only asked that there should have been no other before them? And cannot you see what a girl feels when she consents to accept anything less,—that she is lowered to herself from that time on,—has lost her own ideal of herself, as well as her ideal of the man she loves? And cannot you see how she lowers herself in his eyes also and ceases to be his ideal, through her willingness to live with him on a lower plane? That is our wound. That is our trouble and our sorrow: I have found it wherever I have gone."

Long before she said this to him, she had questioned him closely about Rowan. He withheld from her knowledge of some things which he thought she could better bear to learn later and by degrees.

"I knew he was not well," she said; "I feared it might be worse. Let me tell you this: no one knows him as I do. I must speak plainly. First, there was his trouble; that shadowed for him one ideal in his life. Then this drove him to a kind of self-concealment; and that wounded another ideal—his love of candor. Then he asked me to marry him, and he told me the truth about himself and I turned him off. Then came the scandals that tried to take away his good name, and I suppose have taken it away. And then, through all this, were the sufferings he was causing others around him, and the loss of his mother. I have lived through all these things with him while I have been away, and I understand; they sap life. I am going up to write to him now, and will you post the letter to-night? I wish him to come to see me at once, and our marriage must take place as soon as possible—here—very quietly."

Rowan came the next afternoon. She was in the library; and he went in and shut the door, and they were left alone.

Professor Hardage and Miss Anna sat in an upper room. He had no book and she had no work; they were thinking only of the two downstairs. And they spoke to each other in undertones, breaking the silence with brief sentences, as persons speak when awaiting news from sick-rooms.

Daylight faded. Outside the lamplighter passed, torching the grimy lamps. Miss Anna spoke almost in a whisper: "Shall I have some light sent in?"

"No, Anna."

"Did you tell him what the doctors have said about his health?"

"No; there was bad news enough without that for one day. And then happiness might bring back health to him. The trouble that threatens him will have to be put down as one of the consequences of all that has occurred to him—as part of what he is and of what he has done. The origin of disease may lie in our troubles—our nervous shocks, our remorses, and better strivings."

The supper hour came.

"I do not wish any supper, Anna."

"Nor I. How long they stay together!"

"They have a great deal to say to each other, Anna."

"I know, I know. Poor children!"

"I believe he is only twenty-five."

"When Isabel comes up, do you think I ought to go to her room and see whether she wants anything?"

"No, Anna."

"And she must not know that we have been sitting up, as though we felt sorry for them and could not go on with our own work."

"I met Marguerite and Barbee this afternoon walking together. I suppose she will come back to him at last. But she has had her storm, and he knows it, and he knows there will never be any storm for him. She is another one of those girls of mine—not sad, but with half the sun shining on them. But half a sun shining steadily, as it will always shine on her, is a great deal."

"Hush!" said Miss Anna, in a whisper, "he is gone! Isabel is coming up the steps."

They heard her and then they did not hear her, and then again and then not again.

Miss Anna started up:

"She needs me!"

He held her back:

"No, Anna! Not to help is to help."

X

One afternoon late in the autumn of the following year, when a waiting stillness lay on the land and shimmering sunlight opened up the lonely spaces of woods and fields, the Reaper who comes to all men and reaps what they have sown, approached the home of the Merediths and announced his arrival to the young master of the house: he would await his pleasure.

Rowan had been sitting up, propped by his pillows. It was the room of his grandfather as it had been that of the man preceding; the bed had been their bed; and the first to place it where it stood may have had in mind a large window, through which as he woke from his nightly sleep he might look far out upon the land, upon rolling stately acres.

Rowan looked out now: past the evergreens just outside to the shining lawn beyond; and farther away, upon fields of brown shocks—guiltless harvest; then toward a pasture on the horizon. He could see his cattle winding slowly along the edge of a russet woodland on which the slanting sunlight fell. Against the blue sky in the silvery air a few crows were flying: all went in the same direction but each went without companions. He watched their wings curiously with lonely, following eyes. Whither home passed they? And by whose summons? And with what guidance?

A deep yearning stirred him, and he summoned his wife and the nurse with his infant son. He greeted her; then raising himself on one elbow and leaning over the edge of the bed, he looked a long time at the boy slumbering on the nurse's lap.

The lesson of his brief span of years gathered into his gaze.

"Life of my life," he said, with that lesson on his lips, "sign of my love, of what was best in me, this is my prayer for you: may you find one to love you such as your father found; when you come to ask her to unite her life with yours, may you be prepared to tell her the truth about yourself, and have nothing to tell that would break her heart and break the hearts of others. May it be said of you that you are a better man than your father."

He had the child lifted and he kissed his forehead and his eyes. "By the purity of your own life guard the purity of your sons for the long honor of our manhood." Then he made a sign that the nurse should withdraw.

When she had withdrawn, he put his face down on the edge of the pillow where his wife knelt, her face hidden. His hair fell over and mingled with her hair. He passed his arm around her neck and held her close.

"All your troubles came to you because you were true to the highest. You asked only the highest from me, and the highest was more than I could give. But be kind to my memory. Try to forget what is best forgotten, but remember what is worth remembering. Judge me for what I was; but judge me also for what I wished to be. Teach my son to honor my name; and when he is old enough to understand, tell him the truth about his father. Tell him what it was that saddened our lives. As he looks into his mother's face, it will steady him."

He put both arms around her neck.

"I am tired of it all," he said. "I want rest. Love has been more cruel to me than death."

A few days later, an afternoon of the same autumnal stillness, they bore him across his threshold with that gentleness which so often comes too late—slowly through his many-colored woods, some leaves drifting down upon the sable plumes and lodging in them—-along the turnpike lined with dusty thistles—through the watching town, a long procession, to the place of the unreturning.

They laid him along with his fathers.

9 783734 067488